TRUE

love

WAY

MARY ELIZABETH

Cover design by TRC Designs

Book design by Inkstain Design Studio

Edited by Paige Maroney Smith

First Edition.

For Andrea.

This was always for you.

BOOK BY
MARY ELIZABETH

Innocents

(DUSTY, VOLUME 1)

Delinquents

(DUSTY, VOLUME 2)

Closer

(CLOSER, VOLUME 1)

Sever

(CLOSER, VOLUME 2)

Tramp

(HUSH, VOLUME 1)

Harlot

(HUSH, VOLUME 2)

Kiss of Death

(HUSH VOLUME 2.5)

Criminal

(HUSH, VOLUME 3)

Extra Credit

True Love Way

Low

Poesy

(A LOW NOVELLA)

THE INTRODUCTION

The uncomplicated explanation:

my mind can't be trusted.

It's betrayed me.

How sad.

Chapter 1

DILLON

"**W**ho do you think she is?" I ask.

This girl and her parents showed up fifteen minutes ago in the moving truck that's now parked in front of the empty house next door to mine. With light skin and long brown hair, she's dressed in ripped-up jean shorts and a faded black T-shirt with a design on the front of it I can't make out.

"I don't know," my best friend, Herb, says. He wipes beaded sweat from his top lip.

I rock back on my heels, keeping my bike steady between my legs as gravel crunches beneath my road-worn Vans. The end-of-summer sun hammers down on us from clear mid-afternoon skies.

Kyle, my other best pal, rolls by on his skateboard, briefly blocking my view. "I've never seen her," he says.

"She must be new." Herbert halts his bike beside mine and taps his hands against his handlebars to the same upbeat tune that's been stuck in his head all week.

The house next door is white with yellow trim, and it's been vacant since last September. The previous owners, the Pimentels, were here one day and gone the next. My parents don't like it when I eavesdrop, but I heard them say, 'Mrs. Pimentel took Mr. Pimentel for all he's worth after she caught him dipping his deep-sea fishing pole into somebody else's ocean.

There have been a few people by since the *For Sale* sign went up. Unless they're originally from Castle Rain, no one ever stays long. We haven't had newcomers in a while.

"This place is nothing but townies and old people," my older sister, Risa, always says. "Fuck Washington."

"Do you think she'll be at school tomorrow?" Herb asks.

I shrug.

From the back of the U-Haul truck, a man who looks to be about my father's age appears with a large box in his arms. Beside him, a short, thick woman with long hair, like the girl's, dangles a set of keys in her hand. She has pep to her step, practically floating.

If fat people could float.

"Penelope," the woman calls expectantly. "Do you want to be the first to unlock the door?"

The girl doesn't answer. The lady with the keys loses her smile, and the man with the box scowls.

"She's rude." Kyle scoffs. "I hate her."

I walk my bike from the street to the sidewalk in front of my house. My best friends stay back, kick flipping and tail whipping while I do nothing more than watch.

"Pen," the lady tries again, making the keys sing, swinging them harder than the first time. Her arm jiggles.

No response.

"Penelope," the man stabs. "Don't ignore your mother."

Posted on the steps in front of the house, the girl, Penelope—Pen—*whatever,* is in her own little world. She has a black Discman on her hip and earphones in her ears. With a melody of her own, the new girl next door bobs her head back and forth, oblivious to her parents. Her eyes are hidden behind sunglasses with circular green lenses. At first I think she's mouthing the words to whatever song she's listening to, but then she blows the biggest bubblegum bubble I've ever seen.

My heart does a weird jump-skip-bounce thing.

Pink gum pops, covering her nose and chin. One swipe of

3

her tongue is all it takes to clean up her face. She continues to chew, nod, and ignore.

"Dillon," Herb whines. "Let's go, dude."

I look back at my friends, not as interested in riding bikes all over the town like I was this morning … like I have the last three months. Kyle's face flushes pink, and Herbert's forehead glistens as sweat rolls down his temples. They wait, but impatiently.

"It's the last day of summer," Kyle adds.

I turn toward the new people. Toward Pen.

"It's just a girl," Herbert teases.

Penelope pops another bubble. Her mom walks past her, shoving the key into the doorknob herself. The man with the box, whom I assume is her dad, places the cardboard package at his daughter's feet. Her name is written across the side of it in black marker: *Pen/ Fragile.*

She finally understands and pulls the earphones from her ears. As she stands, wiping dust from her bottom, the girl with the green glasses spots me staring.

I'm greeted with another bubble.

My cheeks scorch red, embarrassed because I've been caught gawking. Instead of burning rubber down the street, I lean forward and rest my arms on my handlebars. The object of my weird fascination kneels and lifts the box. She disappears into the house just as her mom comes back outside.

"Dillon, come on," Herb pleads. "Are you sweet for the girl, or what?"

"Shut up," I say, rolling my bike onto the street. "Let's just go."

"Talk to her," Kyle teases daringly. His dark blonde hair falls in his eyes, covering the gash on his brow from the fall he took earlier today.

I shake my head, trying not to smile. The itch to look back to see if Penelope's come out of her house is stronger than my urge to run Kyle over with my bicycle for messing with me. I don't do either.

"*You* talk to her," I say.

Herb rides onto the sidewalk and jumps off the curb. He lands on his front tire, bouncing twice before setting the rear wheel down and pedaling in circles around me. "Why? You're the one who wants to kiss her."

"I don't wanna kiss her," I say. The sound of the moving truck's doors opening and closing tips my curiosity.

Are they leaving? Is she leaving? Did she forget her gum in the U-Haul?

"Whatever you say," Kyle jokes.

I stay back while my friends race down the road, kicking off our last long ride before the sun sets and the streetlights come on, ending summer vacation. It's been a good one—exploring the woods, building jumps, and swimming in the ocean. Herb, Kyle, and I drove our mothers crazy and gave our street neighborhood a run for its money. We spent every day together, wreaking havoc and causing a ruckus. I'm not ready for it to end, but I want to know more about the girl who showed up out of nowhere.

But I'd rather hide curiosity than deal with crap from my buddies. I press on my neon orange bike pedals, rotating the greasy silver chain, spinning the treaded tires, and push myself forward. Right away my heartbeat quickens, gearing up for the rush I get from using muscles that are beyond tired from riding as fast as I do. The right side of my mouth curves before the left, and the warm wind stings my eyes.

This is where I belong.

Before I get too far, I give in to curiosity and look over my shoulder. Penelope steps out of the house onto the porch in front of a stack of five or six boxes. Instead of picking one up, the girl with Chucks the same color as the sunglasses on her face actually waves at me.

I ride faster.

Girls are weird, even pretty ones who can blow the coolest bubbles I've ever seen.

AFTER EXHAUSTING EVERY OUNCE OF daylight, I start my ride home. Guided by the yellow-orange hue from the streetlamps, I pedal slowly down my street alone. The night's warm, salt-scented and thick, but the burn from the sun is gone. A cat runs across the street in front of me. Someone's sprinklers turn on, misting my face as I roll by. I can hear *Jeopardy!* playing from a television.

I move my bike impossibly slower as I approach my house, stretching out my last few minutes of freedom. The moving truck next door is gone, swapped with a silver Chrysler. I don't see any more boxes on the porch, and there's a wooden plaque above their door that reads *The Finnels'*.

Penelope Finnel.

Pushing my bicycle up the driveway, the security light above the garage powers on, lighting up my entire yard and some of the one next door. At the same time, Penelope's dad walks outside, letting the screen door accidentally slam closed behind him.

He sees me and says, "I'll have to fix that."

"Yeah," I answer, unsure of what else to say. I lean my bike beside my house.

My new neighbor rests against his porch post. He has to be

over six feet tall with dark brown hair and thick eyebrows that make him look scary. Even from here, lit by the security light only, I can see dark veins in his hands and the massive amounts of fur on his arms. Unlike his wife, he's lean. Like his daughter, his skin has been touched by the sun.

"It probably needs a bolt," he grunts. "Like everything else in this damn house."

I think about this for a second and decide to help. "I'm sure my dad has a bolt you can borrow."

Pen's dad looks over at me. His heavy eyebrows come together, like he's squinting. "That's a bright light, boy."

I nod. "Yes, sir."

"I bet it shines right into my room."

I look up at his house. Before tonight, every window was dark. Now they all glow, and even though the curtains are closed, I see a few shadows pass by. I wonder which room is hers.

I hope it's the one across from mine.

"I can't have that light shining in my room, boy," Pen's dad says in a deep voice. "Some of us have to be up early."

"It only turns on when people walk past it," I answer. I stick my nervous-sweating hands into my pockets.

"What about animals?" he asks.

"We don't have any animals, sir," I reply.

Mr. Finnel laughs loudly, booming amusement into

the sticky night air. "I mean raccoons, kid. Cats, stray dogs, possums ... Will cats, stray dogs, or possums turn on the light?"

"Umm..." I start, uncertain if animals will trigger the light. I don't want to lie, but I don't want to talk to him anymore either.

Then the screen door opens and slams shut again, and standing beside the light Nazi is Penelope. Her hair is up now, and from what I can tell, she's not chewing gum anymore. Her knees are dirty, and her shoes are untied. The Discman isn't on her hip, but her green sunglasses are still on her face, even though it's nighttime.

Suddenly, Mr. Finnel's voice scares me out of my own head. "What are you looking at, boy?"

Definitely over six feet tall, the daughter Nazi isn't leaning against the porch post anymore. He's standing in front of his daughter, blocking my view of her.

I straighten my spine and speak too loudly, too quickly. "Nothing!"

He laughs at me again, but his eyebrows are more serious than ever. From behind her father's arm, Penelope peeks out. I can't stop looking at her.

Mr. Finnel's laughter stops. "See something you like, boy? Do you think I'm cute?"

"Wha ... what ... no," I stutter. My heart stops. The guy hates me.

9

Finally, she speaks, soft-spoken and small. "Don't embarrass me, Dad. You're so embarrassing."

The heart Nazi puts his arm over his daughter's shoulders and guides her down the steps to the walkway leading to the Chrysler.

"The boy next door is weird, Pen. Don't talk to him," he warns her with amusement in his voice. "He offered me bolts."

She slaps his arm playfully. "Stop. Let's go get the pizza."

Once they reach the car, Mr. Finnel politely unlocks and opens the car door for the girl who wears sunglasses at night. I stand in the center of my front yard, staring like an idiot. My hands are still in my pockets, and my heart has found its beat again. I should go inside, but I can't get my feet to move.

Then Pen waves at me.

I smile.

The grin Nazi shuts the car door and faces me. His chest almost seems to inflate, and his eyebrows grow angrier. But behind all his boldness, there's a smile he's trying not to show.

"I'm watching you, boy."

ONCE I'VE TAKEN A QUICK shower, I sit at the dinner table with wet hair and shove my mouth full of spaghetti. My sister sits beside me with tiny braids littering her head and lips stained pink from the Blow Pop she had before dinner. Risa's eyes are red, and her smile is lazy. Our parents, who sit across from us, question the skunk smell that oozed from her room earlier.

Risa Decker is this town's very own freak—*slash*—free spirit. With Kool-Aid colored curls and a nose she pierced herself with a sewing needle, my older sister only wears clothes she finds at thrift stores and once tied herself to the tree in the front yard when the city wanted to trim its branches.

She's tried to convince me on multiple occasions that she's Janis Joplin reincarnated, with a flare of Muddy Waters.

Which is weird because Risa was born before he died. I asked Mom.

Risa is five years older than me, but I'm pretty sure I'm smarter.

"It was incense," she vows. Risa starts to laugh but covers it up by coughing.

I roll my eyes and take a bite of garlic bread.

My dad, a small and gentle man, points his fork at his only girl. His glasses sit high on his nose. "It better have been."

Mom, smaller and gentler, nods. "You can be open with us, Risa."

My older sister looks at me and winks. "I know, Ma."

I drink my glass of milk in one gulp.

My dad spins sauce-covered noodles around the fork he was just pointing toward my sibling. "You're Dillon's role model. He's entering a tough age, so the last thing he needs is his sister corrupting him."

Before our father can go off on one of his lectures, Risa brings up the girl I haven't been able to get off my mind.

"Did you see a new family moved in next door? I think their daughter is your age, D."

I nod and swallow hard. "Yeah, I saw."

Mom lights up. "I thought I saw a moving truck parked out front."

"That's right." Dad, having eaten his last bite, sits back in his chair. "I heard the house was purchased."

"Yep," my sister continues. "Rumor is, it's the new football coach at the high school. They moved here from Utah or some shit."

Mom drops her utensil. "Language."

"Anyway," Risa goes on, "you should ask her if she wants to ride bikes with you to school tomorrow, Dillon. She's pretty. Maybe she'll be your girlfriend."

Dad shakes his head, all wannabe-puffy chested and red in the cheeks. He's soft, unlike the bushy-browed man next door.

"He's too young to be dating. Don't you agree, Dawn?"

Mom nods. "Totally agree."

Pushing my empty plate forward, I shove my chair back. The idea of dating was gross to me this morning, but now it kind of makes me mad that my parents think they can tell me what to do. Plus, my sister needs to mind her own business.

"I ride bikes to school with Kyle and Herb. The girl's not pretty. And Mr. Finnel said your security light is too bright, and he's worried possums will set it off," I say, walking away from the table.

I'm at the stairs before my dad, Timothy, the dentist, calls out like he does every night, "Make sure you brush your teeth, Son. You don't want the tooth bugs to bite."

Chapter 2

DILLON

Both of her parents walk her to the door, and after a hush-hush conversation in the hall with Mrs. Alabaster, our eighth-grade teacher, that includes sighing gestures from Penelope and grumpy faces from her dad, the new girl walks into the room. She's hidden behind yellow-framed sunglasses and a peace sign is painted on her face.

Mr. Finnel spots me through the small window in the door and gives me the stink eye before he walks away.

"Everyone, give Penelope Finnel a warm welcome to Castle Rain Middle School," Mrs. Alabaster announces from the front of the class. "This is her first day with us. Please, be kind."

Half-grumbled greetings and whispers about the new girl meet the instructor's request. I make it a point to wave, but stop when Herbert starts making kissing noises from the seat behind me. Shoving my desk back, I smash his fingers between plastic and wood.

"Mr. Decker, please, raise your hand."

I do as I'm told, and every pair of eyes in room twelve turns toward my seat. As blood drains from my elevated hand, numbing the very tips of my fingers, I'm not worried about the funny looks I get from my classmates or the sound of Kyle's laugh two rows over. It's the unsure expression on Pen's face that has me questioning myself.

There's no way she knows I stayed up all night thinking about bubble gum and the green pair of shades she had on way after the sun set.

With her bottom lip between her teeth, Penelope holds her black book bag to her chest and glances in my direction, giving no indication she remembers that I'm her neighbor.

"Take the empty seat beside Dillon." Mrs. Alabaster motions for Pen to move along. "I'm sure he won't mind making your first few days easier until you get the hang of things, right?"

I lower my hand as my cheeks flush. "No, ma'am."

"No, ma'am," Herbert mimics in a teasing tone.

The entire class starts to laugh. Penelope lowers her head,

and long, dark hair curtains her face.

"Enough!" the teacher demands. "Let's not embarrass ourselves and show Miss Finnel that we are not a wild bunch, shall we?"

The silence that fills the room is almost worse than the laughter. The new girl keeps her head low as she takes a few careful steps away from the front of the class. The squeaking sound of her shoes on the tile floor is like nails on a chalkboard, and some of the laughter picks back up when Penelope trips on Pepper Hill's bag she keeps on the floor beside her desk.

"Sorry," Pen whispers. She kicks her foot free.

Pepper scoffs, lifting her ugly pink glitter bag from before the new student's feet. She flips her blonde hair over her shoulder and mumbles, "Watch where you're going, Paula."

"It's Penelope," sudden bravery speaks up. She lifts her chin, uncovering her face.

As if Pen hadn't said a word, the Mean Girl wannabe hangs her book bag across the back of her chair with a grin on her face and turns away from another person she's decided isn't worth her time. Conceited and ugly-hearted, Pepper has this opinion about a lot of people in our class, so it doesn't surprise me she's treating Pen this way.

"What's up with those stupid glasses anyway?" Pepper whispers not so quietly to her friend who's sitting beside her.

With her head held high and her shoulders back, the new girl takes a seat next to mine. She pulls a pen and yellow-covered notebook out of her book bag and doodles on the front of it. As class moves along, she starts drawing stars and smiley faces on her hands. Neither one of us pays attention as Mrs. Alabaster goes over this semester's syllabus.

"I'm going to be an artist when I grow up," Penelope whispers.

She doesn't look directly at me as she colors in a pink heart on the tip of her finger, but I can see her eyes briefly move in my direction from behind the sunglasses she still hasn't taken off.

I don't know her well enough to tell her that her art sucks, so I just smile and say, "That's cool."

Picasso turns in her seat. Dark lenses don't completely black out her eyes, and I can see her long lashes flapping behind them.

"If we're going to be friends, neighbor, there has to be trust. I'm no artist, boy, and you're no liar," she says quietly, not to disrupt the class. "That was a test, and you failed."

My heartbeat picks up, and my palms start to sweat. The right side of my mouth lifts into a smirk, and I can't even help it. "I didn't want to hurt your feelings."

Penelope shrugs and picks up her pen. She scribbles on the empty spaces between her knuckles and says, "That's not possible."

"You don't have feelings?"

The new girl shakes her head. "Not when I'm invisible."

She acts as if I'm the invisible one after that, turning away from me and leaning her head on her palm so that her brown hair serves as a wall between us. Paying attention to anything while Pen ignores me isn't happening. Even when Herb starts to whisper, "Penelope and Dillon sitting in a tree... " I pretend he doesn't exist until he pokes me in the back of the neck with his pencil.

I spin in my blue plastic seat and swat it out of his hand. The orange-yellow number two pencil flies across the room, tip-tapping back and forth from its lead tip to its pink eraser before it finally lands and rolls against some kid's new shoes.

"Dude, that was my only one." Herbert, big for twelve, with dark curls on his head, drops his shoulders and sinks into his seat. "I was just playing with you."

"Wait until I see Mathilda, Herb. You're going to regret it," I say, passing him a pencil. My mom loaded my backpack with more than I'll use this year and next.

My best friend scoffs, shrugging me off like he isn't nervous about the redheaded girl who makes his cheeks blush as bright as her hair. We ran into his crush a few times this summer because we all live on the same street, and he acted as if he didn't hold her hand on the last day of seventh grade before her mom picked her up in a beat-up station wagon.

"I don't even know who you're talking about," the liar says, flipping his new pencil between his large fingers.

"Mathilda Tipp," Kyle pipes up loud enough for everyone to hear, like he might actually believe that Herbert forgot about the girl whom he's liked since he was eleven. "You held her hand last year."

Again, the entire class explodes in laughter. This time it's not at Penelope's expense, and Herbert likes the attention. He soaks it up, throwing crumpled paper balls at Kyle and making up lies about how many girlfriends he had this summer.

"Mathilda who?" he jokes, chuckling with everyone else until Mrs. Alabaster smacks a yardstick against her desk.

As the energy level calms and we're assigned some work to keep us busy, I look over at the one who makes my heart rickety. To my surprise, she's pulled her hair back into a low ponytail and her dark lensed-covered eyes stare right back at me.

"When's your birthday, and why is this town called Castle Rain?" she asks. Pen's hands are entirely covered in scribbled and crappy drawn shapes.

"September twentieth, and because the cliffs by the beach look like castles, and it rains a lot," I say with a nervous itch in my throat.

Pink lips spread into a wide smile, and Penelope says, "That's my birthday, too."

"Seriously?" I ask.

She reaches over and grabs my hand, pulling it across the small aisle between us. Using the marker she drew green leaves on her fingers with, Penelope Finnel paints my thumbnail the color of the trees outside. I don't stop her.

"Yep, my birthday is in six weeks. I'll be thirteen." She colors my next fingernail, and with a sigh, she says, "My mom thinks I should make friends so I can have a party to celebrate becoming an official teenager. Like it's some big deal."

"Being a teenager is going to be awesome," I say.

Pen drops my hand and pulls the hair tie free.

"I meant making friends."

THE GIRL I SHARE A birthday with is alone at lunch, against a tree's trunk in the school's courtyard. I watch her through the dirty cafeteria window where I sit with my pals, who fill every chair around the circular table. In brand new clothes, with wishing-we-could-still-sleep-in eyes, my friends talk about what they all did during summer break loudly. Their laughter is louder.

Turning from Pen, I try to act normal, as if my new neighbor hasn't overtaken my mind. I unpack the all-organic lunch my mom forces me to eat and nod like I know what anyone is talking about.

"You know about *Nipples After Dark*, and you didn't tell us?" Kyle asks, blowing his long blonde bangs out of his blue eyes. "Some friend you are."

Scrunching my eyebrows, I drop my peanut butter and honey sandwich and ask, "What?"

"You nodded when Kyle asked if anyone knows what Skin-a-max is," Mathilda Tipp answers. She eats a small spoonful from her chocolate pudding cup.

My face burns bright, and all my friends look at me with funny smiles as I try to think of some reason—other than the truth—as to why I know about cable's late-night dirty movies. Bad art and bubblegum bubbles cloud my generally good judgment.

Before I admit that I might be obsessed with Penelope, I give them a half-truth.

"I've walked in on Risa watching it."

Kyle pops a fruit snack into his mouth and smiles. "I dig your sister."

Darting the straw into my all-natural juice box, I turn the spotlight away from me by asking my buddy, "How do you know about it?"

He goes on and on for the rest of the lunch hour about being unable to sleep the night before and sneaking into the living room to watch television with the volume all the way down.

"Some nipples are huge and kind of dark-looking," he admits with a proud smirk on his face. "And vaginas are hairy."

TRYING TO FIND MY WAY around school after lunch, the hallway is crowded, and I don't pay attention to what's in front of me as I search for my new class. For one hour a day, all eighth graders switch out of homeroom to an elective course to prepare us for high school. I want to be a doctor when I grow up, and knowing a second language will be helpful, so I chose Spanish. When I got my schedule this morning, I was pissed to see I got cooking instead.

My mom taught me how to use the microwave, so this should be an easy A.

Slowly strolling with my eyes on the numbers above the doors, I literally walk right into Penelope. We bump heads, and the sunglasses that hide her eyes fly from her face to the floor. Some kid kicks them, and they skid to the corner, landing upside down. Grabbing Pen by her arm before she falls to her bottom, I feel her black sweater is still warm from the sun.

"Dang it, Dillon," she says, palming the red mark on her head where our foreheads crashed together.

"Sorry," I mumble, rubbing my own head.

Letting out a heavy sign, Penelope pushes her hair behind her ear and looks at me with unhidden eyes. Brown has never been so dark, eyes have never been so round, and eyelashes have never been so long. Light freckles clutter the bridge of her nose and fade across the roundness of her cheeks. Eyebrows a shade darker than her irises are thicker unconcealed behind sunglasses.

Pretty, I think to myself.

It isn't until Pepper Hill walks between us, knocking Penelope back a step, that the new girl realizes her sunglasses aren't on. She automatically lets her hair fall back into her face, and the smile melts from her lips. Looking back and forth, Pen's breathing noticeably quickens, and the little bit of color in her face turns white. She turns in a circle but doesn't spot what I've figured out she thinks makes her invisible.

"They're right here," I say, quickly walking to the corner where her glasses are.

She snatches them from my hands, slips them back onto her face, and walks into the cooking class without another word. Following her is automatic, and sitting in the chair beside her in class is thoughtless.

"Go away," she groans, safe behind blacked-out lenses. "You're freaking me out."

Scooting my seat closer to hers, I lean in, picking up the faint scent of grass and wind on her clothes. I like the way she talks out of the side of her mouth.

"Do you have a bike?" I ask.

"No," she responds right away, crushing my ego. Pen starts to fill out the questionnaire that has been left on the tables for us to answer. As she's curving the E in Penelope, she looks at me and says, "But I have rollerblades."

Chapter 3

DILLON

With nothing between our houses but yards, Penelope's bedroom is directly across from mine. Her window is covered by plum-colored curtains, and mine by dusty blinds—both of which remain open since we discovered the other looking.

The doorbell rings, and my mom calls me downstairs as I slip on my shoes for school and quickly scrawl on a sheet of paper with a thick black marker. After pressing the message against the cool glass so that Pen can see what I've written, my heartbeat jumps when she appears. Like every morning for the last two weeks, a pair of sunglasses covers her eyes. Today's frames are blue in the shape of stars.

She reads what's on my paper.

Ready?

With a fast nod, the new girl turns and disappears out of her room.

"Dillon, your friends are here, honey," Mom says loudly from the bottom of the stairs. Her voice bounces off the walls.

I grab my backpack from the end of my bed and rush out into the hallway, right behind Risa. Scented like skunk-smelling smoke, which she swears isn't anything illegal, my sister moves out of my way so I can run past her and take the steps down two at a time.

"Give Pen my love," she calls after me with a giggle and a sigh.

Herb's raiding the fridge, and my mom's cleaning something from Kyle's face with a little spit when I rush into the kitchen. It's cool with me that Herbert helps himself to the sugar-free cucumber-lime gelatin I refused to eat for dessert last night, and I dig Kyle's straight spine and lock-kneed posture as my mom licks the back of her thumb to scrub what are obviously freckles from my best friend's chin. But Penelope's waiting for us, so I take my bike's chain and lock from the counter and leave my pals behind.

They're quick to follow.

"Let's ditch the girl," Kyle complains, dropping his skateboard onto the driveway. "She's too slow."

I roll my bike off the front porch and tighten the straps on my backpack before taking a seat on my ride. Herb's already doing a bunny hop off the curb when my neighbor and her parents come out of their house.

"I heard that," Pen jokes. She touches six plastic wheels to concrete and then roller blades in my direction. The dirty red shoes she'll change into when we get to school are tied to her book bag.

"You think my daughter is slow, boy?" Wayne Finnel aka the Dillon Nazi asks. He crosses his hairy arms over his chest and taunts me with creepy eyebrows and bulging shoulder muscles.

I'm the one with a stiff spine and locked knees now.

"It wasn't me," I blurt out.

"Better not have been," he says, flinching when his wife elbows him.

"Leave the Decker kid alone, Wayne," she says with a smile.

Penelope pirouettes from her driveway to mine, twirling so smoothly on blades that her hair sails around her head in a perfect circle. Coming to a full stop in front of my bicycle, her early-morning face lights up behind glasses I wish she would take off.

"Ready?" she asks softly, mimicking the note I wrote.

Beginning in the days when we rode bikes with training wheels, Herb, Kyle, and I have always raced to school. Only a couple of blocks away, it's never taken more than ten minutes to get there. Now that Pen's rolling with us, we've chased the tardy bell almost every day. She likes to take her time, pausing to chase squirrels and smell blossomed roses.

Mom comes out of the house to see us off. She waves toward the house to our left and says, "Good morning, Sonya."

Mrs. Finnel, oversized and over-happy, wags her hand back and forth. Her arm fat swings.

Mr. Finnel flares his nostrils.

"Look, no hands!" Herbert zooms past the house with Mathilda Tipp on his handlebars. Her legs are extended in front of her, and her hands are clutching the rubber grips. Rosy hair swats my friend in the face.

With one last good-bye to the parentals, the rest of us take off behind the daredevil and the redhead. We don't get to the end of the street before Penelope and I are left in the dust. She moves so slowly, I don't bother using my pedals and walk my bike forward while she twirls and dips like a ballerina.

"You can go ahead without me," Pen says.

Instead of trying to convince her for the hundredth time that I don't want to go without her, I change the subject, pushing my bike over the cracks in the pavement.

"Don't tell him I told you this, but Herbert has it bad for Mathilda."

Blue stars slip down Pen's nose, and she pushes them up over eyes I haven't seen again since the first day of school. It's a different style and color of sunglasses every day, never once wearing the same pair twice.

"I can tell," she says.

We stop at the end of the road and look both ways before crossing. The unforgiving late-August sun starts to burn through the gray cloud cover above, shining through full tree branches that line the street, which will be leafless in a couple of months. A yellow-orange school bus full of our classmates drives by, puffing black smoke into the air. As it passes, a cat runs in front of its path, barely clearing the large tires before becoming roadkill.

Penelope screams, grasping onto the front of her sweater where her heart beats beneath. As the school bus continues forward, unaware of its near feline-murdering status, Pen stops, and I stop. The cat is long gone, but judging by the screamer's pale face and heaving shoulders, this isn't about the stray.

I get off my bike and let it crash to its side. Steady on her blades, but breathing like a madwoman, Penelope stares toward the road where the cat almost met its maker. The piercing scream this girl let out still rings in my ears.

"Hey," I say, reaching for her shoulder.

When I touch it, Pen snaps out of the daze and shifts her head my way. The color drains from her face, and her brown eyes are wide under her bluish lenses.

"Are you all right?" I drop my hand.

She takes a deep breath and kind of laughs, shrugging her shoulder. "I was scared."

I stick my hands into my pockets, now noticing how fast my own heart beats. As Penelope chews her fingernails, I curl ten fingers into my palms and keep them tucked in my denim so I don't do the same.

"Where did the cat go?" she asks, mumbling over sore nail beds. "It did make it across, right? Did you see it, Dillon? Do you think it got hit?"

Without thinking, I pull Pen's hand from her mouth and hold it down at her side so she can't make herself bleed anymore. A smear of red coats her bottom lip.

"It ran away," I say. My grip is tight around her trembling wrist. "The cat's alive."

The skating ballerina who quickens my pulse nods her head and swipes the blood from her lip with her tongue. "Okay. Okay."

Since the day she and her family moved into the house beside mine, I've become obsessed with Penelope Finnel.

Purple-orange is her favorite color, even after I told her purple-orange isn't a thing. She ties her left shoe the loop, swoop, and pull way, and the right with bunny ears. Pen opens her bananas from the end, and she eats her eggs with boysenberry syrup.

The girl who wakes up and appears in her window every morning at six-thirty sharp, with insane bedhead, only uses cola-scented lip balm and loves grunge music. She has her mom cut the crusts off her sandwiches, sides first and then the top and bottom. Pen uses the same pink plastic thermos every day at school, even though the cup is cracked. She doesn't blink an eye as fruit punch drips from the bottom, always staining her shirt.

Despite knowing all of that, her bitten raw fingernails are brand new to me. I lift her hand to get a better look at what she's done to herself, rubbing my thumb over her red-hot raw skin and peeling cuticles.

"You're my best friend." Penelope's soft voice forces my eyes from her hands to her blue star-shaped rims. "I'm lucky to have you."

Ditto.

WE SPRINT AFTER THE TARDY bell, skidding to our seats as it rings, and music crackles and buzzes from the speaker box on the wall at the front of the classroom. With smiles on our faces, Pen and I place our hands over our hearts and pledge allegiance to the flag. After morning announcements, we're finally able to sit and catch our breath, and Penelope changes out of her rollerblades.

"You two are pushing it," Mrs. Alabaster says before beginning roll call.

Penelope drives her smile wider at our fed-up instructor and turns her dingy shoelaces into bunny ears. The curve of her lips disappears as she loops, swoops, and pulls the other side, though. An hour into class, when we're supposed to be figuring out what the ratio of something, something, and something is, my best girl hasn't bothered to open her math book. Her head is down on her folded arms, and her hair blankets both.

Mrs. Alabaster notices, but doesn't disrupt sleeping beauty.

Another thirty minutes pass before the bell sounds and we're free for a ten-minute break. Pen doesn't move with the exception of her lungs inhaling and exhaling even breaths. I wait to get up from my seat until every other desk in room twelve is empty.

"Pen," I whisper, reaching out to touch her shoulder.

"Leave her, Mr. Decker," our teacher says. She lifts a piece of chalk and begins jotting down what must be our next task on the board. "Go enjoy your break, young man."

With feet that feel like they're trapped in concrete blocks, I take one slow step at a time away from Penelope. After purposely letting the door slam closed, and before I head down the hallway toward the quad where Herb and Kyle are, I look through the small square window to see if Pen's woken up.

She hasn't, but Mrs. Alabaster put the chalk down and is now rubbing my friend's back. I watch her lips move, but I can't hear or make out what she's saying.

"You coming or what?" Herbert's loud voice echoes from the end of the hallway. "I got candy from the food cart!"

I take a step back from the door, and even though every muscle in my body tightens and struggles to stay right where I am, I turn away and force my legs to move.

Penelope's gone when I get back to class.

"Where is she?" I go cold in the doorway.

Mrs. Alabaster resumes scratching our history assignment on the green chalkboard. The bracelets on her skinny wrist jingle as her hand curves and dips with her scribble-like penmanship.

She doesn't bother to look in my direction and says, "Mrs. Finnel is gone for the day."

My classmates pile in behind me, sugar-rushed and full of energy I don't have. Pepper shoulder checks me on her way to her seat, and Kyle smacks the back of my head. But it's Hebert who stops to mention, "Mathilda saw Pen in the office."

Without thinking, I head out the door to find my girl.

"Dillon, return to your seat," my teacher insists.

I don't turn around, but I don't keep going either. Even with my back toward the classroom, I know every set of eyes is on me. Their silence is awkward, and the hairs on my arms stick straight up as I contemplate my next move.

There's something going on with Penelope, and I know she needs me.

So I run to her.

Only to collide right into her dad.

"Boy," he huffs and puffs. He also has to hold me up straight because his pec muscles almost knocked me out.

I'm a bit woozy.

Shaking my head clear, in the arms of the hairiest man I know, I ask, "Where's Penelope?"

Coach Finnel's dark eyes stare down at me, and I swear he's grinding his teeth behind his tight, mostly-mustache-covered lips.

"You better watch after my girl, boy." His iron-like grip on my arms tightens, and I swear my eyes are going to pop out of my head. "I need to know she's being taken care of when I'm not around."

I nod. "I am, sir."

"Good," he says. "I trust you."

"You can trust me."

He releases me, and as the blood returns to my lower extremities, Mr. Finnel gives me the stink eye I've come to know well.

"Get back to class, boy," he grunts with a slight smile. "Mind your own business. Pen will be there when you get home."

I DON'T WAIT FOR HERB and Kyle after school. With a letter from my teacher to my parents about today's misconduct in my backpack, I jump on my bicycle and ride as fast as I can home.

Unable to breathe and sweating like a cold cup on a scorching summer's day, I leave my bike on the front lawn and sprint into the house and up the stairs to my room.

I run to my window.

Penelope's already at hers.

Hi, her note reads.

She's changed her sunglasses from blue stars to teal triangles.

Hey, I write back.

Yeah, I got it bad. Like Herbert for Mathilda, I've got it very, very bad.

Chapter 4

DILLON

Penelope has scabs on her elbows, a sunburned nose, and she stops every few minutes to pull splinters from her fingers. Her skinny knees are scraped and bloody, and the girl my friends can't stand has pine needles in her morning-messy hair. I want to stop to help her, but...

"She follows us everywhere," Kyle complains. He chops away flimsy, low-lying tree branches with a rusty ax he stole from his dad's garage.

"Yeah, because lover boy over here is sprung," Herb jokes. He slaps the back of my sweaty head and runs past me, kicking a small rock like a soccer ball.

As we explore the wooded area behind our houses, the sun beats down on us from the sky above spruce trees and Douglas firs. Tree trunks and boulders are covered in moss, and the ground is more mud-like than dirt-like. I invited Pen to hang with us because she hasn't been out here yet, but it's obvious I'm the only one who wants her around.

"All I'm saying is she's like a shadow," Kyle says, swinging the dull, discolored steel. "Doesn't she have her own friends?"

"My mom said I can't go out this far," the girl in question yells from fifty feet back. Penelope runs through the scarce, flat ground to close some of the distance between us, but our tail doesn't get far before she stops and grabs her side.

Barefoot, she speed walks through the pain of a side ache but stubs her toe on a half-buried stone on our just-made trail. She cries out, and this time I stop and glance back to make sure she's okay. The moment I do, Kyle and Herb laugh at me.

Squinting through the sunshine, I look up at my friends. They're climbing the side of a small hill I know Penelope won't be able to get up alone. It's covered in overgrown shrubs and weeds; even my boys are having a hard time navigating through it.

Maybe they'll get ticks.

"I'm going to head back with her," I say, pointing over my shoulder with my thumb. "She can't go any farther."

Herb swats some kind of flying insect out of his face, going cross-eyed in the process.

"Quit being a sissy," he says.

I shrug my shoulders and look back at Pen one more time. She has her hand over her eyes, casting a shadow on her face. Red-framed shades cover her eyes, and there's a bead of blood dripping from her knee, down her shin.

"You never hang out with us anymore, Dillon. You're always with the new girl," Kyle points out.

The hill isn't *that* bad, and I invited her to come explore with us, but I didn't tell her to come without shoes. She shouldn't have tagged along if she can't keep up, and it's not my problem if her mom doesn't want her too far from the house. My parents don't care. Kyle's right; I am always with Penelope. Exploring is boy stuff.

"I'm going home!" our follower screams. The sound of annoyance echoes off moss-topped rocks and surrounding trees.

Herb and Kyle laugh again. My stomach starts to ache.

"Good," one of them says loud enough for her to hear.

There's no point in looking back to see if Penelope really goes; I know she does. She's not the kind of girl who throws around empty threats. So when my douche bag pals start back up the hill, I bend down and tuck my jeans into my socks and follow behind them.

I hope they get ticks on their balls.

Over the peak, Herb wants to hunt bears, Kyle wants to hike down to the beach to catch starfish at the base of Castle Cliffs, and I want to go home. But we spend the afternoon among the trees we climb, chase rabbits with the ax, and dig up earthworms to throw at each other like it's summertime again. Our laughter scares birds off branches, and we run, scared out of our minds when we think we hear a snake hiss.

We tell dirty jokes, tease Herb when he admits to accidently touching Mathilda's boob at school the other day, and dare each other to eat mystery berries from a mystery bush. Our faces get dirty, and our hands blister. By the time we head home, we smell like mud and sweat, and Kyle finds a tick on his body.

Unfortunately, it's on his stomach.

"I can't wait until we're in high school," Kyle mentions on our walk back. "Older chicks rock."

"Yeah, because high school girls dig blood-sucking, disease-carrying ticks. Or at least that's what I heard," I tease him.

He scratches the area around his stomach where the body invader burrowed itself into his skin. None of us brought a lighter to burn it off, so he has to wait until he gets home.

"All the babes are going to want me next year," Herb says. Sweat drips his temple. There's a hole in his white T-shirt. "Because I'm buff."

"Too bad you're obsessed with the redhead," Kyle says, talking about Mathilda.

They go back and forth, arguing over who has better muscles and, "What did her boob feel like exactly?"

Meanwhile, my thoughts are spent on the girl who ran out of here screaming. Letting her walk home alone was stupid, and I shouldn't have let these idiots make me feel bad about inviting her. Penelope is the coolest girl I know, and our friendship is … awesome. She's never screamed at me like she did today. I hope I didn't ruin what we have.

Herb tells us he thinks Mathilda stuffs her bra with socks when we clear the woods and step into my backyard. Wayne's outside with his shirt off—probably letting his chest hair breathe—mowing his lawn. When he spots us, he cuts the mower's engine and stares at me.

I walk around the other side of the house to avoid him.

And his hairy body.

The mower starts back up.

"I gotta go home before I get Lyme disease. You coming?" Kyle asks. He's already walking down the sidewalk toward the end of the street where his house is.

"I'm in," Herb says, following behind him.

As awesome as watching ticks burn is, there's someone I owe an apology to.

"Your pants look really special stuffed in your socks like that, D," Risa says. Her witty tone punches me right in the gut.

Pinching my lips together, I exhale slowly and turn around. My sister and Penelope are on the porch, sitting on the top step side-by-side. The setting sun paints their skin as well as the sky in pinks, oranges, and purples, and casts shadows at their shoeless feet. Their skin looks tacky, and each of them has messy buns on top of their heads.

Risa has Pen's sunglasses on.

Penelope digs at me with bare eyes, and it makes the guilt burn so much hotter.

"I'm sorry," I say with a smile I should smack off my own face.

"You're a real jerk for letting her walk home alone," Risa replies. She has a sucker at the corner of her mouth and a mole drawn on her face to look like Madonna. "She could have got lost, genius."

Slowly stepping closer to the house, I hold my hands up in surrender. Pen looks away from me, setting her elbows on her knees and leaning the side of her face in her palm. A piece of hair falls in her eyes.

"Pen," I say, approaching the steps. The crisp scent of sprinkler water swirls in the air around us, and overspray from our other neighbor's irrigation system lightly mists my hot skin.

There's space beside her to sit, but the pang in the pit of my stomach warns me not to.

"Don't worry. I kept your girlfriend company today." My sister smiles. The gap between her two front teeth seems smaller with the oversized sunglasses on her face.

Penelope elbows *like a virgin* in the side, and the tips of her ears turn pink with embarrassment. Her embarrassment becomes my awkwardness, because is it that bad to be called my girlfriend?

Not that she is.

Not that she will ever be.

I take a step back and puff my chest out like I'm tough or something and say, "I don't know why you're mad. You're the one who couldn't keep up."

Her brown eyes snap in my direction, and her pink-tipped ears turn red. Penelope opens her mouth to say something, but bites her teeth together and balls her little hands into fists. Eyebrows that are much thinner than her father's scowl just the same.

Risa shakes her head with a slight curve at the corner of her lips.

"Boys are so stupid!" she says loudly, smacking her knee. "Mom and Dad think you're all gifted, with your awesome grades and ambitious goals. But you're nothing but a typical, stupid boy."

I probably look like a goldfish as my mouth opens and closes, missing a response. The beat in my chest skyrockets, and nervousness crawls up my spine with its skeleton-like fingers.

Benedict Arnold slides her traitorous arm over Penelope's sunburned shoulders and glows with pride.

"Swear off boys, Penelope. Do yourself a favor and stay away from evil, soul-sucking penises." Her smile slowly disappears, and she lowers Pen's red sunglasses and hands them back over to their owner.

There's no mistaking the crazy brewing behind my older sister's eyes. The whites get whiter, the greens greener, and the pupils pupiler. Her grunge rocker boyfriend must have dumped her again.

"Especially if they're in a band," she practically yells.

Penelope stands. I back off some more.

"Because you're all the same, you insensitive pricks!" Risa points her finger at me.

Laughter bubbles from my lungs. I can't help it. This girl surely has a future in theater.

"I like tour buses," she says, now pointing to herself. "I know all the lyrics to the songs!"

"Run," I mouth to Pen.

She listens.

Following right behind her, as I cross the Finnels' front lawn, the familiar sound of oncoming water rushes into my ears and stops me cold. Penelope's smart enough to keep going and clears her porch when eight sprinkler heads pop out of the ground. I'm trapped in the middle of the yard when ice cold water explodes into the air, shooting in my direction.

I hear his evil laughter before I spot Wayne beside the water valve with his arms crossed over his chest.

No doubt there's a smile beneath his mustache.

A SKUNK SMELL OOZES FROM Risa's room and plugs the slender hallway with its scent, and music blasts from her stereo speakers with such heavy bass the house vibrates. My mom's at Risa's door, alternating between turning the locked handle and smacking the door with her palm. Dad's behind her, pushing his glasses up his nose and sighing heavily.

"Let me in, sunshine. We can talk about it," Mom says in a tone as calm as the summer's sea.

"Do us a favor, sweetheart. Put the incense out before the neighbors smell it," my father adds.

With wet hair and soap-scented skin, I walk past my family toward my bedroom at the end of the hall.

"There's other fish in the sea, Risa!" Mom yells over a drum solo. "Jeremy smelled like gasoline and patchouli oil."

Strong rifts and dirty guitar playing stop, replaced by my sister's hysterical voice.

"He smelled like love!"

"You're only seventeen. What do you know about love?" the dentist slightly raises his voice. His glasses slide down the bridge of his pointy nose.

"I know what Jeremy and I had was love," Risa cries out. "Sick, sick love."

Dad purses his lips and scratches the side of his head. "I thought his name was Elvis?"

Mom's eyes widen, and she shakes her head. "That was the last boyfriend, Tim."

My father shrugs his shoulder.

"You don't even know me!" Risa shrieks before the music rattles the house again.

Locked safely behind four walls, I drop my dirty clothes beside my dresser and head over to the window. The sun is down, leaving the sky smeared in shades of purples and blues and the sidewalks lit silver by moonlight. As I lift a single pane of glass, cool air pushes through my holey screen into my room, stinging skin that's been burned by the day.

Penelope's purple drapes are closed, but orange light glows

between and around the two halves. The darkened shape of her body passes by a few times, getting my hopes up, but after thirty minutes, I'm nothing more than the weird kid next door staring at the side of her house.

Grabbing my notebook and marker from my nightstand, I slip on some shoes and leave my room. My parents are still negotiating with Risa, so I'm able to sneak past them and out of the house without issue. Guided by flickering streetlights, I scribble out the message Penelope wouldn't open the curtains to read and climb the steps to my best friend's front door. I hold the message over my rocking heart and knock.

"Do you have no respect for bedtimes, boy?" Wayne answers.

The urge to scribble all over his face with black Sharpie for turning the sprinklers on earlier is strong. My drawing hand twitches, but I stick to the plan and ask for Pen.

Heavy-footed and grumbling under his breath about bad intentions and reefer smoking sisters, the water Nazi climbs the stairs to his daughter's room.

"That freak boy is here," he says. "I don't want you hanging out with him unless an adult is around, and I don't mean the Deckers' either."

"Dad," Pen whines. "Knock it off."

"He doesn't even know how to spell. You're better than

him," he continues.

I turn my sign around and realize in the hurry I was in to save my friendship, I misspelled a word. I'm quick to scratch it out and squeeze the correct spelling on the side just as Penelope appears at the top of the stairs.

I'M SORRY 4 ~~EGNORING~~ IGNORING YOU.

A smile that fights the moon for brilliance spreads across her sun-kissed face, and she takes the stairs two at a time until we're face-to-face.

Penelope pushes my shoulder playfully and says, "Boys are so stupid."

Chapter 5

PENELOPE

"**D**on't panic. Don't panic. Don't freak out," I whisper to myself. My ankles are spread apart, my underwear is around my calves, and my knees are pressed together.

With only a week before my thirteenth birthday, my mom warned me this might happen soon.

"You're a late bloomer, Pen. But it happens to every single girl in the world," she said. "It's natural. It means you're a woman."

Mom handed me a box of Kotex and told me to carry them around in my backpack.

"Better safe than bloody," she said.

I kicked them under my bed instead. There was no way I was bringing pads to school. Pepper Hill already gives me this *you're-nothing-but-a-weirdo* look, and I didn't want my looming womanhood to scare Dillon off. He hasn't ignored me since the day he ignored me, and I'd like to keep it that way.

Dad went all, the Father, the Son, and the Holy Spirit on me when he walked in on Mom and me having *the talk.* I can only imagine what my only friend would do.

I also expected there to be some kind of warning sign that this was coming. It never dawned on me that my flow would show up in the middle of class, in the middle of day, in the middle of the sentence I was writing for our English work.

There's blood on my jeans, and now I don't know what to do.

My eyes burn as they fill with tears, and my jaw aches. Heaviness in my chest that's been mostly tolerable lately flares up and slowly splinters outward. I feel its weight on my shoulders and its stiffness in the bend of my elbows. My fingers curl into a fist, and my too-long nails dig into my thin skin.

Anxiety that won't be swallowed scratches at my throat, and darkness that's troubled me my entire life presses down on my head.

"Why can't I be normal?" I ask myself as hot sorrow spills down my heated cheeks.

There's no hiding behind my sunglasses this time.

Licking salty tears from my lips, I yank itchy toilet paper from the roll and wrap it around my bloodied underwear. After cleaning myself as much as I possibly can, I pull up my jeans and unlock the door.

There's no telling how long it's been since I ran out of class, and Mrs. Alabaster hasn't sent anyone after me, but I can't stay in here for the rest of the day. My book bag is at my desk, and I don't have a sweater to tie around my waist.

Lacing my fingers together under my bottom, I tiptoe down the empty hallway toward my classroom. I don't know how long I have until the next bell rings for break, but I hope it's not anytime soon. There will be no surviving this humiliation.

Approaching room twelve, I stand on my tiptoes and look through the small window in the door instead of walking inside. I'm able to take a normal breath when I see Dillon in his seat beside my empty one. His pencil is down, and his head is turned toward the row of windows along the wall. Sunshine brightens his almost blonde hair.

"Look at me," I say quietly. "Look this way, Dillon."

Best friend telepathy doesn't work no matter how badly I wish it would. I carefully tap the tip of my finger against the thick glass, but the only person who looks up is Herbert.

My heart's beat stops.

Instead of pointing and announcing to the class, "Penelope started her period," like I think he will, my best boy's best pal quietly gets up from his seat and walks over to Dillon. He then whispers into his ear and nods his head in my direction.

My heart beats, beats, beats.

My hands tremble as I think, *Please, come save me.*

Dillon isn't so quiet about getting up. He scoots his chair back, slamming it into the desk behind his. Thoughtfulness grabs his backpack and mine, and without another word, and with his eyes only on mine, he walks past the teacher's desk toward the door.

I take a few steps back so I don't get hit, and when he's standing in front of me, I fall completely into him.

No mud and puppy breath today.

"Where were you?" he asks, rubbing his hand up and down my back.

My cheeks burn, and beneath my orange lenses, my tears free-fall. It kills me to admit what's going on, but I spill lessons learned about womanhood and Kotex and maturity. I tell him about ruined blue jeans and scratchy toilet paper.

"It happens to every girl in the world," I say like my mom did.

My lip quivers.

Dillon laughs.

"I have an older sister, Pen," he says. The boy next door opens his backpack and pulls out a gray hoodie. "I know what a period is."

"I need to go home," I say, lowering my head.

He tilts my chin up and hands me his sweatshirt. "Then let's go."

The good thing about living in a small town is that everybody knows everyone. Dillon and I stop by the office, repeat the tale of my sudden development, and ask for permission to leave early. The principal is able to get ahold of my dad at the high school, who gives him a message to pass to Dillon.

"Boy!" our principal does his best, deep-voiced impersonation of my father.

We wait for the rest of the message, but Principal Snider doesn't say more.

"That's it," he confirms and waves us away. "Get on home."

The one-word memo is enough to keep Dillon on his toes. On the walk home, he doesn't let me get too close to the curb, steps onto the street first after looking both ways three times, and asks me every few feet how I feel.

It's an overprotectiveness that reminds me so much of the man who scared this kid into submission with one syllable. It's a thought that calms the splintering inside me.

"You don't have to stay," I say, opening the front door to

my house. It's never locked.

At the bottom of the porch, Dillon stands with his hands in his pockets. The entire world is orange because of the sunglasses I have covering my eyes, but even I can see how pink the flush on his cheeks is.

"Is your mom here?" he asks, taking one step up.

"Probably not. She volunteers at the senior center until I get out of school."

"I'll stay then," he says right away. "I promised your dad I'd watch over you."

Not sure when "boy" translated into "watch over her," but there's no fighting the smile that spreads across my face.

He follows me upstairs to my room and waits outside my door for a heartbeat before stepping inside. Dillon can see inside my space from his window, but he's never actually been here. I've never had a boy in my room before.

"I should probably…" I start, too shy to continue.

His hand goes right into his blondish hair, pushing the longer stands away from his perfect forehead. With his face shown completely, the nervousness in his sharp eyes and straight lips is on full effect. Edginess blows air out of his lungs, and green eyes that keep me awake some nights roam around my room.

"Do you, like, need help?" he asks, clearing his throat.

"Umm … no," I say, wishing a hole would open beneath

my feet and swallow me.

The tips of his ears are cherry red.

"When Risa … had her—" He stops and stares at the band poster above my bed. "My mom had to help her, you know."

I shake my head.

Dillon takes a breath so big his shoulders heave up and then fall down. "She read the directions to her or something. I can read."

Swallow. Me. Now.

My reader squeezes his eyes shut and takes another deep breath. "I mean, I can read the directions to you. Or I can run home to see if my sister's there."

I'm using this boy's hoodie to hide a period bloodstain on my jeans, and now he's in my room offering to read the Kotex directions to me. This can't possibly get any more embarrassing, and I've never done this before. So instead of jumping out the window to end this crazy life, I reach under my bed for the box I refused to take to school and toss it to him.

WE DON'T LOOK EACH OTHER in the eye for the rest of the week, but it's not because I don't want to.

It's because I should be careful what I wish for.

Chapter 6

DILLON

I step onto the Finnels' porch and stand on their welcome mat before knocking on the yellow door.

"Pen's not feeling well, sweetie," has been Sonya's lie to me every morning since Monday. She'll force a smile on her round face. "Girl stuff."

There's a lot I'm unsure about, but I have a teenage sister who, for one week a month, eats ice cream by the gallon and snaps at me with her teeth if I try to get a spoonful. A lot more smoke than usual also seeps out from beneath her door. Sometimes I wonder if she's possessed with all the crying, and whining, and "You don't know how it feels to be me!" But not even Risa's missed four days of school because of *girl stuff.*

Today Wayne greets me. There's no doubt he's hairier than the last time I saw him.

"What do you want, boy?" His overgrown mustache moves as he speaks. The scent of brewing coffee from their kitchen kicks me in the stomach, causing it to growl.

I straighten my posture and talk clearly, forgetting about hunger pains and enormous arm muscles.

"I'm here to walk Penelope to school," I say.

Mr. Finnel tries to close the door in my face, but Mrs. Finnel shouts from inside the house, "Wayne, be nice to the Decker kid!"

Bigfoot leans against the doorframe and crosses his huge arms over his bigger chest. Thick fur is packed tightly under his thin cotton Castle Rain Varsity Football T-shirt and sticks out around his neck. Dark eyes stare down at me below shaggy eyebrows, and I swear I hear his knuckles crack under his hairy fingers.

"No," he says.

Rubbing the back of my neck, I consider taking my chances against Gigantor to get to his daughter. I'm probably faster than he is, and it'll be worth it, if I can actually find her. Not only has she not been at school, she hasn't popped up at her window either. At this point, there's not anything I wouldn't run through for her.

Mr. Finnel laughs as if he can read my mind.

"She's going to school today, boy. I'm driving her."

My heartbeat picks up, my palms warm, and a tingling pressure builds behind my ribs.

I'll see Pen today, but not as soon as I had hoped.

"I can wait for her if she's not ready," I say, lifting to the top of my feet to get a better look into the house. I've grown a couple of inches since the beginning of the school year, but I need to grow a few more to be as tall as the razor Nazi.

Bushy eyebrows come together, and Wayne takes a step toward me. I take three back.

"Are you trying to get between me and my daughter, boy? Is that what you're doing?"

Afraid to look like a coward in front of the largest human being I know, I square up, but fall short when my words get stuck in my throat.

When I do answer, my voice squeaks.

"No!" I say like a thirteen-year-old boy going through puberty. As of today, that is exactly what I am.

Sasquatch's laugh rocks the entire block, and it sucks because it's at my expense. I'm afraid to say another word in case my voice rattles again, so I stand still and take it.

"She'll meet you there, kid," he says before shutting the

door.

I can still hear him laughing.

ROGER MORRIS TALKS WITHOUT BREATHING.

"You're best friends with Penelope, right? She's kind of strange, right? A little different. A little peculiar. Does she talk to you? She doesn't talk to me. I offered her a cookie once. She still didn't talk to me. Took the cookie, though."

I hardly know the kid, but I'll punch him in his stupid mouth if he says one more bad thing about Pen.

"What's up with the glasses?" he asks, kicking a rock off the curb into the school parking lot. "Why does she get to wear sunglasses in class when the rest of us can't?"

Cars line up inside the U-shaped student drop-off zone in front of the school. As one car drives out, another drives in. The silver Chrysler I'm waiting for hasn't appeared yet, and there are only a few minutes left before we have to be in our seats.

"Her glasses are cool," I say, stretching my neck to see which car arrives next.

It's Penelope.

"They're kind of cool," Roger says. He picks up his backpack from the ground and throws it over his shoulder.

"But she's still weird."

I turn around to knock this kid off his block when I hear Wayne Finnel's voice call my name. There's still a touch of laughter in his tone.

"Get over here, boy," he orders. I swear his mustache winks at me.

I walk around the front of his car, looking at Pen through the windshield as I close the distance between her father and me. The girl with the red heart-shaped glasses on is small, sitting in the front seat with her book bag held against her chest.

Yeti is posted halfway out of his car, with one arm on the roof and the other on door.

"Listen here, boy, and you better listen good," he says, drawing me in close with the magic of his talking, winking mustache. "I want you to make sure my daughter smiles today, got it? Are you listening, boy? Am I making myself clear?"

I nod.

"I want a number at the end of the day, and for every smile, I'll give you one of these." Coach Finnel holds up a snack-sized pack of peanut M&M's. "Have you ever had one of these, boy? They're phenomenal. They're my favorite."

I duck down low enough to see inside the car. "Why is she sad?"

The driver behind the Chrysler honks his horn. Wayne

turns the power of his facial hair on them, and the honker slowly maneuvers his vehicle around us without as much as a glance in our direction.

"It's your birthday today, too?" the horn Nazi asks.

"Yes, sir," I answer.

He nods in acceptance, and we each look over when the passenger door finally opens, and the girl we'd both run through anything to get to exits the car. I'm shocked by her thinner, less-cared-for appearance. Penelope is no try-hard like Pepper, but the shine is gone from her hair, and the color has disappeared from her face. It's only been four days since I saw her last.

She doesn't move as quickly, breathe as surely—her mood is less than birthday great.

My feet carry me right to her.

"Hey, Pen," I say, bending at my knees to get a better look at her hollow-looking face.

"Hey, Dillon," she answers. It's the first time I've heard her voice since she thanked me for reading the directions to her through the bathroom door.

Birthday sadness presses her lips together and reaches up to wipe her eyes from under her sunglasses, but the tear slides down her cheek first.

"Why are you crying?" I ask. "Did someone forget your birthday?"

She shakes her head.

"I got you a present," I say, digging into my front pocket.

They're a little linty, a little sticky, a little warm, but their colors reminded me of her glasses.

"Marbles," she says as they roll from my hand to hers. The right side of her mouth curls up. "I love them."

There's one more marble stuck to a piece of butterscotch I was sucking on earlier. I spit on it, rub it on the front of my shirt, and roll it over.

It's bright red like the color of her shades.

"I didn't get you anything," Pen mentions sadly.

"That's okay."

"No, it's not," she says, lifting her hand to her face. "Have these."

Unhappiness passes me her sunglasses, and I get to look into her cheerless eyes all day.

ONE CAKE. TWO FAMILIES. THIRTEEN CANDLES.

The lights are off, and the air is end-of-the-summer-season still. While our families gather around Pen and me in her kitchen, we're posed in front of the chocolate frosted cake with both of our names written across the top in red icing. There's one melting stick of wax for each year of our lives, casting everyone's shadows against the white walls. Penelope's pink lenses reflect the yellow-orange flame.

She blushes under the tune of our birthday song, holding her fingers in her ears to pretend she can't hear.

"La, la, la, la," she says with a smile I should get two snack packs for.

Herbert, who's standing right behind Sonya, mouths "Pussy" when I make the mistake of looking away from the birthday girl and in his direction.

"Suck my—" I start to mouth back when Coach Finnel steps in my line of sight, shutting me up. My mouth snaps closed, and I sink into my wooden chair.

As our loved ones belt out the end of the jingle, and Kyle adds, "And many more, on channel four," the birthday Nazi points the middle and pointer fingers from his right hand toward his eyes before aiming the same fingers at me.

"I'm watching you," he lips.

My eyes widen, and I scoot closer to the girl who's only five hours older than me.

"Make a wish," Penelope's mother says. She licks chocolate from the spatula she used to frost the cake.

There's some stuck to the corner of her mouth.

"You can have this wish," I say, carefully pushing the cake

closer to Penelope.

She shakes her head, smiling a smile that spreads from cheek to cheek. "I'll take next year's wish."

Before the white-and-blue striped candles melt completely, I inhale a deep breath and make my request.

I wish that Pen would take her sunglasses off around me—always.

The candles don't stand a chance against the will of my wish. When all thirteen flames are out and we're left in the dark room turned smoky, Mr. Finnel is the first to speak.

"I can't believe you took the wish, boy."

SEPTEMBER AND OCTOBER THANKFULLY FALL into November, and December merrily arrives. One year drops into another, and come January, Castle Rain lives up to its name. It feels like the downpour will never end. Washington's covered by a thick layer of gray clouds, our streets flood, and the ocean overflows onto the beach.

Nothing stands a chance against the constant rainstorm. My shoes and socks are always wet. My hair never dries. My fingers prune. Water leaks from the roof and sometimes seeps through cracks around the windows. Dad's placed pots on top of the refrigerator and in the hallways to capture the drip, drip, drops. He's patched a few holes in the house, but another replaces it just as fast.

"Can you find your way to school today, D?" Risa walks into my room without knocking and asks.

I look away from Penelope's curtain-covered window and turn toward my sister. Sopping wet rainbow hair dribbles color-tinted water to her feet. Soaked clothes stick to her skinny body, and black mascara is smeared all around her eyes.

"What happened to you?" I laugh, pulling my beanie over my head.

"The Beetle won't start. I tried to fix it, but I think I made it worse." She shrugs, wringing her hair on my carpet.

"Is it raining?"

She shakes her head. "No, but it's wetter than a whore's panties."

I kick my sister a towel from the floor and grab my backpack before passing her at my bedroom door. She smells like dank grass and smoke, and after getting a closer look, Risa's eyes are bloodshot, and the smile on her lips is lopsided.

"I'll ride my bike," I utter.

Under the influence holds up two fingers and replies, "Peace."

Waterlogged grass squishes under my shoes as I walk

through my lawn over to Penelope's. My breath turns white with each exhale, and the pulse inside my chest speeds up when I approach the front door.

Since the week of our thirteenth birthday, I have lost count of the amount of days Pen's seat has sat empty in class.

The weather keeps us from riding to school on bikes and blades, like we do when the sun's out, so most days I don't know if Pen's going to show up until the pledge starts and she's not at my side. Other mornings, like today, when the rain stops long enough for me to make it onto her porch, I'm told excuse after excuse.

"She's got a touch of the flu," Sonya lies.

"Pen has a doctor's appointment today, honey."

"My little girl's staying home, but will you get her homework?" she's said with a forced smile.

I cross my fingers behind my back and knock.

Mrs. Finnel opens the door, oversized in king-sized sweats and a sweatshirt. The normal fake grin she usually greets me with is missing, and the bags under her eyes are dark enough to pass as bruises.

Sonya exhales heavily and drops her shoulders before moving to the side to let me inside the house.

"Maybe you can get her out of bed, Dillon," she says with exhaustion in her voice. "Because nothing we do is working."

I pull the beanie off my head and stand at the bottom of the stairs, unsure of what to do. Penelope's mother closes the door with her foot, shutting out the dim natural light. The house is closed up, stuffy with wet-scented air blowing out of the heater vents. With the exception of the chugging coffee maker, it's silent.

"You can go up there," Mrs. Finnel says. She walks toward the kitchen. "Wayne isn't here, sweetie."

The man of the house made his rules very clear to me when I started to come over on a regular basis: Stay out of Penelope's bedroom, and don't ever touch my television control.

"I'll know if you do, boy. I'm always watching," he said.

Ape-man doesn't know about the first time I was in Pen's room, and Sonya keeps him in the dark about the few times she's let the rule slide. The door has to stay open, and we only listen to music and flip through *Rolling Stone* magazines — it's blameless.

This feels different.

The door is cracked, and I can see the shape of her body under a pile of blankets on the bed before I step into her bedroom. The purple curtains that hang over her window are tightly closed, and Pen's room is nearly pitch-black.

A part of me wants to tear the drapes down entirely for keeping me from this girl, but I only open them enough to let some gray light in.

"Penelope," I whisper from the edge of her bed.

Mostly hidden deep beneath quilts and sheets, deep-set in a cotton pillow, she inhales and exhales soundlessly, and there's dark hair fanned across her face. Her chocolate-covered eyes move behind her thin, blue-veined lids, and the roundness of her cheeks flush pink.

"It's time to get up," I say a little louder.

The laziest girl in the world rolls to her side but doesn't wake up.

I tug the blankets away from her face, exposing the length of her throat and the tops of her bare shoulders. More of Pen's long hair lies across her prominent collarbones, and her rosy lips part.

A flash of heat forces me to take a step back.

Instead of touching her again, I kick the bed. "Get up," I say boldly. "We're going to be late for school."

Nothing.

"Pen."

"Pen."

"Penelope!"

She snores.

I kick.

Her forearm slumps above her head.

She snores again.

"Please, wake up," I finally beg, taking a chance and touching her side.

Long eyelashes flicker against her lightly freckled cheeks, so I shake sleeping beauty. Softly at first, but with more force once her eyes strain to open. Grogginess triumphs, and then not even rocking this girl makes a difference.

Taking a step back, I spot a glass of water on her nightstand and consider dumping it onto her face when Pen pulls the blankets over her head. Ten little, red-painted toes show at the end of her mattress, curling in before they relax. Small ankles and exposed calves make me so nervous I almost run out of the room. Instead, I pull all the blankets off the heaviest sleeper I know.

She's sleep lines and pink panties.

I squeeze my eyes so tightly shut I may never open them again. Blind and searching for a way to escape, I hold my hands out in front of me and quickly shuffle toward where I think the door is. My shoe kicks the bedframe, and I trip over my backpack.

She's soft-spoken and curious.

"Dillon, what are you doing?" Penelope asks. There's a drop of laughter in her sleepy tone.

Sonya said the room Nazi isn't home, but it would be just

my luck that Wayne would show up while I'm in his daughter's room when she's in nothing but a sleep gown and underwear. While most of me wants to see her face because it's been a few days, the tiny part that wants to live shoves me toward the door.

She's begging and sad-sounding.

"Don't leave me," Pen says tenderly.

I stop, but don't turn around. I don't open my eyes.

"I had a dream that you were here," she says. "Then some soulless jerk pulled all the blankets off me, and it was you."

"You haven't been at school," I say in the dark.

The springs in her mattress bounce and squeak, and I listen to her yawn.

"You can turn around," she says.

Penelope sits on the edge of the bed; her bare feet dangle an inch above the carpet. She has tangled hair and dark circles under eyes that are almost as shady as the ones below her mom's. The pale-yellow nightie covers every inch of skin to her knees, and this girl is slouched, like she's about to collapse back into dreamland.

"I came to walk you to school," I say.

Drowsiness yawns again as she stretches her long arms above her head, but then she stands to her feet. My nervous heart pounds against the inside of my chest.

"Throw me those jeans," Penelope says. She points to the

pile of clothes on the floor beside the door.

I toss the faded denim to her and turn around as she slips them up her legs.

"I need a shirt and a hoodie," she says. The zip of her zipper zipping makes me nervous all over again.

Passing her whatever from the pile, I say a quick prayer to the man above when she goes into her closet to change. While she's in there, I straighten out her bed and fluff the pillows. My mouth feels like it's full of cotton, so I drink the glass of stale water I almost used to wake Pen with in one gulp.

Penelope comes out of the closet with the hoodie on, but with the actual hood tucked in. Her hair is stuck inside with it, and the hoodie's string is pulled longer on one side than the other. Expressionless with her palm over where her heart beats, this impossible girl sits on the bed and looks up at me with helpless eyes and sweat above her lip.

"I don't know if I can go," she says. "You have no idea how hard it was to get dressed."

I set the glass down and ask, "What's the matter?"

She's shrugging shoulders and tight lips.

Searching around the room for anything that might help, my eyes land on the most obvious answer. She's surrounded by the things that make everything better, but they're out of reach from the bed I have a feeling she hasn't really left since the last time I saw her.

Red frames fit snugly above her ears and on the bridge of her nose, and black lenses cover her glossy eyes. I pull her long hair out of her hoodie and set the hood straight. After correcting the strings, I straighten the sleeves and pull it away from her neck so she can breathe.

"Better?" I ask.

This girl wipes sweat from her face with the back of her hand and nods.

Her hair is bedhead knotted, and if it were the weekend and we were only headed to the beach or for a hike in the woods, I wouldn't mention it. But I don't want Pepper to have more reasons to make fun of her, and Penelope's still a girl. She cares about how she looks.

I think.

While she puts her socks and shoes on, I sit behind Pen in bed and brush the tangles out of her hair.

"You better not tell Herb and Kyle I'm doing this," I say, pushing the bristles through her wavy strands.

Her laugh is small, but it makes me feel ten feet tall.

HER HAIR SEEMS FLUFFY, BUT she doesn't look in the mirror at all while she brushes her teeth. Slowly fading sleep lines mark the side of her face, and dirty untied shoelaces almost trip her as she walks.

I follow her down the stairs with our backpacks over my shoulder. Pen holds on to the rail with both hands, stopping every couple of steps like this is actually painful for her. She glances up at me, and I can see her dark, wide eyes over the red rims of her sunglasses.

There's something wrong with this girl, but I don't know what it is.

"Baby, you're out of bed." Sonya, who was staring out into space as we came down the stairs, slowly lowers her coffee mug.

She carries her large body around the counter and approaches us before bringing Penelope into her arms. Her daughter lays her head on her mother's shoulder and exhales softly. I stand back, unsure of what to do, while Sonya soothes her only child by running her hand down the length of her fuzzy hair.

Mrs. Finnel turns her face into the side of sorrow's head and whispers, "Are you sure you want to go to school today?"

Pen nods.

Sonya takes a deep breath and stands straight, pushing her daughter out in arm's length. They go back and forth about the need for breakfast, and what about lunch? The older of the two offers to drive, but Penelope wants to walk.

As Pen and I rush out the front door, she refuses instant oatmeal and a bruised banana.

"Mom, I don't want anything. I just want to get to school," she insists, closing the door behind us.

The dim outside light doesn't bring much out in Pen's complexion. She's almost as gray as the dense clouds hovering above the tops of trees, and moisture in the air makes her fluffy hair frizzy.

She's reaching for her rollerblades when a drop of rain plummets from above and lands on my forehead; smaller ones mist my face.

"Crap," Pen starts. "It's going to rain again."

"The sidewalks are under water. You shouldn't blade anyway," I say, wiping away raindrops from my face.

She shoves her sunglasses to the top of her head and meets my eyes with large pupils and tears that are about to fall heavier than the rainstorm. With her palm on her forehead, Penelope rests against the house and says, "I'm not really up for a ride in the car, Dillon. Maybe I should stay home."

"Wait here," I say, running through the sloshy lawns, past

my sister's mint green Volkswagen, and up my front porch where my bicycle is posted against the rail.

Rubber tires bounce down wooden steps and roll across puddles and wet grass. A light sprinkle becomes a heavy drizzle in the minute it takes me to ride my bike over to Penelope. I have to get this girl out of here before Sonya realizes the sky is about to open.

I'm not up for a ride in the car either.

"Jump on," I say with my bike between my legs. My backpack sits high on my shoulders.

Penelope lets her red shades fall back over her eyes, and she actually smiles. "Where do I sit?"

"Right here." I pat the handlebars.

"Are you sure?" she asks. Pen swings her book bag over her shoulder and walks this way.

I keep the bike steady as my neighbor steps onto my front tire and sits on the chrome handlebars. Her bag hits me in the face, and the sudden weight change wobbles both of us. My passenger screams, leaning too far to the right, and then too far to the left.

"Stay straight." I laugh, standing to give us a push-start.

Beside mine, her knuckles turn white from gripping the bar so tightly. As we pick up speed, Penelope's hair tickles my face, and the drizzle turned heavy shower soaks our clothes and falls into our eyes.

She's loud laughter and pretty smiles.

"Go faster, Dillon. Faster!" she shouts as we race down the street.

We run over pond-like puddles, washed-up sticks and leaves, and the back tire kicks up wet dirt and small rocks. The bottoms of my shoes press hard into my bicycle pedals, and the muscles in my legs burn.

I breathe in her laughter and rainwater.

Penelope tilts her head toward the clouds and extends her arms at her sides.

Swerving my bike side-to-side, misery turned easiness soars like a bird.

Chapter 7

DILLON

Mrs. Alabaster can't get rid of us fast enough.

On the last day of school, she shoos Penelope and me out of class, throwing our report cards at our backs as we run down the hallway one last time. Rushing through double doors, we race toward the bike rack where my bicycle is locked up.

She and I breathe in bona fide summertime air and ride away together over speed bumps through the parking lot—officially high school students. After ditching the rollerblades for good, Pen flies on my handlebars every day she's well enough to roll herself out of bed in the morning.

Completely trusting me not to wreck, she extends her arms like wings and angles her face toward the sun. The girl, who keeps me up for entire nights at the window, shouts the same words every time we ride.

"Faster, Dillon. Pedal faster!"

Wind that smells like pollen flows through her long, wavy hair. Bright sunshine makes each brown strand look almost red. Penelope's laughter's a tune that's been stuck in my head for months, and I'm glad to choke on pollen-scented, nearly red hair to hear it.

The swish, swish, swish of rubber tires striding over pavement gets louder the closer Herbert and Mathilda catch up to us from behind. Penelope glances over her shoulder, and I look up to see sunlight shine through the yellow lenses of her yellow star-shaped sunglasses. Peach-colored lips curve up as our competition passes by. She and the redhead reach out for each other, touching fingertips—The Handlebar Sisterhood.

Sailing on his skateboard, Kyle grips onto Herb's backpack and rolls with him.

"Hold on," I say to Penelope over the sound of speed.

At the mercy of natural instinct and memory of the street I've lived on my entire life, I stand up and lean down low. I squeeze my eyes closed and draw power from every muscle in my body to turn pedals around faster. My passenger's high-pitched scream drives me to thrust harder, go faster; sweat drips down the side of my face, and my lungs starve for air.

We pass our rivals, and Pen shouts, "Suckers!"

They blast past my house as I slow down and sail into the driveway, triumphant but out of breath.

Pen jumps off my bars, and I drop the bike over oil stains before collapsing onto the grass, gasping for oxygen. Stars for eyes stands over me, blocking the sun. She has our report cards in her right hand and a fading smile on her lips.

"I should look at this before my parents ask for it," she says, crumpling beside me.

I'm not surprised to see a few A's have lowered to B's, and once perfect attendance is now marked with tardiness. My citizenship is no longer excellent, and there's a small note for my parents in the comment box.

I am concerned about Dillon's recent behavior and decline in academic urgency. He's often tired in class and easily distracted. Mr. Decker turns his assignments in late, and his quality of work suffered in the end. May I suggest he work hard on his summer reading list and concentrate on preparing for high school? If he can stay on track, Dillon has a very bright future ahead of him.

Penelope's barely passing report card also has a note from Mrs. Alabaster.

Summer school.

"That's not happening," the almost flunkie says, shoving her bad grades into her book bag.

Later, after my parents chew me out about my report card, I'm sent to my room for the rest of the night. They don't know there's nowhere else I'd rather be, and I go willingly, faking shame. Penelope's waiting for me, waving her small hand. We don't move for hours.

CAN YOU USE THE PHONE?

From her bedroom window, Pen reads the note I press against the warm glass, and she shakes her head. It's after two in the morning and my vision blurs, but I eat candy bars and drink cans of soda to stay awake.

NO, her note replies.

I sketch a sad face and hold it up for her to see.

This is our nightly routine. Penelope's sluggish during the day because she can't sleep at night, and I raid the kitchen for whatever sweet foods and drinks we have so I can stay up with her. More times than not, I crash when my sugar does, but sleeplessness can stay up until the sun rises.

Those nights usually lead to the days she doesn't go to school.

Not always.

Sometimes she's too sad to get out of bed.

GO TO SLEEP, she writes.

Sipping the bottom of a warm, flat soda, I ignore the note like I do every time she holds it up and crush the aluminum in my hand. I toss it onto my dresser with the other ones I've finished tonight. Months ago, I changed my room around so that my bed sits under the window. The mattress beneath me only feels like it becomes softer as the minutes slowly tick by. My eyelids are heavy, and my eyes burn between drawn-out blinks. I yawn, and from here I can see Penelope sigh.

HERB KISSED MAHTILDA TODAY, I write.

Pen's eyes widen, and she smiles. She looks down to write in her notebook.

THAT'S GROSS!

Disgust isn't what I felt when I saw my best friend kiss the redhead behind the gym after lunch today. I looked at the world in shades of green, and when I went back to class, only Penelope's lips were in color.

I was jealous.

HAVE YOU EVER BEEN KISSED? she writes.

My heartbeat picks up, and exhaustion moves aside by the rush of red-hot adrenaline that shoots through my body. I sit up straight, hoping she can't see the blush that bleeds from my cheeks to my chest.

NO WAY, I write back. **HAVE YOU?**

She quickly shakes her head back and forth, forth and back.

Tense muscles in my shoulders relax, and I exhale. My heartbeat slows down as the talk about kissing drops into silence. I watch Penelope chew on her nails, and she looks back. As tiredness I can't fight off pulls me under, the last thought I have before I fall asleep is about how glad I am that Pen's never been kissed.

HERB, KYLE, PENELOPE, AND I spend the day at the beach, boogie boarding and diving through salty waves. We eat sandy sandwiches and capture starfish between rocks at the base of cliffs shaped like castles. As instructed, when the sun starts to go down, I grab Pen and our towels and run home.

"Don't be late, boy," Wayne warned me before we left. "My daughter better be here to celebrate this country's glory."

Our bare feet pound on the heated concrete, and our shoulders sting from the sun's burn. We both have more freckles across our noses than we had this morning.

It's the Fourth of July, and people from every house on the block are out front with their grills and lawn chairs, enjoying our nation's freedom. Evening air smells like hamburger grease and the vinegar in the barbeque sauce on chicken and ribs. Firecrackers pop and smoke bombs make everything foggy.

After I snatch a slice of watermelon from my mom's contribution to the block party, we follow Risa out back to light Penelope's sparklers.

"Are you guys ready for high school?" my sister asks. An unlit joint hangs at the corner of her lips, and her toes are dusty. Risa's long blonde hair is parted down the middle and ironed straight to look like Janis Joplin's. Penelope painted a peace sign on her cheek this morning to match the ocean-faded one on her own face.

"Yep," I say, throwing the watermelon rind into the trees.

My partner in crime shrugs her reddened shoulders, twirling her sparkler's magenta papered end between her fingers.

Leaning against a heavily barked pine tree, Risa cups her hand over the end of the joint and lights it with her other. The open flame flickers an orange glow against her face, and the twisted end of her habit scalds bright red. My sister blows dense white smoke over her shoulder before tossing the silver Zippo to Pen.

"I mean, I'll try to watch over you, but I have my own things going on, you know," she says.

When Risa gave our parents her report card, they tried

to tell me that the teachers at Castle Rain High love the elder Finnel child so much they want her to stay longer. I'm not an idiot; Risa failed twelfth grade, so she has to repeat her senior year.

She'll be a super senior. I'll be a regular freshman.

Failure waves her burning joint between Penelope and me. "But you have each other."

I roll my eyes, waiting for some *don't be weird* comment from Pen that doesn't come. She's preoccupied with her sparkler, flicking the lighter's strike wheel, sparking the flint but unable to light a flame; yellow embers reflect on her blue-framed shades. Offering my help, I light it in one shot.

"We'll be fine," I reply to my sister. Penelope dances between us with a pink-twinkling fire stick.

"High school's different, D. Even in this piece of shit town." Dark ash falls from the joint. Risa's eyelids droop, and a lazy smile forms on her lips. "I heard that school in Neah Bay closed. Rumor is they're busing them into Castle Rain until something's figured out."

I light a second sparkler for Pen.

"So what?" I say.

My sister laughs. "So what? Those reservation boys are huge, and they're troublemakers. I can't imagine they're going to like it when they're uprooted from their hometown and transported an hour just to go to school. But that's what the *man* does. When people get comfortable, the government breaks apart families and ruins lives. That's why I say fuck the authority. I'll go to high school for five years if I want to. I won't conform!"

Penelope takes a break from sketching stars with sparkles to cross her eyes under cobalt-tinted lenses and twirl her finger beside her temple, like Risa is coo-coo coo-coo.

The scent of skunk and wet grass hangs heavily in the air, smoking out the smell of burning coal and sunscreen. I have another sparkler in my back pocket for Pen, but the more my sister hits the herb, the more outrageous she becomes.

"The wars," Risa says, lowering her voice. "They're all a conspiracy."

I side-eye Pen, who covers her mouth with her palm to keep from laughing.

"Which war?" I ask.

"All of them," paranoia replies. "President Clinton ordered the hit on World War II."

Embers fall from her joint, and she waits for my reaction, puffing smoke circles from her mouth. I'm about to carry Pen out of here over my shoulder when the ultimate conspiracy theory calls out for his daughter.

"You better not be out there with that freak boy!" Mr.

Finnel booms from his backyard, practically rumbling the ground beneath my feet. "Boy, you better not be out there getting fresh with my girl!"

"President Clinton sent him here to ruin your life, too," my sister laughs, squinting as she smokes another toke.

Penelope drops her firework and snuffs it out with the toe of her sandal-covered foot. Pushing sea-salt caked hair out of her face, the girl with sunburned shoulders runs up and presses her lips to my cheek before she disappears between the trees without a word.

I slap my hand over my face where she left a kiss as heat flashes through my body, from the tips of my toes to the ends of every strand of hair on my head.

"Handle that one with care," Risa says. She winks, but it's with both eyes.

So, she just blinks.

MOM AND DAD SMELL INCENSE on Risa right away and call a family meeting on the front porch away from the block party.

"Have you no respect for the law?" My mom stomps her foot. Her blonde hair bounces. "Have you no respect for your lungs? Have you no respect at all?"

My father has his Hawaiian printed shirt buttoned all the way to the top like a cholo on vacation. His glasses slip to the end of his nose as he leans toward me and sniffs. I take a step back with my hands held up.

"I did not inhale," I say with a smile.

My sister flips me the bird, and I run down the steps to sit beside Penelope on the damp lawn. Tables, chairs, barbeques, and smokers have all been cleared from the street. The sun is down, but the air is still summertime thick. Pen's barefoot, and her dirty hair is pulled back away from her tanned face and skinny neck.

Freckled cheeks go red, but she doesn't look at me.

"Hi," I say.

"Shhh," she responds. Penelope drops her hand, palm up on the grass between us.

With the prickle of his only child's lips still on my face, Wayne rushes into the street with a firework and a lighter. Pen's smile bends high when the fountain erupts like a volcano, gushing silver and gold magma into the air. It whistles and pops, bursting with colors that brighten the dark street. Illuminating the faces of my family and hers with white light, it dims as fast as it catches the world on fire.

Mr. Finnel is there to replace it with one that shatters the night like a strobe light. Between blinding surges of intensity, I lower my hand beside Pen's and immediately feel the warmth of how close she is.

My pulse drops in sync with pulsating brilliance and keeps the beat when it burns out.

Taking advantage of the few seconds of darkness between flares, fountains, and wheels, I scoot closer to the girl next door.

Our pinkies touch.

There's no air.

My ears ring.

My vision's spotty.

Red, white, and blue lights screech as they lift for the stars, and there's no stopping me now. I grab her hand—warm and sticky with nails she bites until they bleed—and tie our fingers so closely together not even the hand holding Nazi's glare can make me let go.

Chapter 8

PENELOPE

"How long have you been sad, Penelope?" the female doctor in a long white coat asks.

I shift back on the examination table, crinkling the bleached tissue paper underneath my legs. Mom wipes away tears she tries to hide from her eyes, sitting in a blue plastic chair in the corner of the small examination room. The scent of rubbing alcohol stings my nose, and images of ocean life painted on the walls in bright colors don't make me feel majestic or safe like they're supposed to.

"You can be honest with her, sweetie," my mom says, forcing a smile. She clutches her large leather purse to her chest.

My eyes swing back and forth across the room, unable to find a spot to focus on. Schools of fish, a winking octopus, and the grinning blue whale look back at me, mocking my unease with their perma-happiness.

"Do you want to play with my stethoscope?" Dr. White Coat asks in a high-pitched, generic tone. She and the whale have the same smile.

"I'm almost fourteen." The palms of my hands tingle, and my chest feels like it's full of fluid.

Red-lacquered lips fall into a straight line. "You're right, I'm sorry."

I've spent time trapped in offices like this one since I was five. Every doctor I've ever seen asks the same questions as the one before them. They wear the same stiff coats, speak in identical patronizing tones, and each promises to make the spinning agony inside me disappear.

They all shine lights into my eyes.

"Just look straight ahead," Dr. Stethoscope says, aiming her penlight through the lenses of my shades. Her breath smells like rubbing alcohol, too. "This would be easier if you'd take your sunglasses off."

My heart's been spied on by countless pediatricians.

"Are you nervous?" She lifts my wrist and counts the beats manually, just in case she heard wrong.

I always become a pincushion.

"We're going to run some blood tests, Penelope. This is normal, and it will only pinch a little."

Mom holds my arm down while I scream. It doesn't hurt, but stretching my lungs feels good.

Every Rorschach test is different, but I always give the same answer.

"What do you see in this one?" Dr. White Coat asks. She exhales heavily through her small nose, and her ear-length haircut gets uglier the longer I'm made to look at it.

The black ink blob on the white card looks a lot like my dad's shaggy chest when wet or two people holding hands.

"Murder," I answer dishonestly.

Mom smacks her forehead.

Dr. Mushroom Hairdo lowers the test card and says angrily, "What?"

Shrugging my shoulders, I kick my dangling legs out and crinkle more tissue paper beneath me.

"Murder."

"You see ... murder?"

"Penelope, please, don't do this again. Dr. Laura is here to help you, baby." Mom's round eyes plead with me from her seat in the corner between the door and the blood pressure machine.

It's the exact expression her face twists into each time I'm dragged into fake oceans to be studied, poked, and questioned. They throw words around like *anxiety*, *helplessness*, and *depression*. My eating, sleeping, and social habits are questioned, dissected, and analyzed.

"How many hours a night do you sleep?"

"Do you eat at least three times a day?"

"Are there people your age you feel close to?"

For the first time there is, but I don't want to talk about Dillon Decker. Words about brilliant birthday marbles I keep in my pockets—five in each side—won't pass my lips. I can't hide the blush that spreads across my cheeks when I think about the way his sweaty hand felt holding mine, but they'll never know. Mom tells Dr. Nosy about the boy next door, but when she looks at me for confirmation, I don't confess happiness on handlebars.

"Have you ever experimented with drugs and alcohol?"

"Do you want to hurt yourself?"

"Are you sexually active?"

I cross my arms over my chest and look up at the white ceiling through my orange lenses, refusing to answer anything.

"Do you hear voices?"

Only yours, I think to myself.

"Do voices in your head ever tell you to do anything you're not comfortable with?"

My eyes drop down to my mother's. She sits on the edge of her chair, expressionless with a sea turtle behind her head full of dark hair. As I wait for her to tell this quack I'm unhappy not mental, I notice the stiff posture in her shoulders and lack of breathing and realize the woman who gave me life might actually believe there's crazy behind this sadness.

When she finally speaks up, it's nothing I haven't heard before.

"Depression runs on my husband's side of the family," she says, taking a breath. "Both his mother and sister suffer from it, but they didn't develop symptoms until adulthood. Penelope started showing warning signs as a small child."

Dr. Jerk Face nods.

"Psychotic behavior," Mom continues slowly, "has never been an issue, but Pen does have obsessive tendencies. My daughter doesn't sleep at night and rarely eats entire meals. Because these depressive episodes occur more often as she gets older, she has missed a lot of school, and her grades have suffered."

I almost start screaming again to make her stop talking.

"The new school year starts in three weeks, and I'm worried about the way she's going to deal with the pressure of high school. I mean, she has her sunglasses…"

I pound my fist into the examination table, and the fluid

feeling in my chest hardens and prickling panic trickles down my arms into the tips of my fingers. My lips tingle, and my teeth snap together and grind.

"Penelope never did well around strangers. As a toddler, the tantrums she had in public were frightening. She would cry herself into unconsciousness. Other times she threw up on herself or pounded on her chest until she bruised because she said it hurt on the inside. People would look at us like we were monsters."

Mom allows grief to fall freely down her cheeks.

"Watching her little face turn blue from how afraid she was … I still hear her screams." She stops to ponder for a moment. "After a while, my husband and I took turns running errands so that one of us could stay home with her. When she started kindergarten, it was apparent how unaccustomed to human interaction she was. Tantrums started again, and most days I would have to sit in class with her so she wouldn't cry. Although, she still didn't participate, and after the first month they wanted to drop her."

Dr. Laura passes my mother a box of tissues, which she takes but doesn't use.

"The day before they were going to kick her out of school, my husband bought her a pair of pink sunglasses from a gas station. He told her they made her invisible, and she believed him."

I pound my tight fist into the padding once more and start to shake my head, knowing exactly where this conversation goes next.

"Penelope," the pediatrician starts, "have you considered trading the sunglasses for something that will actually help?"

"Nope," I answer quickly.

"You have to understand that you're only putting a Band-Aid over the real issue. Depression has a history of becoming worse with age, and you're self-medicating with what you believe makes you invisible. But I can prescribe something that will treat your true symptoms."

"No."

"This isn't your fault, and I can help. One tiny pill before you go to bed and you won't have a problem going to sleep anymore. School will be easier because you'll be able to concentrate, and medication will dull the ache inside your chest. There won't be a need to be invisible anymore, Penelope."

Squeezing my eyes shut, I swerve my thoughts to the only person who's never made me feel unseen and focus on the kindness and care Dillon offers me until my grip on the edge of the table loosens. My lungs fill with air as I take a breath, and my jaw aches as it relaxes.

I look up as Dr. Laura passes my mom a prescription.

"SHE'S BEEN UP THERE FOR a week, Sonya. What's wrong with her?"

Dad just walked through the front door, and he and Mom are already fighting. His muffled voice travels through the floor and walls from downstairs into my room. Kitchen cabinets slam closed, jolting my panicky heart. From the middle of my bed, peeking out from underneath a pile of heavy blankets, I listen to them argue like I have for the last seven nights in a row.

"Football season's about to start, and the team needs me. I can't be home all day. You're here, so act like the adult and make our girl get up," Dad barks, slamming the utensil drawer shut. Sterling silver forks, knives, and spoons clank together. The sound digs into my bones.

Normally soft-spoken and non-confrontational, Mom cries out, and a moment later glass smashes. I push myself up against million-pound gravity and drop my numb legs over the side of the bed. My head feels too large for my shoulders, and my skeleton too soft to support the weight of my body.

"This isn't about a little girl who thinks she's invisible, Wayne. She needs more than sunglasses!" Mom shouts. Another glass breaks.

Stepping toward my bedroom door with wobbly knees and

gritted teeth, each step is harder to take than the one before it. I wait for the floor to fall out from underneath me or for the walls to cave in, but I safely reach out for the gold doorknob and turn it.

Lights from the first floor brighten the dark hallway. I don't leave my room, but without the door between us, my parents' shouts are clear.

"What's happening to our daughter is serious," my mom continues. "She's scaring me, Wayne."

The longer I'm on my feet, the heavier I feel. My tired shoulders slump, and sweat beads on my top lip. Heat radiates from my scalp, making my dirty hair greasier. Exhausted lungs act as if they're jammed in too small of a space, like my ribs have shrunk all of a sudden. To keep from collapsing, I lean against the doorjamb and dig my toes into the beige carpet.

"Medication is out of the question. She's too young," Dad says with finality in his tone.

The sharp, cutting smell of grilled onions twists my empty stomach. Saliva pools in my mouth, thick under my tongue as my jaw aches bad enough to cause my eyes to water. Dad cuts through reheated steak, scraping his fork and knife against the blue plate I know he's using; it's the same one he uses every night.

"But what if it helps this time?" Mom asks. Broken glass crushes between her shoe and the linoleum, grinding into smaller pieces.

Silence rings in my ears, so I step back into my dark room and close the door with a small click of the handle. Sliding back under the blankets on my bed would give me the only thing close to ease from bitter guilt that's eating me.

I ignore my life-givers when their argument starts again and pull apart my plum-colored curtains. With every star in the sky on fire and the moon spitting white light over Castle Rain, I'm able to see Dillon looking back at me like it's in the light of day.

The only boy to ever hold my hand smiles easy and presses his palm against his window. Pretending his fingers are between mine, I press my hand against the cool glass and try to smile so he knows that I miss him.

But I can't.

All I can do is cry.

Chapter 9

DILLON

"They're not too big or too small and perfectly arched. That freckle the shape of a snowball on the left one is my favorite, and I'm so glad these don't hang low. I've seen some that dangle, and it's disgusting. Yours are definitely not awful."

Risa and Kyle sit crisscrossed in front of each other. My sister rubs my friend's *perfect* earlobes between the pads of her pointer fingers and thumbs, and he's wide-eyed and red in the face, eating it up.

"How old are you?" Risa scoots closer to my friend; their kneecaps touch.

"I just turned fourteen," he answers, staring directly at my sister's purple lollipop stained lips. "I'll be fifteen in, like, eleven months."

The girl I share DNA with pushes a strand of blonde hair out of Kyle's eyes before she presses the tip of her nose against his.

"We're only five years apart," she says. "Have you ever been kissed, boy?"

He sucks in a sharp breath and shakes his head fast.

It's the last weekend of a summer that went by too quickly, and we stretch every second left together. When the Finnels and my parents mentioned going out to dinner earlier, Penelope and I convinced them to leave us home with Risa. Once receiving a *boy, do I look stupid to you?* look from Wayne, and after he teased me with a few packs of peanut M&M's for smiles I still count, he actually agreed to leave us here.

Kyle rode his bike over when the Chrysler reversed out of the driveway, and now the four of us sit in a semi-circle in my sister's stuffy, incense hot-boxed bedroom. Risa's the only one smoking, but my head is fuzzy, and my mouth feels like it's full of cotton balls.

Penelope has her head on my shoulder and her fingers tied so tightly with mine, I can feel her heartbeat between our knuckles. She tilts her head back, showing me drowsy eyelids over reddened eyes under circular shades.

"Have you ever been kissed?" she whispers, talking out of the side of her mouth like she always does.

"Shut up," I say, nudging her gently with my elbow.

Risa pulls away from the boy with the perfectly curved ears and lifts the citrus-scented grass wrapped in burning paper to her lips. The end of her joint chars red-orange, and I watch as my pulse flies, and the itch to laugh scratches the roof of my mouth.

Our babysitter blows a dense stream of grayish white smoke into Kyle's face, but Pen and I suck in the kickback. It tastes almost as good as it smells, and I catch the girl at my side lick the flavor from her lips like candy.

"Can I try?" she asks. Penelope sits up straight, slanted toward Risa.

Her long brown hair grew longer during the sunny season Pen spent mostly in bed. The ends are cut uneven and lighter in color, and curls that used to bounce when we ran between trees or through sand at the beach now fall flat and frizzy. Her hands are skinnier than they were on the Fourth of July, and when she takes off her sunglasses, lack-of-sleep purple bruises are under her eyes.

As she reaches for my sister's habit, the bones in her elbow stick out. Thin fingers wiggle like she knows what she's asking for, like she even knows how to hold it.

"I don't know, Pen. Your dad will kill me," Risa says, shifting away from Kyle to sit upright. Her spine straightens, and she hides what's left of her joint in the cup of her hand.

"He won't know," curiosity pushes. Scooting on scrawny knees, Penelope kneels beside our caregiver. "I only want to know what it's like … just once."

Scratching above my right eyebrow, cool sweat drips down the back of my hot neck and the ceiling in this smoky bedroom suddenly drops down on me. I push my dirty hair out of my face and blow air I shouldn't have inhaled in the first place out of my prickly, nervous-for-her lungs.

"This stays between us," my sister says as she passes her dependency to the girl I had to force out of bed this morning.

Kyle and I trade a fast look; his eyes are red, round, and as curious as Penelope's.

Sometime last school year, a local policeman with huge arm muscles and sunglasses that reflected like mirrors came to class and preached about the dangers of marijuana.

"It's a gateway drug," he said, passing out D.A.R.E bumper stickers we later stuck to the bathroom stalls. "Weed is a trailblazer for broken dreams and a life on the gritty streets."

A life without a home is the last thing on my mind as Pen stares at what she's gotten herself into. Spellbound by ribbons of smoke, she holds the joint up and stares at the smoldering end before the corner of her mouth curves up.

She touches her lips to the twisted end and inhales, shutting her eyes as she does.

Moving closer to craziness, I watch the way her pink lips wrap around the gateway to broken dreams and wish it were my lips she's kissing. Penelope exhales without coughing, and I inhale everything she lets go of, slowly nudging closer so I get it all.

"Wanna try?" She licks her lips again.

My heart thuds, thrashing against every pulse place in my body. The air around us shakes, and the ceiling lifts back to where it belongs.

"Do it with me," Pen offers, holding life on the gritty streets out for me.

She's silly grins and *come on, come on.*

Trashing lessons learned from cops on a school day, I smoke what she gives me just to feel what she does but cough, because I'm nowhere as smooth as Pen naturally is. Kyle takes what's left from my hand and hits the joint we all watched Risa roll on her SAT practice book. We're able to pass it around our circle once more before it burns ash, and then we can't stop laughing.

Penelope and I hold hands and blow hair out of each other's faces. I push her sunglasses to the top of her head, refusing to look at her eyes through pink lenses anymore.

"My face is numb," she says.

"I can feel my heartbeat in my brain," I say.

"You have a brain?" my comedian asks.

Smoke clears out of the room through a crack in the window, and the last day of summer lowers into the last night. Lying on the bedroom floor shoulder-to-shoulder, Penelope and I look up at the collection of local band posters, autographed dollar bills, and ripped liquor labels stapled to the ceiling while Risa and Kyle talk in hushed tones and whispered voices. It's not until they go silent that we care enough to look up to find out what they're up to.

My sister is kissing my best friend.

"What the—"

Pen's lips press against mine.

Leaning back on my elbows, Penelope holds my face between her shaky hands and pushes her tight-lipped mouth against my relaxed one. Our noses smash together, and I'm pretty sure my teeth cut skin and I taste blood, but her kiss is mine.

She's slow breathing and bolder than me.

Bravery's tongue parts my lips, and I push up on my hands, but Penelope shoves me down flat. The back of my head crashes with the carpet, but our mouths don't break apart. We open a little wider, move our tongues in small circles, and kiss for the first time with our eyes on each other, holding hands.

"SHE DEVELOPED OVER THE SUMMER," Roger Morris says, nodding toward the girl who kissed me on my sister's bedroom floor last night.

The only course Penelope and I have together is first period biology, and because she was hard to get out of bed this morning, we were late riding to school. Now we can't sit together because the good kids, who managed to make it to class on time, took the seats. We took what was left.

I look across the biology lab where Pen partnered with Mathilda Tipp. Hidden behind a pair of red- framed sunglasses, she and Herbert's girlfriend compare schedules.

"What are you talking about?" I ask, wondering how much I'll have to pay Mathilda to trade seats with me, hoping I have enough.

"Her boobs, dude. The weird girl grew boobs, and they're kind of big."

My mind goes blank, and I don't think.

I act.

I elbow Roger Morris in the face. His nose cracks on impact, and he drops to the floor, knocking his stool over and pushing our table into the backs of the kids who sit in front of us. The entire class looks over their shoulders to see what the ruckus is about. Penelope stands to her feet, holding her hands over her mouth in shock.

I see them.

Boobs.

A teacher, whose name I don't know yet, drags me out of his laboratory by the collar and walks me down to the office himself.

"There's always one kid who tries this crap on the first day of school," he says, pushing me into a wooden chair beside the door with the plaque that reads *Principal.*

The high school administration office is small, busy with students rushing in and out wanting to change their schedules, and teachers complaining about the new school year with stale-smelling coffee in paper cups and folders under their arm.

I watch the entrance like a hawk, waiting for a certain P.E. teacher to storm in, knowing I can't stop thinking about his daughter's chest now that I've noticed they're there.

"Boy!" Wayne shouts, walking in like I knew he would, behind his daughter and her new additions.

Looking down at the floor, I'm too ashamed to face Penelope or her dad, especially when I hear Pen giggle.

"There's nothing wrong with defending a girl's honor,"

Coach Finnel says. His gym shoes appear in my line of sight. "Tell me what happened."

I shake my head, but lift my eyes to his. He holds out a pack of M&M's so that only I can see the small yellow packaging.

"Penelopehasboobs," I mumble.

"Huh? Speak clearly, boy. I can't hear you."

The girl I can't wait to kiss again stands behind her father with a crooked smirk on her lips, and my eyes fall from it to her round chest.

I just say it.

"Penelope has boobs!"

Chapter 10

DILLON

"We should talk," Dad says, folding his hands together on top of his desk. "And I have to be honest with you."

Sitting across from him in his office, I lean my head back and look up at the ceiling fan spinning around, and around, and around; a gold control chain clinks against the light bulbs' glass cover. Cool, spun air chills my heated face. It's Saturday, and Penelope and I have spent all day building sand castles at the beach and sucking on blue-raspberry snow cones.

"I don't want to take up a lot of your time, Son, but your mother got an interesting phone call while you were at the beach with the Finnel girl. After the—" he coughs "—ordeal on the first day of school, it became apparent I've put this lesson off for too long."

"What?" I sit up straight and give him my attention.

Dad pushes his silver-rimmed glasses up his nose and clears his throat. "Well, someone saw you kiss Pen today and called to make sure we are aware."

"Oh." Sinking into my seat, I swallow my heartbeat and stare down at my feet.

"You're going to be fourteen next week, so what you're going through right now is normal. I went through it when I was your age, too."

My cheeks burn sizzling red.

"I want to apologize if you feel like you're going through this change alone, Dillon, but you're not. Mom and I are here for you, and I'm sure Risa can answer any questions you have about your body if you're not comfortable enough to come to us. She's a girl, but she's a good sister and went through puberty at an early age, actually."

The dentist sort of dazes off, his expression becomes blank, and his eyes seem far away. He's probably reliving the basket case my sibling became when she first had her cycle.

"Dad, it's cool. We don't have to talk about this," I say, ready to run from this room.

He leans toward me, knocking over a pencil holder shaped like a lateral incisor. Yellow-orange number two pencils spill and roll over the edge of his desk. Looking at me from over his spectacles, my father beckons me closer.

"Have you grown hair in any odd places?" he whispers, as if anyone other than us will hear.

Gripping the wooden arms of the chair, I close my eyes and hope to blend in with the cracked brown leather. Heat spreads from my checks, down my neck, past my elbows, to my fingertips.

Just last week Penelope lifted her arm in front of Risa and me and pointed to her armpit, laughing as she said, "I never get enough to shave off."

My sister tried to convince her to let the solo strand live, but Pen pulled it out and made a wish as it flew away in the breeze. I didn't feel the need to show her where I grew hair over the last year.

"Have you had any abnormal dreams? Does your body change when you think about girls? About Penelope? Is there anything you want to tell me?"

When I don't answer, too embarrassed to say a word, my life-giver opens the top drawer from the black filing cabinet behind his mahogany desk and pulls out a small plastic medical model of what looks like the lower half of a woman's body.

"You're smarter than most kids your age, Dillon, so I won't insult your intelligence by showing the replica of the male reproductive system. As you can imagine, it has the same parts as you."

He turns around the anatomy model he does have to show me what's inside, and I almost scream.

"This is the female reproductive system, Son. I may only be a dentist, but technically, I am a medical doctor. During the next hour or so, I am going to explain exactly what all of this means, and most importantly, when you're ready to have sex—"

Jumping to my feet, I trip over my untied shoelaces and stumble out of the office door. I take the stairs down two at a time, running past my sister as she comes through the front door and I run away from it.

"How was the talk?" she asks sarcastically as I sprint around the house.

A month since I busted Roger's face, I'm still getting used to Penelope's developments. Her reproductive system is more than I can handle. Wayne would snap my neck for even knowing what the plastic version looks like.

"Boy!" the anatomy Nazi calls out my name.

A fence doesn't separate our backyards, so he catches me tearing through the grass toward the trees that line the end of our property. The deep-tone of his voice scares me, and I get tangled in my dingy laces before I fall face first, skidding long enough to get grass stains on my white T-shirt.

"What?" I say with a mouth full of dandelions.

"How many smiles today?" Couch Finnel asks, not at all concerned with the dirt dive I just took.

Wiping blades of grass from my mouth, I sit up and say, "Lost count after fifty-seven."

From his back door, King Kong nods and turns back into the house.

"You owe me a lot of candy, old man," I mumble under my breath, standing to my feet. "Pay up, sucker."

The murmur Nazi suddenly reappears and says, "Did you say something, boy?"

I shake my head and disappear between the pines to find the girl with the star-shaped glasses.

PENELOPE'S ANKLE DEEP IN FRESH mud, dancing with bright sunrays that flicker through openings in the tree branches. There's a wildflower above her ear and dried clumps of dirt stuck to her legs. Swaying back and forth, kicking her feet up and then back, the only girl who gives me abnormal dreams waves me over with a smile that threatens to take over the world across her face.

I kick off my shoes and socks and hurdle in beside her, flinging watery mud way over our heads. Coming down like a chunky waterfall, it lands in our hair, on our faces, and across stars enough to blind her.

To the rhythm of our excitement, caked in sludge and covered in grass stains, we jump up and down, splattering soaked earth across tree trunks and mossy rocks. Pen screams, I shout, birds flee, and squirrels scatter. We step on each other's toes and bump heads, but nothing stops us from making this puddle ours.

Shaking her head back and forth, invisibility shades soar from her dirt-freckled face and mud sails from the ends of her filthy hair. I watch her dance, covered in soil, free from whatever she hides from, and realize it's been two weeks since I've had to talk her out of bed before school. Fourteen days have passed since the last time she missed a day of school, and this is the happiest I've seen her, ever.

Big brown eyes look up at me, and Pen circles her arms around my neck. With dirty lips beside my ear, she whispers, "You make me so happy."

DILLON

Searching through piles of clothes on her bedroom floor, I find a clean pair of pants in one stack and her left shoe under another. I grab a shirt from the closet and toss all of it at the end of her bed.

"Penelope," I say, opening her purple curtains to let sunlight in. "You have to get up."

She's small under a mass of blankets, dressed in the same pajamas she was in yesterday morning. Sleep lines warp the sides of her face, and her hair sticks to her chapped lips. This girl only has enough energy to lift her small hand and wave me away.

"Go away," Pen mumbles.

I pull the covers further away from her body, hoping some fresh air and a little vitamin D will give her what she needs to get up.

"Come on, I got your clothes picked out. Where's your brush so I can help with your hair?"

Stepping over to her stereo, I turn on whatever played last in the CD player and search through dresser drawers for a pair of sunglasses while incoherent lyrics and scratchy guitar chords hum from the small speakers.

"Turn it off," sleepiness groans, covering her head with a pillow.

After choosing a blue pair of circle-framed glasses to match the shirt I hope she likes, I yank the pillow from over her face and ask one more time for her to please get out of bed.

She sits up, but my heart sinks into my stomach when her sore eyes manage to open and look up at me.

"Don't you get it, Dillon?" she says, struggling to keep her head straight. "There's a reason why you're my only friend. Why haven't you figured this out yet?"

I drop the shades on her nightstand and say, "But today is our birthday."

Pen collapses back onto her mattress and hides under quilts and darkness. "Get out of my room."

Chapter 12

PENELOPE

Mom barges into my room, letting light from the hallway in, stinging my barely opened eyes. I kick off the blankets, drenched in my own sweat, but can't bring myself to get out of bed. Muscles in my arms and legs feel like they're made out of cement, and my bones out of metal pipes.

"We can't keep doing this. I got you out of school for another day, but they expect you to be in class tomorrow."

"Leave me alone," I say, covering my face with my hands.

"Not this time, Penelope," Mom answers. The sweet sound of her voice tingles inside my chest, but when she brushes the hair out of my face, I turn away from her hand.

Molded to my bed, I hold on to my purple sheets and squeeze my eyes shut so I don't cry. The weight of oxygen is torturous, and as much as I want my mom, the sound of her footsteps on the carpet splits my head wide open.

I turned fourteen a week ago and still haven't blown the candles out on the cake.

"At least take a shower and come downstairs with me. We can sit in front of the TV all day, Pen, but you can't stay in this room for another day."

Pushing my face into the mattress, I bring my legs underneath me and curl into a ball. Every strand of hair on my head hurts, and I can hardly breathe.

"You don't understand," I cry out. Hot tears soak into the soft cotton under me. "Nobody gets it!"

Instead of leaving the room like she normally does when I yell, she jerks on the end of my sweatpants and then on the back of my sweatshirt. Mom tries to touch my face again, but I quickly and painfully roll to my other side.

"I'll get up later," I lie. "Let me sleep a little longer."

"No, you've slept enough."

Mom wraps her fat fingers around my wrist and pulls me upright. Darkness that's made itself a home inside my body and mind sizzles and roars, shooting pain through my limbs and knocking air from my lungs that comes out of my mouth as a piercing scream. I try to yank my arm from my mother's grip, but she only holds on tighter.

"It hurts," I cry, reaching for my bed's wooden headboard before she lifts me completely up. "Stop."

"Tell me what hurts," the lady who carried me in her stomach for nine months says as tears fall from her round face. She doesn't stop forcing me away from the only thing in this house that gives me comfort.

My feet touch the carpet, and my fingers slip from the headboard. I dig my fingernails into my mom's hand when I slide from the mattress completely, and scream until what feels like the whole room shakes as fear from leaving my space eats my heart.

"Everything!" I shout. "Everything hurts."

I fall to my bottom and use my body weight to anchor myself to the floor, crying and kicking and not wanting to be anywhere but in here. Ruthlessness pulls my head back by my hair when I try to bite her fingers, and she drags me across my bedroom floor by the neck of my sweatshirt.

"Please, Mom, please. You don't know how bad it is," I say, choking on my words, choking on this life.

She doesn't answer, managing to heave me into the hallway where I kick the walls, knocking down framed school pictures, wedding photos, and a wooden crucifix. My dirty hair sticks to tears across my face, and the balls of my feet hurt from striking them into the drywall. Heavy cotton saws into my throat as I'm pulled into the bathroom. The shower water is already running, and the small space is full of steam.

"Calm down, Penelope," my mom whispers soothingly, bracing me alongside the sink. She hugs me against her body, squeezing tight enough to hold my pieces together for a second.

I shake my head back and forth, clenching my teeth together, hating her touch even though it helps ease the hurt a little.

"I can't breathe," I say, sucking oxygen that doesn't reach my lungs in through my mouth.

My lips tingle. My fingertips are numb. My vision spots.

"I'm dying," I say, feeling my heart beat too quickly, like it's going to explode, like it's going to burst out of my chest.

"You're not, baby," she swears, reaching up the back of my sweatshirt to place her palm on my bare skin. She rubs her hand up and down my spine, whispering how much she loves me into my ear. "I won't let you ever die."

Fully clothed, Mom helps me into the bathtub and climbs in behind me. She cradles my body against her soft chest, pushing my wet hair away from my face and neck. Sobs calm to hiccups and shaky breaths, and warm water brings back feeling in my fingers and toes. As we sit under the shower's downpour, my mommy tells me again and again that everything is going to be okay.

"It won't always be like this, Pen."

I don't believe her.

PROTECTED BEHIND A PAIR OF green-lensed shades, my hair is damp at the roots and dry on the ends, and my stomach aches after eating the first full meal I've had in days. Mom and I stayed under running water until it turned cold, and when we got out, she didn't let me go back into my room. Forbidden from one safe spot, I wait for the other to get home from school.

Barefoot and sitting on the Deckers' front porch, salt-scented air blows in from the ocean that's only a few blocks away. Leaves have begun to turn yellow as autumn returns with the breeze. Warm, end-of-September sun warms my clean, coconut body wash smelling skin. I feel like I'm jammed inside a flimsy bubble, looking out at everything around me, but I don't itch with panic, and my heart beats like normal.

Dad doesn't want me to take any medication I was prescribed, but Mom promises they're fine once in a while.

"Our secret, okay?" she said before I dropped the white pill onto the tip of my tongue.

When the form of the only boy who matters appears at the end of the street, I block the bright sunlight from my eyes with my hand to watch him walk my way.

Pulse points race in a great way.

As I curl my toes over the wooden step below me, dry wood splinters and pushes against my soft skin. I stand so that he can see me and lift my hand to carefully wave, still sore from my earlier panic attack and days in bed.

Dillon stops seven houses down and squints against the same daylight that shines off his dark blonde hair to look back at me. He's taller every time I see him, like he grows an inch every minute we're not together.

"Freak boy next door is getting big," Dad said last week, noticing, too. He chugged milk chocolate creatine and then added, "But I can still kick his ass."

With his backpack high on his shoulders and the laces on his right shoe untied, both corners of his mouth curve up and he starts to run the rest of the way home. The closer he gets, I can see the softness in his face has sharpened, and the band T-shirt he wore on the first day of school that fit perfectly now seems small.

Not at all winded from running half a block, Dillon slows down in front of his house and walks across his lawn, shaking his head so that his long, wavy hair falls back into place.

"Where's your bike?" I ask, stepping onto the concrete walkway.

His green eyes stare down at me; the shape of his body blocks the sun from shining in my face.

"Two bikes were stolen earlier this week from school, so I don't ride it unless you're with me. I heard it was those rez boys," he says, scratching above his eyebrow.

My head feels too heavy for my body, and my eyes want to close, so I sit back down and take a deep breath.

"You okay?" Dillon asks, stepping closer to me.

I shake my head, fighting back tears.

"Is anyone home?" He steps onto the porch beside me in filthy, untied Vans and nods toward the front door.

"I don't think so," I say.

There are no cars in the driveway, and Risa hasn't come home from school.

Thoughtfulness holds his hand out for me and says, "Come on."

Dillon follows behind me as I walk through his house and up the stairs, one slow step at a time.

"If you fall, I'll catch you," he says, not having a clue as to how much it makes me want to cry.

I've only seen his room though my window, but as soon as I push open the door and the sweet, soapy smell of comfort washes over me, achiness in my stomach soothes and stiffness in my shoulders eases. I inhale deeply through my nose and don't hold back when relief falls from my eyes.

This simple boy has a simpler bedroom. Unlike mine, there's not a single pile of dirty clothes on the floor. His bed is made, and the walls are mostly bare, with the exception of a few framed posters.

Moving across the room to the twin-sized bed, I crawl under a navy comforter, take off my glasses, and place my head on Dillon's flat cotton pillow. Dropping his backpack and kicking off his shoes, the boy whose bed I've invaded shuts the door and closes the blinds until the room is a perfect shade of dark.

He sits at my feet and asks, "Why are you crying, Penelope?"

"Because I'm sad," I say, allowing that never-leaving sadness to soak into his red pillowcase.

Slightly slouching, he nods before saying, "Is it true you're depressed?"

Old springs in the bed creak under the weight of our bodies, but I have never been more comfortable in my life. As tiredness weighs down my eyelids, warm tears continue to roll down my face, and I can't find it in me to be embarrassed or relieved that Dillon has finally figured me out.

Dad has it all wrong. The boy next door isn't a freak, I am.

"Yeah, I am."

THE NEXT TIME I OPEN my eyes, my dad is standing over me, slowly waking me up with a mustache-tickle kiss on my forehead. In a hushed tone, he says, "You're too young to spend the night with boys, sweetheart."

For a second I don't know where I am. My eyes roam around the room, and as my dad lifts me out from under the warm blankets, I spot Dillon sleeping on the floor beside his bed and remember our tiny talk and how good it felt to be wrapped up in what's his.

So good that I reach for the corner of the navy comforter and take it with me as my father steps over the boy who pressed his lips to my forehead before he did.

Cradled in my dad's arms, I breathe in the scent of the football field and pretend to sleep against his hard chest as he carries me down the stairs. At the bottom, Dawn's voice breaks the silence.

"Is she doing okay, Wayne?" she asks. Mrs. Decker covers me entirely in her son's blanket.

"Sonya said today was rough, but she'll be fine." Dad's voice rumbles against my ear.

The front door opens, and cool air stings my face when my father steps outside. I crack open my eyes and blink against the brightness of the yellow porch light. Moths and other night flying bugs swarm around it, and stars blanket the night sky above it.

"If you need anything," Timothy says, alerting me of his company. "Let us know."

"Just tell that boy of yours that I owe him," Dad says. I smile.

Carried over both driveways, through another front door and a different set of stairs, I'm put to bed in my own room. The second I'm left alone and the hallway light glowing under my doorjamb shuts off, I jump out of bed and rush over to my window.

Dillon looks back at me from across the lawns, holding up a note that reads **BE MY GIRL**.

Chapter 13

PENELOPE

"Is Dillon Decker really your boyfriend?" Pepper Hill asks. She flips her lengthy blonde hair over her slender shoulder and pops pink bubble gum into her mouth.

With long eyelashes, glossed lips, and perfectly straight teeth—confident, flawless, and happy—I stare at the girl sitting across from me in the school library and wonder why I wasn't born more like her and less like me—awkward, defective, and doomed.

"We've been going out for a few months." I shrug my shoulders and sit back in my chair, flipping my wiry brown hair over my bony shoulder.

"Huh," she replies, looking at me but not noticing that I'm an actual person and not a plaything for her and the group of Pepper Hill wannabes who hang with her. "I bet he only asked because he feels sorry for you."

Why doesn't she understand he's my only friend?

"Thanks a lot, Pepper," I say, closing my math book and dropping my pencil. I'm no longer interested in completing the stack of makeup work I've accumulated from the days I've missed.

Her blue eyes open widely, and she waves me off. "No offense or anything, but the glasses are weird. And you're never at school. Dillon's super smart, and you're…"

"I'm smart," I reply instinctively, blushing as soon as the words pass my lips.

Lucifer tilts her head to the side and smiles. "Okay."

After pushing my red circle-framed glasses up my nose, I open my book bag and shove my things inside. I make it a point to avoid Pepper, but she doesn't keep it a secret that she wants what's mine and seeks me out when I can't be found. Bathroom gossip and unintentional-intentional shoves in the school hallways from Pepper Hill and company is one thing. Knowing she is perfect for Dillon is another.

Pepper might be right, and it'll only be a matter of time before he realizes it.

"Do you guys kiss? Have you done *it* with him?" she asks, breaking library rules and laughing loud enough to knock dust off the books.

"You're gross," I mumble, zipping up my bag.

She reaches out and grabs my hand. Her side bangs hang over her left eye, and she smells like cotton candy. I probably smell like muscle rub, and my hair is in the same ponytail my boyfriend helps me tie it in every time we're rushing out the door for school.

"Getting it on with Dillon wouldn't be gross. Seriously, do you even look at him?" spitefulness asks with a tinge of red coloring her cheeks. "He's gorgeous, Penelope."

We've been official for five months and haven't rounded first base, but I'm not telling her that.

She smacks her hand against the surface of the table. Like fingertips tapping on the underside of my sternum, anxiety ignites a fluttering panic in my chest.

"Don't do that," I say, pushing my chair back to leave.

Pepper hits the table again. "This?"

I rub my hand over the spot above where my heart kicks and remind myself that she can't hurt me if she can't see me.

Escaping between shelves of books and school appropriate posters that read, *Reading is Magical,* I keep my head down and continue toward the exit with the drum of anxiety banging in my head, which only thuds louder when the enemy passes between a row of science books and me.

She turns and stops in my pathway, crossing her arms over her chest, colored in different shades of red behind my glasses.

"I think you should break up with Dillon. For his own good."

"I think you should get out of my way," I reply in the strongest tone I can manage.

Pepper Hill takes a step toward me. "What are you going to do if I don't?"

Thoughts of chopping off her stupid hair and whipping her in the face with it cross my mind, but before I get the chance to grab some scissors, the boy she wants to steal from me appears at the end of the non-fiction section. His smile falls once he notices I'm cornered by evil.

I try to walk around my tormentor to get to him. She steps in my way, refusing to let me pass. Shoving her into the bookshelves is my next move, but Dillon reaches for me first.

"What are you doing, Pepper?" he asks, pulling me to his side. Brightness holds my hand, positioned just a step in front of me.

"Nothing," she lies, dropping the wicked act and smiling sweetly.

Once she finally goes away, I lean against books about

space and genetics and whatever else science has to say and stare back at the boy whom I should break up with for his own good.

"Why do you like kissing me?" I ask. "Wouldn't you rather kiss girls like Pepper Hill?"

He shrugs. "Because you're my favorite."

"My dad gives you candy to make me smile, that's weird." I scoff, surrounded by the scent of cracked binding and old ink on aged paper.

"I never said your dad isn't weird." His silly grin bends higher, and I want to push his hair away from his eyes.

Dillon doesn't realize how great he's become and how utterly the same I am. Everyone wants to be his friend, and they tolerate me because I'm always around. I know the day will come when he gets over staying up with me all night at our windows.

What boy really wants to brush some crazy girl's hair in the morning because she can't do it herself?

And in a few years, Dillon will graduate high school at the top of our class and leave for college.

I'll be lucky if I pass the ninth grade.

"I got you something." The boy next door opens his backpack and pulls out a long yellow feather. "The art kids are making something with them."

As happiness buzzes inside me, I say, "You stole it?"

"They had a lot. One won't be missed," he says, handing it over to me.

Holding the quill between my fingers, I rub the feather across my lips; soft fibers slide along my mouth and tickle my nose. Dillon reaches out and pushes my shades to the top my head like he does every time we're alone together. As I look up into his beautiful green eyes, I think about what Pepper Hill said and wonder why I didn't come up with it myself.

After everything he does for me, giving him this is the least I can do.

"Dillon?"

"Yeah?" He stares as his gift passes my lips.

"Do you want to have sex?"

SHOCKED AND BEYOND RED IN the face, Dillon side-eyes me the entire walk from the library to my math room. Before he continues to his honors English course, his mouth opens like there's something to say, but he snaps his lips shut and practically shoves me into class before walking away.

I take a seat in the back and pull out the book to a class I don't have a chance of passing before the end of the year.

"Did you get any makeup work done, Penelope," Mrs.

SheBlendswiththeRestofThem asks.

Tearing one assignment I managed to complete from my three-ring binder, I hand it over but don't bother coming up with an excuse as to why the other practices are incomplete. Mrs. NoName taps her brown leather pump on the dirty tile floor and shakes her head.

"This isn't going to cut it, Miss Finnel," she says in a disappointing tone.

"Sorry," I mumble.

Other students notice our educator isn't at the front of the classroom instructing. They look over their shoulders, glancing back and forth from Mrs. InsertNameHere to me, hanging on our every word.

"How many chances can I give you? Why isn't education a priority? Do you care about your future, Penelope? Do you want to go to college?" Disappointed goes on and on.

I watch her thin lips move, but I don't listen, only nodding when she pauses for a response.

"Blah, blah, blah, blah." Mrs. Blah jabs her finger into the assignment I gave her. "Blah. Blah."

"Yeah, ma'am," I say, distracted.

"I'm going to have another discussion with your father." She blinks quickly, throws her hands up, and walks away.

Mrs. PolyesterSkirt has a run in her stockings.

One by one, my fellow scholars face the front of the classroom, open their math books to page blah, and start today's lesson. I attempt to keep up, but like my earlier lecture, finding X and rounding to the nearest tenth bleeds into a bunch of ... blah.

"Mrs. Bixby is such a drag."

Two desks over on my right, Joshua Dark sits low in his chair, flipping a blue pen between his fingers. Near black eyes look back at me, surrounded by olive skin and short spiky hair. He's occupied the same seat all year long, but Risa told me to avoid the reservation kids, and Josh Dark is their leader.

Smiling politely, I pretend to busy myself by solving the ratio of whatever.

"Do you understand this shit?" He picks up his belongings and moves to the desk right beside mine. "Need help with that stack of late work?"

He smells like cloves and cinnamon gum, and I notice gold specks in eyes I thought were black. Larger than any other boy in our grade—even Dillon—Josh's arms are triple the size of mine. When he reaches over for my overdue assignments, his hands are almost the same size as the sheet of paper.

"Damn, girl, you are behind." He picks up his pencil and answers all my problems.

When the hour's up and it's time to go home, Joshua Dark

has finished more than half of my makeup work and packs the rest with promises to have them done by tomorrow.

"No big deal," he says, lifting his backpack over his massive shoulder when I thank him.

I don't ask why he's in this math class if he's such a smarty-pants; his menace to society reputation precedes him. Rumor is he beat up the principal at his old school, and he deals drugs to small children at playgrounds. Mathilda Tipp said she heard he and his gang robbed a bank once, but going by the moth-eaten holes in his shirt and old shoes, that's probably not true.

Josh walks behind me out of class and then towers over me in the hallway. Passing me a crumbled piece of paper, he says, "If you need help with tonight's homework, give me a call."

"Why are you being so nice to me?" I ask as his seven digits burn in my hand.

Bad news nods toward the classroom and says, "Bixby's a bitch."

I roll my eyes. "She's nothing compared to my English teacher."

"Mr. Koster?" he asks. "Bald, fat, and smells like—"

"Colby jack cheese," I finish his sentence.

"Exactly." Josh laughs. "I have him, too. First period."

We compare schedules and discover we share the same teachers at different times during the day. While exchanging strange encounters we've had with each of them, I don't notice the hallway's empty, and we're the only two students left until Dillon comes looking for me.

"We're waiting for you, Pen," he says, out of breath.

Josh takes a step back, losing the smile. Dillon grabs my hand, moving between the dangerous, bank robbing, homework maestro rez boy and me.

"Sorry," I say, squeezing his fingers.

Dark eyes fall on me. "You apologize a lot."

Rolling mine, I introduce trouble to kindness. "Dillon, this is Joshua Dark. He helped me with my math assignments. Josh, this is my boyfriend, Dillon Decker."

There is no response from either one of them at first, but kindness shouldn't be confused with weakness.

"Stay away from my girl." Bad, blonde, and bold squares up, showing a side of himself I've never seen before.

Unfazed, Josh smiles and walks away, saying, "See ya, Penny."

Chapter 14

DILLON

My dad stares at me like I just told him there's a dental theories' seminar for nerd dentists like himself he wasn't invited to.

No, better than that.

His face reminds me of that time he realized a grown man had stolen his lucky molar spreader from his office after an extraction and was forced to buy a new, unlucky one.

"Are you sure you're ready?" Dad clears his throat, shutting the door so that Mom doesn't hear our conversation.

Sex is natural, it happens, and it's a part of becoming a man. Dad told me all of this when he was naming parts on a plastic uterus, and now he wants to know if I'm ready. I wasn't ready for hair to grow on my balls, but that happened.

I wonder how many M&M's Coach Finnel will give me if I make Pen smile during sex.

Those should count as double.

"Considering Penelope's condition, Dillon, committing to a physical relationship with her isn't very wise."

"She's sad sometimes," I say, swallowing my anger. "Not dying."

Pulling the rolling chair out from behind his desk, he sits and takes his glasses off. Dad pinches the bridge of his nose before continuing. "There's more to it than that, Dillon. Especially in children, and that's exactly what the two of you are."

"I'll be fifteen in five months," I say, sitting straight to seem taller, even though I stand nose-to-nose with this man.

I wait for my father to present a pamphlet on depressed teenagers or a plastic model of the human brain and prepare myself for a lecture about things I don't want to hear. Instead, he unbuttons the cuffs on his light blue dress shirt and rolls up his sleeves.

"Your friend is very sick, Son," he says in a serious voice. "And it's an illness she won't likely grow out of."

"I can deal with it," I insist. Penelope's mine to deal with, and I know her better than he or anyone else does.

"No, I don't think you can." Dad leans back and crosses his arms.

Sitting in front of a wall covered with framed degrees and other awards he's received from his field of expertise, there's no doubt the man who gave me life is smart. I give him a hard time but take the advice he gives me more times than not.

This isn't one of those times.

"You're a little young to be in such a serious relationship, but it's obvious it makes you happy. Until lately, it's remained mostly innocent."

Listening to him talk—like he knows what being with the girl next door is like—makes me want to pull his two front teeth out with a pair of rusty pliers. Without Novocain.

"Since the Finnels moved in, your mother and I have witnessed your priorities slowly take the backseat for Pen. We're well aware of how intense first love can be, but I think it's time we intervene."

Pushing my hand through my hair, I exhale a frustrated breath. "Risa's in love every other week, and you don't say anything to her."

A small smile cracks Dad's sorry resolve. "Your sister is a free spirit, and I mostly support her journey through self-discovery."

"She's a pothead and a high school flunkie," I reply, rolling my eyes. Guilt instantly smacks me in the mouth, and I don't say another word, afraid of the sting.

Knowing that my dad might be right bites, too.

"And you're normally not, but your progress report arrived in the mail yesterday."

A few disappointed teachers warned me that my grades were sent home for my parents to see. Every day since then I've checked the mailbox, hoping to swipe it from the postman's bag before it was delivered, but all that arrived were bills and grocery coupons. Deciding my instructors are rotten liars, I gave stalking the postman a rest.

Wrong move.

"Your mother also mentioned noticing your bedroom light on at all hours of the night, which would explain why you're late to school so much."

My pulse throbs in my fingertips as I say, "I'll work on my grades, and I won't be late anymore."

Dad slips his spectacles back up his narrow nose and blinks behind the thick lenses. "I've never felt like I need to enforce any kind of strict rules with you, Dillon. And I like Penelope, but..."

Before the gavel lands, I stand and rush to the door, saying as I go, "I'll let Pen know we can't have sex. Thanks for the talk."

Dipping out the front door into the May sunshine, I cross

my driveway and then the Finnels', careful not to step into the oil stains Risa's Beetle has left on the concrete. As I step onto the neighbor's front porch, I don't bother knocking before I walk inside. The "ring the doorbell before you enter my kingdom" Nazi isn't home, and Sonya says I'm welcome into her home anytime.

"She's upstairs," Penelope's mother says from the kitchen, licking what looks like brownie batter from her finger.

Taking each step slowly, I decide that I'm never going to my dad for advice again. What does love have to do with sex, anyway? And who is he to judge Penelope's sadness? He's the guy who cried every time I lost a tooth as a child because he said my teeth were so perfect the Tooth Fairy didn't deserve them.

"Bad news," I say, pushing open Pen's bedroom door.

"Shh." She holds her finger to her lips.

I stop in the doorway, brightening the dark, stuffy space. Her walls glow orange from firelight burning from dozens of tea light candles she lit and placed all over. The blaze starter sits crisscross in the center of her bed, palms up on her knees with the tips of her middle finger and thumbs touching.

"Huuummm." Penelope's eyes are closed, and her bare face is expressionless.

Enough flickering candles to burn the entire house down cover every flat surface in the room. I quickly count a row of twenty on her dresser in front of her stereo, another ten sit on the windowsill, seven burn on the nightstand, and three twinkle on top of her English book on the floor beside a huge pile of clothes.

"What the heck are you doing?" I ask, closing the door behind me. Before we burn alive, I blow the candles out and open the bedroom window to let some air in.

"Hey!" she exclaims, falling flat on her back. "I was so close that time. You need to respect the dead, Dillon."

Waving a purple pillow under the smoke detector so it doesn't go off before the smoke clears out, I ask, "Close to what?"

"Summoning Kurt Cobain's ghost. I want him to use my voice to communicate to his fans one more time."

Throwing the pillow to the corner of the room, I sit on the edge of the bed, satisfied that I've saved the entire block from a fiery death.

In an old band T-shirt with a few plastic rosaries around her neck, Pen has the rocker's albums at her side and his music quietly playing in the background.

"You shouldn't light so many candles or offer your body as a vessel to lifeless musicians," I say.

"He wouldn't be dead if his wife didn't kill him." Disappointed brown eyes look up at me.

"Didn't he shoot himself?" I ask.

Pen waves me off. "You've come with bad news?"

I nod and say, "My dad said we shouldn't, you know …
do it."

The spirit caller sits up, and her long, wavy hair falls behind
her slender shoulders. Crucifixes hang low over the roundness
of her chest. Three days have passed since she mentioned losing
our virginity to each other. Since then, thoughts about the girl
who sometimes cries for no reason invade my brain in a new
way.

I memorized the shape of her lips and how the top is
plumper than the bottom. She has freckles dusted across her
chest, and some fall in the form of a diamond right under the
hollow point at the base of her throat. Long eyelashes sweep
along her pale cheeks when she blinks, and I like the way she
talks out the corner of her mouth.

When we kiss, I'm more aware than ever of the way her
developments push against me, and how her fingers lace around
the back of my neck. Pen took my hand under the table at lunch
the other day and placed it on her bare thigh. I was too afraid
to do anything, and my fear was the only thing that stopped me
from slipping my palm up and down her leg like I wanted to.

"What do dads know?" she says, brushing the back of her
hand across her forehead. Her shirt creeps up as she lifts her
arm.

Jumpiness bounces in the pit of my stomach. I close my eyes for a second, chasing away thoughts of bare navels and yellow panties peeking out from under jean shorts.

"He's kind of a doctor," I say, swallowing hard.

"But he doesn't know about us," she answers easily, resting her chin on my shoulder. Penelope looks up at me from under her dark lashes.

This girl's closeness makes my palms sweat, and my heartbeat picks up.

"We love each other, right?" she whispers.

It didn't make sense when my dad mentioned it before I dashed from his office, but hearing the word *love* from Penelope's lips makes everything seem clear.

I've loved her since bubblegum bubbles and moving trucks.

I love her for red heart-shaped glasses.

I love her because of the way she looks flying on my handlebars.

I love her.

"WHAT'S WRONG WITH PENELOPE?" HERBERT asks, nodding his head toward sorrow's form under a tree in the school courtyard.

Pen has her face hidden between the knees she has pressed

to her chest. I knew today was going to be tough when I pulled her out of bed this morning and saw dark circles under her eyes and tears rolling down her pale cheeks, but it's getting worse as the day goes on.

Veiled behind blue lenses, she's not invisible; the world is. She's not speaking to anyone but me, and when I picked her up from class before lunch, she was asleep with her head down on the desk.

"Nothing's wrong with her," I say sharply. My friends don't know. They haven't put two and two together and realized Pen's not normal.

Joining my girlfriend under the old oak, I kneel down beside her.

"I don't think I can go to class, Dillon," she says. Her voice sounds hollow between her legs.

"One more class and we can leave together."

She shakes her head, turning to the side so I can see her face. Liquid grief slips from her eyes, and her lips tremble when she says, "I'll go find my dad. He'll let me sleep in his office."

"You've made it through most of the day. Another hour is nothing," I say, drying her face with my fingertips.

Lifting hopelessness to her feet, I tuck her under my arm and walk toward the English building where Pen's last course is. I watch her smaller green Chucks step beside my black and white ones as I talk about things that make my girl happy. Like ghosts and the feathers I keep taking from the art studio.

She holds on to my shirt when we reach the last class on her schedule.

"This is it, and then we have all summer, okay?" I say, peeling her fingers back from my clothes before kissing her knuckles.

"I'm not going to pass this class in one day. It's not a big deal if I skip." Penelope's bottom lip quivers. She lowers her head so I can't see her face.

The pang in my stomach I get when she gets this depressed kicks in, turning my insides out. Instead of doubling over and crying out like my girl does when things get too bad, I kiss the top of her head and push some of her frizzy hair behind her ear.

I'm about to walk down the hall toward the honors English class in the next building I'm passing by the skin of my teeth when Joshua Dark walks past us and opens the classroom door. He holds it open with his foot and says, "You coming in, Penny?"

She looks up and halfway smiles at the boy she's been warned over and over again not to talk to. I almost change my mind and tell Pen we should ditch and go home now, but when she nods her head and steps away from me, the words are stuck in my mouth. Before she's too far, I grab her hand and squeeze her fingers.

"One more hour," she reminds me with a real smile.

The hurt in my stomach disappears into the classroom, but Josh doesn't follow behind her. He moves his dirty shoe from in front of the doorjamb and lets it close. With only a few feet between us, hot anger rushes through my limbs, and I want to smack the silly grin off his punk face.

The bell signaling the beginning of class screams from the ceilings, ringing in my ears. It's enough to snap me out of the blind rage eating me up, and I walk away, already counting down the next sixty minutes.

"WHERE IS SHE?" MATHILDA WONDERS out loud, picking at the ends of her hair. "Let's get this summer started."

My bicycle's unchained and ready to ride my girl home flying. Herb, Kyle, and the redhead are ready to go, rocking back and forth on two and four wheels. Despite wanting to go home before we even got to school this morning, Penelope's nowhere to be seen. An hour has come and gone, and she's never late.

Tilting my bike against the chain-linked fence, I push my hands into my pockets and anxiously wait for her to appear through the double doors she comes out of every day. Each time they open, my heartbeat skips, hoping it's her. It's not.

"Dude, we're the only ones here," Kyle says.

I look around and finally notice the courtyard's nearly empty. She could have left class and gone home, but Pen's normally good about letting me know when something like that happens. If she ditched class to sleep in Coach Finnel's office, he would have woken her up to ride home with us. Penelope still would have been here by now.

"I'm going to look for her," I say, walking away from my friends.

"We'll be here," Mathilda calls out.

I don't bother checking in with Pen's dad before I head toward her math class. Something about the half-smile she gave Josh on a day she can do no more than cry tells me exactly where she is. Walking through the double doors she didn't come out of with my heartbeat stuck in my throat, when I see her leaning against a row of lockers, talking to him like I didn't have to push her out of her house this morning, nearly makes me choke it up and spit at her feet.

Pen notices I'm at the end of the hall and stands straight. A part of me is relieved to see that her face is still past pale and that her shoulders are slumped.

"Crap," she says, waving good-bye to Josh Dark and

walking toward me. "I'm sorry. You should have left."

"What's going on?" I ask when she stops in front of me.

"Nothing," she says, looking over her shoulder before continuing. "Josh helped me turn in a bunch of classwork. It raised my grade to a D-. I was thanking him."

Lifting my eyes above Penelope's head, the homework helper walks down the hall in the opposite direction. Instead of chasing him down, I take my girlfriend's hand and lead her outside, far away from trouble.

"I passed math because of him," Pen says in a dismissive tone. "I'm sure he just felt sorry for me. He probably won't even remember who I am next year."

With our fingers linked and our friends in sight, I don't tell her that I hope she's right.

Chapter 15

PENELOPE

"**A**re you guys in kid-love or love-love? Because there's a difference, you know."

I shrug my sun-kissed shoulders, not knowing what to call the warm, swirling sensation Dillon gives me on the inside. I'm only certain that it's my favorite feeling in the world.

Risa puffs smoke into the sticky, summertime air. "Has he seen your boobs?"

My eyes open wide under my orange circular lenses, and I cross my arms over my chest. "No!"

Officially out of high school, my boy's sister has been

on the road this summer, following some indie band all over the Pacific Northwest. She came back two nights ago with dreadlocks, a studded nose, and a small tattoo on her lower back. Risa brought me back a shirt. It made me feel nice to know I was in her thoughts while she was sleeping in the back of vans and brushing her teeth in gas station bathrooms.

"D told me you want to have sex, Pen. That's such a big, big thing for such a small, small girl. Do you know what it's like to be with someone like that? To share your body with another person?"

"I don't know," I answer, waving her habit out of my face. "I've seen it in movies."

Her newly knotted hair is tied back, and the diamond in her nose sparkles in the sun. She has on a pair of my pink-framed sunglasses, and the gap between her teeth is pretty behind her red-stained lips.

"What's the rush?" she asks. "You guys are so young. Wait it out a while."

With her words going in one ear and out the other, I wipe sticky sweat from my hairline and look over at my yard where my Dillon levels a fresh patch of concrete below our porch with my dad. The two of them have spent the last week breaking up what was there before with sledgehammers and other power tools, burning under the summer sun and bickering back and forth about teenage sissy muscles and gross chest hair.

"I swear his mustache reached out and touched me," my boy said last night after a long day of working beside my father.

"Girls on the marching band have more strength than the freak kid next door," Dad later complained.

Lifting heavy curls from my neck, I tie my hair into a bun on the top of my head and stretch my legs out in front of me. Dillon stands before his hard work, red in the face and squinting against the sunshine. His white T-shirt is soaked in sweat. My breath catches when he hooks his fingers under the hem and lifts his shirt off.

"Stop looking at him like that," Risa jokes, pushing my shoulder forward.

I can't. I don't.

He's heavy breathing and shimmering skin.

That boy is all mine.

The object of my affection looks up, meeting my eyes between our yards. Pulling my bottom lip between my teeth, I cross my legs, curl my toes, and wave.

"Sex is cheap, Pen. Making love is prettier," high as a kite mumbles between hits.

Dillon throws his shirt over his shoulder and motions me over.

He's ten different tones of blonde and muscles that weren't there two weeks ago.

Up on my bare feet, I hop across the hot concrete onto itchy grass that tickles between my toes. I didn't notice when I was sitting next to Risa sucking up secondhand smoke, but her addiction has gone straight to my head. Giggles bubble in my chest, and my entire face tingles. The closer I float toward Dillon—walking past my father, not caring if my hair smells like pot—the harder my heartbeat dances.

"We're busy, Penelope," Dad grunts. He mixes a bag of concrete in a wheelbarrow.

Lifting my shades to the top of my head, sweaty and sun licked winks down at me and says, "Ignore him."

A cool ocean breeze flows through our backyards, sea salt scented and refreshing enough to raise the hair on my arms. Loose strands of my hair whisk across my face, sticking to the Cherry Cola balm on my lips.

With a bead of sweat falling from his right temple, Dillon pushes unruly curls behind my ear and says, "I love you like no other."

My crazy heart shakes and shimmies, and a more tender part of myself tingles. It takes everything I have not to lick the drop of moisture sliding down the side of his face in front of my dad.

Wiping it away with the tip of my finger, I stare at the tiny bead of fluid and consider rubbing it across my mouth. It falls free, soaking into the lawn before I get the chance.

Dillon takes my hand and walks me around the newly laid slab of concrete over to the one they did earlier this morning on the other side of the porch. What will soon be an area for my father to barbeque dries slowly in the humid heat, dark gray in color and perfectly flat.

My boy kneels, pulling me down with him to our knees. Before I can question what we're doing, he holds his hands out in front of him and spreads his fingers. Knowing exactly what he's up to, I hold my smaller hands up beside his. We drive our palms into the wet cement at the same time and push until our fingers are almost covered.

"It's so cold!" I laugh out loud.

We lift our hands at the same time and look at our permanent mark on Coach Finnel's summer project. Dillon runs to the end of the yard, but I stay and stare at our prints, thinking about everything his hands do for me. They grip the brush he uses to comb my hair when I can't do it myself. His two large palms and ten long fingers grip his bicycle's handlebars and ride us wherever we want to go. His knuckles pound into my front door every morning, despite how mean my father is to him. These hands hold the pen he uses to write me notes across our lawns.

Best of all, his hands hold mine.

"Hey, are you okay?" Dillon asks. His voice lost its carefree tone, and his smile and bright eyes have been exchanged for a scowl.

I smile, hoping it eases the look of concern from his face.

"I'm fine." I stand to my feet and wipe the sticky cement onto my denim shorts.

Dillon takes a step closer. He has a small broken branch in his right hand.

"Are you sure? Because we can get out of here."

I shake my head, forcing cheer into my voice. "That's okay."

Concern's shoulders noticeably relax, and some of his smile returns, instantly lighting up his face.

"Your dad is going to be pissed," he says, kneeling back down and pushing the tip of the stick into the concrete above our handprints. "But who gives a shit?"

Dillon scribbles our names above our hands, the date below them, and then he draws a small, lopsided heart between them.

With his arm over my shoulders, and mine across his bare, sweaty lower back, we're proud of our contribution to the future Finnel cookout area.

Then my boy's sister suddenly stumbles out of nowhere, pushes us over, and takes the stick. In long, warped letters she writes RISA HEARTS WEED onto an untouched slab. After sling shooting the branch across the yard, my hero goes home.

Speechless, Dillon and I tense when my dad appears from the other side of the house. In tube socks that reach his knees and shorts that don't, my dad's face is red, and his dark curly hair is frizzy.

"Am I working alone, boy? Do you want me to die under this sun? Is this a part of some master plan to end my life and steal my family?" There's a touch of humor in my father's tone, and I'll guess there's a smile under his mustache.

Then he sees what's happened to the backyard's addition.

"Boy!" he roars. "I leave you alone for five minutes and you ruin everything."

Dillon drops his arm from my shoulder but lifts his hands in surrender.

He's wide-eyed and full of excuses.

I take a few steps back, secretly loving when these two go at it and wait for my dad to see the real issue here.

Coach points to my handprints and says, "You have some cute hands, boy."

Dillon rolls his eyes.

"Risa hearts weed," Dad reads. He stands straight and focuses on his archenemy. "What the hell does that mean? Is it some kind of gang talk? Are you a homeboy? Should I be concerned for my daughter's safety?"

This time I roll my eyes.

"I didn't do that," Dillon exclaims, backing up as my dad moves toward him. "It literally says my sister's name."

Dad looks thoughtful. "I thought I smelled weed earlier. She's in town?"

Dillon nods. "She just got back."

Who does he think I was sitting with on the Deckers' porch all morning?

Dad nods. "I better have a talk with your parents."

My boyfriend throws his hands up. "Do whatever you want."

Dad turns back to his ruined work. "I have one more question for you, boy."

"What is it?" Dillon asks.

"Why is there a heart between your hands and my princess'?"

The neighbor kid was right. My dad's chest hair does look like it's going to reach out and grab him.

SUMMER ENDS AND STORM CLOUDS move in, coloring the world in the same gray hues as my mood. On a rainy day in September, I turn fifteen and celebrate with Dillon hidden in the woods. We skip cake and ice cream and don't come home until a million stars and a quarter moon light the ground.

When we break free from the trees, our parents have their flashlights out and their yelling voices on.

Dawn cries, "It's one in the morning. I was about to call the police!"

Our families split us up, forcing us into our own homes. Mom's decorated the kitchen with the same birthday banner she used when I turned fourteen.

"You slept through your last birthday, remember?" she answers when I ask why.

Fifteen unlit candles decorate the homemade cake, and whatever she made for dinner sits cold on the stove. Yellow balloons tied to the table chairs are already losing their ability to float, and I sympathize with them. Days have been low for me lately, too.

Dad grabs a beer from the fridge and pops the top off. He won't look at me.

"I'm going to bed," I say, walking past a birthday celebration I didn't want in the first place.

I spent my day of birth in the arms of the only boy who can help me wish away the sorrow plaguing my insides. We hid under one hundred-year-old oaks, protected from the rain beneath their large branches with the sound of waves crashing against Castle Rock in the background.

I slept, we kissed … He wouldn't touch me, even when I begged.

"It doesn't need to be special," I said, overcome with greedy need. "We can do it right here. For our birthdays."

Dillon didn't bother himself by saying no again. He closed his eyes and leaned his head back against the thick bark.

"What were you thinking, Pen?" Mom asks as I walk away. "Why would you leave and not tell us where you're going?"

With my hand on the stair's banister, I say, "I told you I'd be with Dillon."

"But you also said you'd be home before dinner," she replies.

Dad throws his empty beer bottle into the sink and opens the fridge for a fresh one. It breaks, and my mom sighs. Not willing to stick around and listen to the argument brewing between them, I head up to my room with the words, "If she was consistently taking her medication, this wouldn't be happening," following behind me.

My boy appears in his window after me and is the first to write a note.

I DON'T CARE WHAT THEY SAY.

MY SOPHOMORE YEAR IN HIGH school plays out the same way my freshman year did. I don't have any classes with Dillon because he's smarter than me. The kids in my classes stay ten feet away because I'm the weird girl with the sunglasses. Teachers stop trying after the first semester when they finally realize it's better spent on someone else. On the days I make it to school on time or at all, I often talk Dillon into sneaking away early. Sometimes he can't, so I hang out in my dad's office and sleep until it's time to go home.

"Here," Joshua Dark places a sheet of paper on my desk and takes his seat in the spot beside me. "I knew you weren't going to do it, so I did the homework for you."

I slide the assignment closer and smile at the algebra problems I, in fact, didn't do.

"Thanks," I say.

Josh places his hand on the back of my chair. He smells like cinnamon and soapy laundry detergent. Still labeled as trouble, the rez kids continue to bus in from Neah Bay. They grew impossibly bigger over the summer, and my dad spent the first few weeks of school recruiting them for the football team. Some, including Josh, also don't look so … poor.

I haven't seen one hole in any of Joshua's clothing, and it

seems like he has on a new pair of shoes every day.

I kick the red pair he has on today with the side of my foot and say, "Did you get some awesome job or something?"

This bad boy winks at me and says, "Something like that."

I turn in the work he did for me, like I did yesterday and the day before and the day before that. Truth is, the only reason I'm passing this class is because he does enough work for two. It's a secret our teacher hasn't caught on to yet or just doesn't care about, and one I haven't mentioned to Dillon.

Josh moves his hand from the back of my chair to the back of my neck and rubs his thumb back and forth. Straightening my spine, I look around to make sure my boyfriend can't see this, even though I know he's sitting in a class across campus.

"We should hang out sometime, Penny."

Pretending to need something from my book bag, I bend over so that Josh's hand falls back to the seat. There's nothing but a few extra pairs of sunglasses in case the teal pair on my face somehow breaks, my sack lunch, and another yellow number two pencil identical to the perfectly good one already on my desk.

"Is there something wrong with this one?" Josh asks, holding up the first pencil when I present him with the second.

I shrug. "I like this one better."

Disturbance tears a corner from his homework and scrawls

something down. He passes it to me before sticking my pencil in his shirt pocket.

It's his phone number.

"I have a boyfriend," I remind him, brushing the contraband from my desk.

Joshua tears off another corner and writes his number down again, this time in blue ink.

"Call me when you want to come to my side of town."

"YOUR DAD'S GOING TO BE home soon," Dillon says, blushing and so kissable. Lying against my pillows, he holds himself up on his elbows.

I crawl across my bed, kneel beside him, and take his hand in mine. "Don't say anything, okay?"

Bright green eyes look up under long, dark blonde lashes. His breath hitches, and his freckled cheeks tint red.

"And close your eyes," I say, nervous under the thousand pounds of pressure his stare forces down on me.

I've asked for this over and over, but his answer is always a never-changing no. He doesn't have to say so. I know he won't touch me because of my forever state of sadness. But I want it, and I know it'll make me better, just like his handholding and kisses do.

The thought of Dillon touching me where it tingles is nearly enough to make me scream. To have his bare skin pressed against mine will do more than any pill Mom passes my way behind Dad's back.

I know he thinks about it.

It's when he blinks a little slower and kisses me a little harder. It's when he has to step away and adjust his pants like I don't know what he's doing. When Dillon stops breathing and lets me kiss from below his ear across his throat, I know he wants it, too.

I place his hand on my chest, and his eyes snap open—wide open.

He doesn't remove his palm. "Pen."

"Are you scared? Because I'm not," I say.

Dillon shakes his head, slowly blinking.

Letting go of his wrist, I toss my sunglasses to the other side of the bedroom and lift my shirt over my head, showing Dillon Decker my bra for the very first time.

I unhook the pink cotton and let it fall down my arms.

Neither one of us takes a breath.

Slowly and with a shaky hand, Dillon touches me on his own.

"The greatest," he whispers.

Carefully lowering me onto my back, Dillon lies at my side. We kiss, but I want him to *really* touch me. Turning myself into his side, I hitch my leg over his and move my hips up so he knows it's okay to get closer.

He won't.

"Why are you afraid of me?" I ask as his kiss brushes down my neck to my collarbone. "We love-love, Dillon. It's enough."

His eyes look up at me while his lips move further down my chest. I watch as they skim over my shoulder and lower down the right side of my right breast.

Slowly, slowly, slowly his mouth gets closer to my nipple until he's finally there. Warmth surrounds—wet and tongue and licking. Fire shoots between my legs, and I have to use my own hands to cover my mouth.

Dillon's gentle at first, but then his hand squeezes harder, and he sucks deeper. I can feel his tongue circling and kissing. He switches sides, and the abandoned nipple shines in the low light. Fire shoots again. This time I moan, and Dillon smiles against my breast.

Hot—everything is hot as a fever. I can taste what having sex with him will be like. He's strong. His movements are tough. He would handle me, love me … take me.

I can't wait another day.

I circle my hips against his leg and whisper, "Dillon."

"Now?" he asks, lifting his head.

He's pouty lips and wanting this, too.

Until the slamming door of a silver Chrysler echoes from the driveway up to my room.

Dillon jumps up and throws my bra at my face. We're all over the place, limbs and shirts and legs. He pulls my shirt over my head while I try to snap my C-cup back in place.

When our backs hit the bed, my bedroom door opens, and a very suspecting football coach gives us both the "boy" look.

"Nothing!" Dillon yells, despite never being asked a thing.

The pillow over his lap is a dead giveaway.

Chapter 16

DILLON

Penelope and I turn sixteen on a rainy morning in September. Deep gray clouds rumble and boom, mimicking the noise in my head.

"Don't make me spend my birthday here," she says through the phone. "Take me somewhere safe."

"Okay," I say and end the call.

My eyelids are heavy, and lack-of-sleep aches deep within my bones and muscles. I know skipping out on another birthday will break my mother's heart. The horrified look on her face as she clutched the cordless phone in her hand last year when my girl and I emerged from the woods is something I'll never forget.

"How could you, Dillon?" she later screamed at me. "Do you know how terrified I was?"

I kick my comforter off and sit up, stretching my sore arms above my head before I get out of bed and grab clothes from my dresser drawers. Once I'm dressed, I spill whatever's in my backpack onto the floor and pack a flashlight and a couple of extra hoodies for Pen.

She'll forget to bring her own.

Before I walk out the front door, I pack a few bottles of water and some food from the refrigerator so we have something to eat during the day and snag the red throw blanket from the couch.

Hopelessness waits on the sidewalk in front of my house in yellow rain boots holding an oversized black umbrella above her head, wearing pink sunglasses.

She passes me the umbrella, and we walk side-by-side with no destination in sight. We end up at the beach just as the sky opens up and soaks the world. The ocean fights back, slamming angry whitecaps against Castle Rock hard enough to crumble the cathedral.

The birthday girl runs ahead of me, kicking up wet sand behind her. Pen spins with her arms extended at her sides and her face meeting the rain.

"Happy sixteenth fucking birthday!" she shouts to the sky. "This year will be better, right? This is when it all gets figured out."

I run after her, dropping the umbrella for slowing me down.

"Then why do I feel like I'm dying?" She falls to her knees and drops her face into her hands.

I wrap the damp blanket around her body and raise my girl to her feet. With rain falling into my eyes and sobs breaking from between Pen's lips, I lift her into my arms and carry sadness as fast as I can to the cliff at the end of the seashore. A small, cave-like opening at the base of the bluff is just enough to protect us from the storm and the ocean.

"I know it's your birthday and you can supposedly cry if you have to, but don't," I say, lifting Pen's drenched sweater over her head along with her thin T-shirt and bra.

She shivers, half-naked in dim light from outside, and continues to cry because she's right. Sixteen won't change anything. Whatever she has is getting worse with age, and if that means this year will be worse than last year, I'm afraid.

"I can cry if I want to," she says with chattering teeth just before I pull my dry hoodie from the backpack over her tiny frame.

"That's true, but I think our time in this cave will be better spent if you're not making things wetter with your tears."

She smiles. "You had the lyrics wrong."

I tilt her chin up and rub the back of my thumb across the corner of her curved lips. "That's better."

After I change my hoodie, I make Penelope eat a granola bar and a cup of applesauce. A slow stream of tears continues to fall from her eyes, but it's nothing new. All she does is cry lately.

"Are you tired?" I ask, moving strands of wet hair away from her face.

My own exhaustion has taken a backseat to the concern and heartbreak I experience whenever I look at this girl. How helpless I am around her has made a home deep inside my gut, and I can't shake how guilty it makes me feel.

She trusts me enough to let me have her love. Penelope comes to me when she needs help.

But I can't save her.

I can't make the tears stop.

Nothing I do anymore works.

I lean back against the rock wall, and Pen lies beside me on the sandy ground, resting her head on my lap. Rain continues to hammer down from the sky, and the ocean crashes to the shore. An hour passes before Pen's breathing evens and she falls heavy at my side. It's not until then that I close my eyes and finally sleep for the first time in over twenty-four hours.

WE DON'T WAKE UP UNTIL the next morning.

This time my mom does call the cops.

Chapter 17

DILLON

"What's Pen's deal with the rez kid? I thought you told her not to talk to him," Hebert says between bites of pizza.

I look up from my lunch toward my friend across the table. Mathilda Tipp's beside him, checking her makeup in a small mirror; her blue eyes look over the top toward me.

"Why?" I say, knowing this has something to do with the reason my girl's not in the seat next to me and nowhere to be found.

"I saw her walking with him earlier and was going to kick his ass, but redhead over here wouldn't let me."

Mathilda snaps her mirror shut and drops it into her bag. "You guys do realize Penelope's a real person, right? She can have friends."

"Word is Josh Dark is a dealer," Kyle says, digging a white plastic spork into a questionable looking school-issued fruit cup.

Herb, Red, and I wait for him to explain, but he continues to eat odd colored peaches and pears.

"What kind of dealer? Does he deal cards at poker games?" Mathilda asks.

"Or deal fine arts?" Herb adds.

Kyle pushes his tray away and sits back in his chair. He shifts his eyes back and forth between the other two occupying our table and me.

"Umm, no," he says in tone that suggests we're idiots. "He deals drugs."

While Mathilda questions Kyle about the information he just dropped on us, everything around me literally stops. With the sound of my own heartbeat echoing in my ears, I rub my hands over my face and close my eyes until the surge of rage washing over my head crashes and I can take a decent breath again.

"There she is, D. Don't tell her I told you. I don't want her mad at me." Herb chews on his pizza, and Mathilda pretends to look through a magazine she quickly pulls from her bag. Kyle crosses his arms and waits for the show.

Pen and I have never had a fight, but I feel like fighting now.

My girl hides her face from me behind a curtain of her hair and green-framed glasses, but she smiles softly to everyone else. Before she has a chance to pull the chair away from the table, I kick it out. She sits, not bothering to say hello.

"Why were you talking to Josh again?" I ask irately and lowly, so that only she can hear.

Herbert coughs.

"He's my friend," she says defensively, scowling.

And just like that, Pen breaks my heart.

She doesn't call many people friends. It's hard for her to admit that Herb, Mathilda, and Kyle are her friends, but she so easily admits Joshua Dark is?

As I scoot my chair back, it screeches against the tile floor. I get up and walk away from the girl I love because I can't stand to look at her.

I need space.

Just for a moment, I need some air.

Heading toward the back of the school where I know I can be alone for a while, I'm relieved when I look over my shoulder and Penelope hasn't followed me. The lunch bell rings, and since I was dropped from honors history after the first semester for too many late assignments, I have the basic American history class with my girl right now.

I don't go.

"Hey, you," Pepper Hill says, showing up out of nowhere. "Fancy seeing you here. I thought this was my secret spot."

She digs inside her purse for a pack of cigarettes and pops the orange end of one between her red lips. With the paper box still in her grip, Pepper cups her hand over the end of the smoke and lights it with a pink lighter.

"Wanna try?" she offers, blowing an acidic gray, offensive smelling fog-like smoke into the air.

My dad gave me the lecture about tobacco, so I know about all the dangers of smoking. But I'm angry, so I do it anyway and fall hard for the instant calming effect and head change it gives me.

I take a deeper hit, filling my mouth and lungs with the disgusting taste of tar and acetone.

"Slow down before you get sick." Pepper laughs.

She takes the half-smoked cigarette from me, and with her standing so close, I can see why Pen's jealous of her. Pepper's stunning in a blinding type of way. Her hair's a different color blonde than it was when we were younger; I can see the natural color growing out closer to her scalp. Unlike my girl, this one wears a lot of makeup, and she smells like a gross love spell.

"We can meet here every day, if you want," she says, shaking her pack of cigarettes.

I know it's wrong, but if Pen can do it, so can I.

"Okay."

"NOT TODAY, DILLON."

"Can I go up and see her?"

Sonya sighs. "Dillon, not today."

Penelope hasn't been to school in almost two weeks, and I haven't been allowed to see her. Coach Finnel was over to speak to my dad last night. They talked quietly about doctor visits, episodes of unstoppable crying, and the pros and cons of medication she's supposed to be taking.

"Will you tell her I love her and ask her to call me as soon as she's feeling better?"

With tired eyes, more so than my own, Mrs. Finnel smiles. "You know I will, honey."

Not bothering with my bike, I leave it in the middle of the driveway with my heart and start the lonely walk to school. I didn't sleep at all last night, like the night before, afraid to leave the window in case she showed up.

Sleeplessness wraps itself around my body, squeezing the

life right out of me. Like looking through a fishbowl, my depth perception is off, and my reaction time is slow. I trip off a curb onto the street in front of a car, jumping out the way before it hits me. The driver honks her horn before speeding away.

By the time I make it to school, I fall into my seat and can't keep my eyes open. I fold my arms over my desk and drop my head, dead to the world. An hour later, the sound of the bell is in my dreams, and someone shakes my shoulder.

"You can't keep this up, Mr. Decker. One more time and I'm calling your parents. Get out of my class."

I lift my head, and my psychology teacher, Mr. Moore, is walking away from me. Collecting my things—including the assignments I didn't do while I slept—I stumble out to the next class. I should wake up after lunch.

WHEN I GET HOME FROM school, she's waiting for me, bright-eyed and barefoot at my doorstep. Penelope runs as soon as I'm within sight and slams into my body, pressing kisses all over my face. It feels good to touch her, and I'm happy to see her. I'm glad that she's feeling more like herself, only too tired to show it.

"What's the matter? Are you okay? Dillon, talk to me." Looking at me through green circular sunglasses, she places her palms on the side of my face and forces me to look at her.

"I'm just tired," I say, taking one of her hands and leading her into the house, up to my room.

Falling face down onto my bed, my eyes automatically close.

"It's a job to be my boyfriend, isn't it? I'm a hassle." Her weight presses down on the mattress beside me.

If I could make the words leave my mouth, I'd tell her that I get it, and that I love her regardless. I understand she's sick, and I'm here and never going anywhere. Exhaustion keeps me from explaining she can count on me.

Penelope takes off my shoes and pulls a blanket over my body. She lies beside me, but not as close as before, and I hate the distance. A single word about how much I missed her today or that I like her glasses refuses to pass my lips. When she starts to cry, I want to wipe her tears away but can't.

Before I fall asleep, the one who keeps me up at night whispers that she loves me.

"I'm sorry I do this to you. I'll try harder to be better," she says softly.

When I wake up, I'll tell her I love her, too, unconditionally. My love for her is absolute. I'll explain I stay awake with her every night because I want to, because I care, because she's my girl.

No matter what.

Tonight, I'll be by the window, and everything will be like normal. Tomorrow, we'll walk to school together, and everything will be okay. If she'll just stay here with me, when I wake up, she'll know.

"YOU SMELL LIKE CIGARETTE SMOKE," Penelope whispers.

I press my lips to the top of her shoulder, slowly lowering her bra strap.

"No, I don't," I say against her soft skin.

She lifts her arms so I can pull the black lace down her arms. "Yeah, you really do."

I meet Pepper Hill behind school every day after lunch to smoke, giving my girl a different excuse each time.

"I left my backpack in the cafeteria," I'll lie. "There's something I need to get from ... wherever."

There's more to it now than getting back at my girlfriend after our first fight. Pen's been doing well for the last few weeks, but I still worry, and smoking helps me deal. I don't like lying to her, but it's better than admitting there's something I share with her worst enemy.

"Maybe it's from the party," I say, removing my shirt.

Today is my parents' nineteenth wedding anniversary, and

they're hosting a party. Everyone's drunk, and after sneaking away with Pen, Risa promised to be our lookout.

This could be the night.

Pushing her legs apart, I lower myself between her thighs so that Penelope can feel exactly what she does to me. Her head falls back, and her pink lips part as I press my bare chest against hers, lighting the room on fire.

Pressing myself against her warmest spot, with only our jeans between us, I feel her nipples harden against my skin and a shallow breath is pushed from my lungs.

"Take them off," I say, panting.

Penelope reaches between us and unbuttons her jeans.

"Not your jeans. Your glasses." I pull them from her face and throw them off the side of the bed, hoping they break so she can't put them back on for the rest of the night.

Unhidden and exposed, Pen turns her head to the side, as if she's suddenly embarrassed for me to see her. She closes her eyes and grips onto my sides, nearly breaking skin with her nails.

I kiss where her heart beats beneath.

Then lower.

And lower.

Unzipping her jeans, I lower them down to her hips before Pen lifts so I can pull them all the way off, leaving her in nothing put a blue pair of underwear with a small white bow on the top elastic.

She hides her face behind her hands and sucks in a sharp breath when I kiss the inside of her knee.

"Is this okay?" I ask before I go any further, afraid of pushing this fragile girl too far.

With her eyes still closed and my sheets gathered in her grip, the girl I have grown up loving nods her head and bites her bottom lip.

Holding my breath, I slowly slide the light blue cotton down her smooth, slim legs until she is bare, and I can absolutely see all of her.

Refusing to breathe in case I miss something, I slowly move my trembling hand toward what I've never touched before. Penelope's back arches from the mattress the moment I do, and my lungs thrash for air.

"You can tell me to stop anytime," I say, trying not to gasp.

Following the directions her body and her face give me, I move my hand slower, faster, deeper … right there—too hard.

I press my forehead against hers, and we inhale and exhale heavily with our eyes only on the other.

Then her entire body goes stiff, and her legs close on my hand. Pen bites her bottom lip to keep from crying out. Her cheeks turn so, so red, and her skin is so, so hot. I can feel every muscle in her entire body tense as she goes higher, and higher, and higher.

Until she finally soars and carries me with her.

Afterward, there's something about the light in her eyes and the bend in her smile that tells me things will never be the same.

Chapter 18

PENELOPE

"**I** want this."

"Baby, are you sure?" Mom asks, eyeing the light pink shirt I hold up for her to see.

"Yeah, it's cute. I'll get the yellow one, too."

"Cute?" she asks, dumbfounded. "Please be sure, because this was a far drive, and if we get home and you don't—"

"I'm not going to change my mind," I cut her off, smiling at my choices.

My mom holds her hands out for the clothes I would normally never wear from a store I've never stepped foot in before today and takes them to the register with a worried expression on her round face. There are four more bags of purchases she questioned me twice about both before and after she paid for them.

Handing me the fifth bag, she shoves the receipt into her purse and says, "This is too stressful. Let's eat."

I order a salad that I have trouble eating because my mother scrutinizes every bite, like I have an eating disorder not a brain disorder.

"Eat all of your vegetables," she says, waving her fork at me between bites of lasagna. "They're good for you."

I pop a cherry tomato into my mouth and smile.

The woman who brought me into this world wipes her mouth with a white cloth napkin and says, "Today has been good, right, baby? Everything's okay?"

Nodding my head, I push a sprout of broccoli to the side of my salad bowl and pierce my fork through a slice of cucumber.

"It's been great. I'm good," I say, stabbing a chunk of avocado next.

Suffering through silence isn't something I have to worry about, but Mom does. For her sake, I should talk about school or maybe confide in her about the rez boy I've become good friends with over the last couple of years.

I don't because she'll tell Dad. Considering how different he and Dillon are, they both agree the bussed in kids are trouble.

Coach Finnel doesn't mind if Joshua Dark plays on the football team, but he won't allow a so-called criminal to befriend his offspring.

I've heard the rumors about Josh, but I don't believe them.

"How's Dillon, honey?"

"Good, Mom. Dillon's good."

Which is the problem. The boy next door has always been too good for me, so this is my attempt to be more on his level.

I know this might be a disaster.

"You look beautiful, baby. It's a nice change," Mom says honestly, reaching across the table for my hand.

"Thanks, Mom."

"Dillon's going to love it."

"I hope so."

"Your dad, on the other hand, won't be too happy about his only daughter growing up."

PENELOPE

"**S**he's not allowed out of the house looking like that."

Crippling panic seizes my insides, leaving me utterly immobile.

This is exactly what I was afraid of. If my dad doesn't like it, what are Dillon and the other kids at school going to think?

"Wayne, don't be ridiculous," Mom snaps, moving in between my father and me.

From his spot on the couch, he aimlessly flips through television channels, like this isn't terrifying for me. I'm going out on a limb, scared out of my mind, and he can't even put the remote down to comfort me.

"She looks like she's eighteen, Sonya. I have enough trouble keeping that freak boy next door away from her."

He has no clue how hard he's failing.

"She's sixteen. She looks sixteen," Mom insists, stomping her foot.

"That boy isn't allowed over anymore. You're not allowed near him, Penelope." Dad's mustache moves when he talks.

I want to rip it off his face.

Feeling like a complete failure, I turn my back on the man who refuses to show vulnerability for five minutes and run upstairs. I slam my bedroom door closed and flip on my stereo before the echoes of my parents' argument can be heard through the walls.

Before I crumble, I rush over to my window and shut the curtains, too embarrassed to let Dillon see what I've done to myself.

It was a mistake.

Chapter 20

DILLON

"You can't keep this up forever, you know." Risa holds on to my elbow, searching my eyes with ones the same color as my own. "I know you love her, but you need to start loving yourself, D."

With a thermos of coffee for myself and a second for Pen, I drag my feet across my lawn and then hers. Like I have a million mornings before this one, I knock on the Finnels' front door three times before Sonya opens it, and I step into what's become a second home to me.

"Need a refill?" my girl's mom asks in a chipper tone I wasn't expecting. She carries her heavy body over to the coffee pot.

"Not yet," I say, taking the stairs up to Pen's room.

Before she's out of sight, I look to the kitchen and catch her beaming like someone just told her the moon is made of vanilla soft serve.

Since I was up at the window last night alone, I've prepared myself for the hard time Penelope's sure to give me this morning. The episodes of depression she suffers from are more frequent lately, but her behavior leading up to and during them remains mostly the same. I can predict and handle her moods better than anyone else at this point.

"Time to wake up, Pen. I brought coffee." I open her door, but stop before stepping inside.

"What do you think?" she asks.

I think she looks like Pepper Hill.

Standing in the center of her bedroom, she spins so I can see this new look from all angles. My girl's dark brown hair is now an almost blonde color. Instead of leaving it long and curly like she has since I met her, it's perfectly straight and cut a few inches below her shoulders.

Dressed in a pair of pre-washed purple Levi's and a white tank top, she's going to show the entire school skin only I've seen until now. And instead of wearing the beat-up pair of Chucks she has for the last year, Penelope slips her feet into black flats.

She's beautiful, but I don't understand.

Her face falls. "Do you hate it, too?"

I enter the room and kiss her cheek, stunned by the smell of fruity perfume on her skin.

"I don't hate it. You look pretty."

"You think I'm pretty?"

"Yes, I almost don't recognize you."

My girl happily presses her glossed lips to mine and takes her java from my hands.

For a change, I sit in bed while she runs around the room, trying on a few sweaters with price tags still attached. She chooses the black cotton one and throws the others onto the closet floor. Penelope sprays hairspray in her hair and then asks me if I like the gold or silver necklace better.

"Gold," I say, hoping I answer correctly.

Convinced I've lost my girl to this Pepper-like replica, before we leave, Pen kicks off the flats and shoves her feet into a pair of Converse, giving me hope she's not totally changed.

I watch her the entire way to school with her new pink book bag held high on her shoulders, kicking the same rock for a block. I assumed she would eventually grow out of being a tomboy—everyone said it wouldn't last forever—but I thought Penelope was more like Risa and less like Pepper Hill. She smells like a botanical garden and has lip gloss on her lips, and today is the first time in two years that I haven't been the one to brush her hair.

She's straight out of a magazine and brand new to me.

Maybe I feel insecure.

Maybe I hate this.

"Penelope, you know you're good enough, right? You're perfect to me no matter what you look like."

She turns her head and strands of hair blow across her face. "Oh, yeah?"

I grab her wrist, stopping our stride in front of the school. I lift the sunglasses she hasn't ditched yet, and I look into her eyes. "Yes."

"Is that why you smoke with Pepper Hill every day behind school, because I'm good enough?"

I **LEAVE FIRST PERIOD TEN** minutes early and run down the empty hall toward Penelope's English class. Waiting outside the door with my hands in my pockets, guilt is like lead in the pit of my stomach and panic I can't shake creeps up and down my arms.

The bell rings, and I'm pushed against a row of lockers

behind me, where I wait for Pen to file out of class. A short girl
with glasses, a tall guy with a letterman jacket, and one of the
rez kids burst out the door first, followed by another twenty
faces that blur together.

"This is my locker, man," someone says at my side.

I move out of the way without looking, and then another
passing student bumps me in the shoulder.

"Sorry," whoever mumbles.

My next course is on the other side of the campus. I need
to head that way now if I'm going to make it to my seat before
the second bell rings. With the way school's been going, I can't
afford to be late. My grades are up, but I'm down to one honors
class.

High school and my future goals—college and medical
school—take a backseat to my broken heart and the look of
betrayal that crossed Pen's pretty blushed face after I admitted
to spending time with Pepper.

Bodies in the narrow hallway begin to disappear. Penelope
still hasn't left her class, but other students start to go inside. I
wonder if she got by me or if she left school completely while I
suffered through civics.

One last student wanders out of the classroom with his
nose in a book, not watching where he's going. I grab his elbow
and nearly scare him right out of his skin.

"Is Penelope Finnel still in there?" I ask.

He pushes a pair of wire-framed glasses up his nose and says, "Who?"

Shoving him away, I head into the room and find her still seated in the far corner. She has her head down over her folded arms, and judging by the steady rise and fall of her breathing, she's asleep.

I approach the desk and kneel down beside the one who has my heart, smiling at the sound of Pen's soft snoring.

"Can you ask her to move? This is my seat," some chick with a squeaky voice asks.

I don't bother looking up and brushing locks of hair away from the girl next door's face. Her lips are parted, and her dark brown irises move behind her blue-veined eyelids.

Unfolding the arms of her sunglasses so she can put them on right away, I whisper her name.

"Wake up, baby," I say quietly.

Her lashes flutter at the sound of my voice.

"Come on, Pen. We gotta go."

She sits up and wipes the corner of her mouth on the back of her hand with makeup she's never worn before smeared under her sleepy eyes. She takes her shades from me and places them on her face without cleaning it away.

We're the only students not where we're supposed to be,

and neither one of us says a word until we pass through the school's courtyard and stop in the middle quad. Her next class is one way, and mine is the other.

"Want me to walk you to class?" I ask, unsure if I should touch her or not. I hook my thumbs behind the straps of my backpack instead.

"I'm not an invalid, Dillon," she says, turning to move away from me.

"Why would you say that to me?" I ask, catching her wrist. I feel like I'm looking at a person I don't know.

She shakes her arm free from my hold and takes two steps back.

"Maybe we should break up," she says coldly with no expression on her face, but tears start to fall from under her purple lenses.

Closing the space between us, I take her face between my hands and wipe her sadness away with my thumbs. I bend at the knees so we're eye to eye, wishing she would leave the sunglasses at home for once.

"We're not breaking up, Pen. Not over this. I'm sorry I didn't tell you about Pepper, but I swear it doesn't mean anything."

She shakes her head, licking misery from her lips. "Why don't you get that you're too good for me?"

"Because I'm not," I say, pulling her against my body.

Her arms wrap around my back, and I tilt her head back to kiss the corner of her mouth.

"Please don't do this," I beg, bringing her bottom lip between my teeth before letting go and kissing her.

It takes a moment, but her lips part and our tongues touch. Penelope's fingers clutch onto the back of my shirt, and I slide my hands into her hair. Overwhelming need flows through my veins, heating my body until I feel like I'm going to explode. Moving my mouth down the side of her neck, I slowly push her until she backs into a wall.

I press a kiss to the soft spot below her ear and whisper in a breathless tone, "Why don't you get that *you're* too good for *me*?"

PENELOPE'S NEW LOOK BRINGS NEW ATTENTION.

The same people who have called her weird for the last four years suddenly find her worthy enough to talk to.

"Cute glasses," they say as she walks down the hallway with me at her side.

"I love your hair color," some gush. "Where did you have it done?"

"What brand is that lip gloss, Penelope? It seriously looks

amazing on you," Pepper says, stopping at our table during lunch.

The bend in her smirk and the way she winks at me as she gets up and walks by raises the hairs on the back of my neck. I know it's wrong, but I still find time during the day to sneak away with Pepper and smoke a cigarette or two between classes. I've even given her money to buy my own pack from the hookup she has.

It's the only thing I have that's mine, and I need the temporary relief from the constant gloom of being with someone who suffers from depression.

Soaking up the attention, full of smiles and fake laughs, Penelope entertains it all. She exchanges numbers with some of the girls in our grade and makes plans to see a movie with a group of others.

She tosses the phone numbers away with the trash and never actually makes it to the movie theater, because once school is over and it's just she and I, the act is up.

I don't know if it's because she tries so hard during the week not to be exactly who she is, but nights are hard and weekends are nightmares. She's not only sad anymore, she's full of rage and impossible to handle.

"Come on, I've let you see me," unpredictable and insatiable says, trying to get her hand down my shorts.

Pen and I escape April showers hidden inside the cave buried at the base of Castle Rock. I kiss her until my lips bleed and touch her until she shakes beneath me, clawing at my arms and sides. After we've spent the afternoon half-naked and attached, sleeplessness crashes into me, and all I want to do is close my eyes. Penelope's wide-awake and begging for more.

"Can we just hang out for a while? I didn't get any sleep last night." I lie back in the cool sand and run my hand through my hair.

"Neither did I." She scoffs.

"Obviously," I say, looking up at the roof of the cave.

She throws a handful of sand at me; tiny granules fall into my hair and eyes. I sit up, spitting beach sand out of my mouth and brushing it away from my face.

"Why won't you have sex with me?" she asks, throwing another handful. "Are you scared?"

"Stop," I say, shaking sand from my hair.

She stands and kicks it at me before bolting out of our hiding place. It takes a moment before my eyes stop watering, and I can see again. By the time I shove our blanket and flashlights into my backpack, she's halfway down the beach and running, so I don't chase her.

Part of me wants to go back into the cave and not come out until I've slept for twelve hours, but I force my feet to move through rain-wet sand and head home. The walk seems to take hours, and I'm barely moving by the time I approach our houses.

"You're not earning any of these today, boy," Coach Finnel says. From his front porch, he holds up a small pack of chocolate peanut candies.

I walk to the end of my lawn and ask, "Is she in there?"

He nods once.

Lacking the energy to fight with her anymore, I go inside as a bolt of white electricity strikes from the sky. Thunder follows, cracking hard enough to shake the ground.

Mom comes running out of the kitchen with a dishtowel in her hand as I enter the house.

"Were you out in this storm, Dillon?" she asks, stopping in front of me.

"I was at Castle Rock with Pen," I say, dropping my backpack to the floor. "We had a fight."

"Again?" my sister comments in a sarcastic tone from the couch behind me.

Dad trots downstairs with his lips in a straight line and his brows scrunched together like he's worried about something.

"You walked home in this rain? Are you crazy?" Mom's hazel eyes open wide.

"His girlfriend is," Risa sing-songs.

Surrounded on all sides by my family, I lean back against the front door since it's obvious they're not going to let me upstairs.

"Why didn't you use the pay phone to call one of us, for heaven's sake? Your lips are blue!" the woman who brought me into the world shouts.

Scrubbing my hands over my face, I drop my arms to my side. "I walk home from the beach all the time. What's the big deal?"

Mom shakes her head before throwing her arms in the air and turning back to the kitchen. Dad takes a step forward, and my sister shuts the television off.

"The big deal is that you've returned home soaking wet after you took off this morning without our permission. The note you left said you were at the Finnels', not the beach during a rainstorm. You're allowing Penelope's sickness to break you down, and my son is unrecognizable. For your mother and me, it's a very big deal," Dad says in a tone edging hysterical.

His chin trembles, and I have to look away, unable to face the pain I've caused. It's only then do I notice my clothes are drenched and sticking to my skin. My hands tremble, my teeth chatter, and water drips from the ends of my hair.

"I didn't realize it was raining..." I start.

"When's the last time you slept, D? You seriously look like

a zombie," Risa says. She stands from the couch and carries a blanket over, wrapping it around my shoulders.

They don't understand.

When has my sister ever taken responsibility for anything in her life? Two years out of high school, she still doesn't have a job and gets by on our dad's tab. Risa's probably high right now, and she wants to talk to me about mistakes she thinks I'm making?

My parents don't know what it means to love someone to death like I love Pen. Their relationship is based on pot roast dinners in the slow cooker and who can guess the answers during *Who Wants to be a Millionaire* first. They have matching robes and too many decorative pillows on their bed. The only thing I've ever seen them argue about is the one time my mom left the cap off the tube of toothpaste.

Lifting my chin in a sad attempt at saving face in front of anyone today, I say, "If you're done talking to me like I'm stupid, I want to go to bed."

With the exception of the rain beating down on the roof and thunder rolling after lightning strikes, the house falls silent.

No one stops me when I drop the blanket and head to my room. With every intention of sleeping until morning, I close my door and kick off my shoes, purposely avoiding my window in case heartache is there.

Instead of falling right into bed, I make the mistake of closing my blinds first and catch the look on her face before parallel panels shut between us.

Don't open them.

Don't do it.

I pull the string and know immediately I won't be shutting my eyes anytime soon.

WHY AM I SO BROKEN? her note reads.

I pick up the cordless phone and hit *Redial* because her number is the only one I ever dial.

When she answers, I say, "You're perfect to me."

Chapter 21

PENELOPE

After waking up on my bedroom floor with my knees pulled to my chest and my hair stuck to my face, the nightgown I've been in for a week is bunched around my waist, and I don't have any underwear on.

This is the only coherent thought I'm able to process before the weight of my own madness crashes down and strangles the life from me.

Tears I have no control over pool in my burning eyes before falling to the carpet under my head. Sludge-like blood pushes through my cement-like veins, and my fading heart beats inside a cage of bones.

Forcing my arms to bend, I scratch at my throat, hoping to make holes to breathe through because my lungs don't work.

I roll over to my back, choosing to suffocate rather than to live a life in the dark.

This has to be what dying feels like.

Otherwise, why would God be so mean?

DILLON

Herbert drives his mom's Honda into the driveway with Mathilda in the passenger seat and Kyle in the back. All four windows are rolled down and the music is up, blaring absence lyrics and heavy beats until he kills the engine.

"Guess who got his license today?" he says, sticking his head out the window.

Redhead waves as I approach the car, and Kyle reaches to shake my hand through the open window.

"What are you guys up to?" I ask, shoving my hands into my pockets.

I turned sixteen eight months ago, and the thought of getting my license hasn't crossed my mind once. It makes me wonder what else I've missed.

"Where's Pen?" Herb asks. "We're heading to the beach, jump in."

Shifting my eyes to her closed bedroom window, I rock back to the heels of my feet and shake my head. "I don't think she's up for it."

"Does that mean you can't come? Is she your mommy now, or what?" Kyle asks, laughing like it's some kind of joke. "You never hang with us anymore."

I slap my hand on the top of the red Civic and take a step back, unable to bring myself to explain what's really going on with the girl next door.

"I'll catch up with you guys later. Maybe I'll have Risa drop me off over there tonight," I lie, hoping to appease them enough to leave without giving me a guilt trip.

A smile spreads across Kyle's face. "Tell your sister I said what's up."

Chapter 23

PENELOPE

A different day.

A different doctor.

A different prescription.

Chapter 24

DILLON

I haven't seen Penelope in eight days and don't leave my room unless I have to, in case she wakes up.

"Dad and I are going to grab something for dinner. Do you want to come?" Mom asks. She's a small voice behind my locked bedroom door. "Getting out might make you feel better."

Lying on the floor under my open window, I throw a baseball up and catch it in the palm of my hand before throwing it again. Red threads sewn into a rubber casing spin as it goes up, up, up and as it comes down, down, down.

"Dillon, will you please let me in?" the woman who gave

me life asks. She tries the handle, jiggling the brass knob and then knocks. "Are you even awake?"

I sit up, letting the ball drop to the floor. It hits the carpet with a soft thump and rolls to the center of my room.

"I'm not hungry," I say, scrubbing my hands over my face before standing to my feet.

The setting sun colors my bedroom walls in pinks and oranges, and the warm summer air drops in temperature with it as the largest star in the sky sets in the west. Looking out my window, disappointed to see that Pen's is still shut, I walk away with an ache in the pit of my stomach and unlock my bedroom door.

Mom slowly enters my space, dragging her thumb over the surface of my dresser and making a face at the layer of dust that rubs off. Her hazel eyes widen at the pile of clothes in the corner and at the mass of dirty dishes I haven't bothered to take down to the kitchen.

"At least I know you're eating," she says, stacking empty glasses and plates so she can take them away.

Sitting on the edge of my bed, I say, "It's not that serious."

Penelope could be her daughter.

With two handfuls of my dirty irresponsibilites, she opens her mouth to speak. I brace myself for the same lecture I've heard a few times this week already, but drop my shoulders when she snaps her lips shut.

Unable to make anyone happy, I feel like I'm being torn in two. My heart is with the sad girl next door who can't leave her room in a prescription pill slumber. Sonya won't show me mercy and refuses to let me see Pen at all. My parents force me to go to school every day without her, and they hide the house phone so I'll stop calling the Finnels'.

The last thing I want is for Penelope to think I've abandoned her, and I want my parents to know they can trust me. One thing prevents the other, so I'm stuck going to school and coming home only to lock myself in my room.

Mom shifts from one hip to the other. Her light-colored hair is pulled back, and there's discomfort in the dark circles under her eyes.

"Mom, I'm fine," I say, hoping to ease her worry.

She sighs heavily. "Please, come to dinner with us. It will make me feel better."

Pushing away from the mattress, I agree to go and take some of the dirty dishes to lessen the burden. Light returns to the color of her eyes, and a smile spreads across her small face. For just one moment, the thought of leaving the house and not eating a meal alone lightens my mood.

But it all falls like the glass in my hands when I hear Penelope scream.

"Dillon!" my mom calls after me as I run out the door, crushing pieces of broken glass beneath the soles of my shoes.

The desperate, ear-splitting pitch of my girl's cries and screams gets louder as I rush down the stairs and out the door behind my father who ran from the kitchen. Tripping down the porch steps, I catch myself and race over to the Finnels'.

Pen's barefoot in pajamas with nothing less than brutal craze in her eyes, pulling on the back of Wayne's shirt as he tries to walk around the house. Her toes dig into the grass, but her father is stronger and able to pull her onto the driveway. Dirty feet turn bloody when she stubs them on the concrete, and she falls to her bottom when her nimble fingers come free from the dark blue cotton.

Sonya stands at the opening of their front door with her hands over her mouth and tears falling from her eyes. Mom walks past me to comfort the neighbors turned friends.

With my heartbeat gone still, I try to go over to Penelope, but my dad holds his arm out in front of me.

"Get inside," he orders in a stern tone I've never heard from him before.

"Dad, please. Dad! No, you can't, Dad!" Penelope sobs, but Coach Finnel doesn't listen. Even when his daughter crawls after him on her hands and knees and grabs onto his ankle.

"Let go," he says. Wayne has a medium-sized cardboard

box in his hands.

I watch Pen's knuckles go white and can't stand back any longer as my eyes fill with tears. Shoving my dad's arm away, I go to her despite his protests and drop to my knees beside the girl who crushes souls. She doesn't react to my hold circling her, but something in me snaps back into place, and I feel complete with madness in my grip.

Unreachable's fingertips dig into her life-giver's calf. Wayne doesn't shake her off or drag her forward like he did when she pulled his shirt. Looking down at us with dark eyes and a blank stare, he simply waits for her to let go, like this is nothing more than a bratty girl throwing a temper tantrum.

I can feel the quake in her bones and hear the fear in her tone.

This is no fit.

It's hysteria.

"It's me, Penelope," I whisper into her ear, slowly placing my hand on top of hers.

She falls from her knees, and I pull sadness between my legs with one arm around her middle and the other slowly pulling her fingers free.

"Come on, baby. Let go," I say, holding so tight there's no space between our bodies.

Suddenly, she does and turns in my lap, clinging to me with

wild strength and cries, "He broke them."

Free from his only child's grasp, Mr. Finnel walks over to the metal trashcan stored on the side of the white house and lifts its lid, dropping it to the driveway. Pen hides her face in my neck, coating my skin with her warm tears, unable to handle what her dad does next.

I watch as he dumps what's inside the box upside down over the trashcan and cry with my girl when I realize what it is.

A rainbow of broken arms and shattered lenses falls from the box, some still reflecting the sunset and others keeping their different shapes. Green circles, yellow ovals, purple, red, and blue fragments of Penelope's bravery vanish into the garbage with empty milk cartons and last week's leftovers.

"Oh my gosh." I hear my mother say from somewhere behind me.

Wayne shoves the empty box into the metal can on top of the ruined sunglasses and places the lid back on.

"Go home, boy," he says, lifting Pen from my arms.

Penelope's outrageous fight stops, and she goes still. He carries her like a baby against his chest, past my parents, and then past his wife before they disappear into their house.

Slapping angry tears from my face, I stand to my feet and run to the house and up to my room.

I have a box of my own I keep under my bed.

"You need to let the Finnels deal with their daughter, Dillon. You don't have any idea what they're going through," my dad says, standing under my doorway.

Inhaling a deep breath through my nose, I wait for him to move out of my way.

He has no idea what *I'm* going through.

"You're not leaving until you calm down," he says, taking a step toward me.

Because I'm taller and stronger than my father, it's the only opening I need to get past him. He doesn't try to stop me, and I ignore my mother's protests when I run past her as she comes into the house.

Standing in the middle of their yard with rage and hurt running down my eyes, I throw handfuls of counted smiles at Wayne's front door. Small packages of candy collide with their home, scattering across the paint-chipped wooden porch. When Penelope's invisibility crusher comes outside to see what's going on, I pick the box up and throw it at him. What seems like hundreds of yellow packs explode between us, and together we watch our attempt at her happiness crash to the ground.

It's only a fraction of what he owes me.

Chapter 25

DILLON

"I love you," she whispers.

We're tangled limbs and naked skin, breathing heavily and touching curiously. My bare back stings under the summer sun, and her pale, undressed chest practically glows. A cage of stark white bone, red blood and muscle, and blue veins protect the fragile beating heart beneath. I brush my lips over the diamond-shaped collection of freckles at the base of her throat and push my knees up, opening hers around me.

She's tired-wild and lifeless-living.

The dense wall of trees around us protects her from being seen, and the blanket over the grass keeps her comfortable.

Far enough out into the woods, only the wildlife will hear her screams.

She's all that matters and safe with me.

Sliding my hands up her thin stomach and over her round chest, my girl tilts her head back, and her brown eyes move under her translucent lids. Chapped lips part, and a sound so small escapes I don't know if I heard it and question my own sanity.

"Are you sure this is what you want?" I ask, unbuttoning my shorts.

Penelope's long lashes flutter, and she opens her eyes against sun rays so strong red blotches slowly appear on her outstretched arms. She has green blades of grass in her grip, holding on to Earth so she doesn't fly away as I slowly push my fingers into her warmest spot.

My girl circles her hips over my hand, and I shove deeper, like either one of us knows what this really means.

Leaning over her small body, I kiss the length of Pen's neck and pull her earlobe between my teeth.

"We can stop whenever you want," I say, licking the single tear that bleeds from the side of her eye.

"I don't want to," insistence answers with a breathless voice.

Pressing my forehead to her temple, I watch as this girl takes what she needs from my too-willing fingers and sends birds soaring from tree branches with the forceful melody that her lungs release as bliss captures her body in its tight clench.

A light sheen layers her already humid-sticky skin as she comes down, and I slip myself from her soaked center. Color that only returns to her face when we do this flushes her cheeks, making her look more like the girl who used to draw on her hands and wear heart-shaped sunglasses than the one she's turned into, perfect looking on the outside but decaying within.

Pen turns her face into my neck and begs, "Please, Dillon. Please."

Her thighs shake on the outside of mine and ground-gripping hands push and pull at me. I hold myself above her, and my heart hammers as I pull myself free from my black boxers. Penelope uses her feet to push my shorts she can't get off fast enough down to my knees.

"Be easy," I say, lowing my head to her chest to breathe for one second.

Penelope tangles her fingers in my long hair, pulling my head up and kissing my mouth with a hectic kind of urgency. She drags her teeth down my throat and loves me so hard there I feel blood vessels break and bruises form.

Taking her hands and pinning them to the ground, I can't help but notice she's the most beautiful thing I've ever seen. Her chest and stomach heave up and down with heavy gasps and gulps of air, and her hair is curly and littered with leaves and broken blades of grass. Dirt and rocks are stuck on the underside of her palms, and a black ant crawls over her wrist before falling onto our blanket.

"Everything's okay," I say, watching ever haunting burden pool and spill from the whites of her eyes. "It's just me."

Releasing her from my hold, I slip my arm under her head and cradle hopelessness close as I push myself where she's wanted me for so long. Pen's arms circle around my back, and she shuts her eyes as I try to push inside.

She's tense muscles and loud gasps.

I hold her hips down and move slowly, terrified to hurt the girl I love the most. Pen turns her face into my arm and sinks her teeth into the soft skin there. Tiny beads of blood pool where she's broken me; Pen licks them away.

Too wound up to feel pain, I let her wound me however she needs to get through what my body does to hers.

"I'm sorry. I'm sorry," she cries as I fall under and deeper.

Gripping her long hair in my hand, I stop when I'm as far as I can go and fully surrounded by craziness and drop my forehead to hers. Sadness holds my face between her palms and wipes tears away from under my eyes while hers flow freely.

"It's just me," she whispers, warm under the bright sun.

We move together, getting lost in sensations we've never felt in secret beach caves. Our hearts mend with blood-soaked rope and sync beats so they match. The blanket beneath us bunches under our bodies, and I dig my toes into weeds and wet dirt to be closer, to get deeper. *There has to be more of her to feel.*

Pressure towers, and I know what's coming. Shaking my head because I'm not ready for this to be over, I push our joined hands into the grass beside Pen's head and cry out. Her palms fall from my face and slide down my body, touching moving muscles and heated skin.

When winding pressure releases, the world around us explodes, sending trees, grass, and dirt past the clouds. I close my eyes and let the universe destroy itself while I get lost in Penelope, forgetting about depression and disappointment and uncertainty.

She's all there is and everything I need.

It starts to slow down, and everything begins to fall back into place. Propping myself on my elbows to keep from collapsing on sorrow, I look around to see every tree and patch of grass where it belongs.

Then I look down and find brown eyes staring at me under dark eyelashes that shadow her flushed face.

Penelope giggles, and I feel like I might start to cry again.

She never giggles anymore.

"THEY'RE STARING AT ME."

Looking around the courtyard, all I see are other students in a hurry to get to their next class. In the first few weeks of our senior year, I can't afford to be late every day like I have been since the eighth grade, and we need to make the most of the next nine months.

Penelope can't mess around, or she won't graduate, and I need to stay on track for college.

"No, they're not," I say, running my hand through my hair.

"I must be lying then, right?" she fires back, pushing her perfectly blondish hair behind her ear before walking away.

Our classes are in the same direction, so I follow her, but I don't bother catching up. When Pen's moods spike, either for the good or bad, there's no talking her out of the way she feels or convincing her that she's wrong.

Shoving my hands deep into the pockets of my slim-straights, I watch her hips sway from thirty feet ahead of me in the pair of dark colored Levi's she's wearing. Her sandals flip and flop against the bottom of her feet, and the chunk of hair she missed curling this morning makes me smile because it reminds me of the Pen she used to be.

"I've been looking for you."

Turning around just as Penelope walks into her economics class, I come face-to-face with Pepper Hill. Overcome by the scent of huckleberry and a spoonful of sugar—thanks to the perfume she must dip in before coming to school every day—I take a step back.

"What's up?" I ask, burying the concern I feel for my girl.

The right side of Pepper's rose lipstick-covered pout lifts. She pulls out a pack of Marlboro Lights from her purse so that only I can see and asks, "You look like you can use one of these. Are you in?"

Quickly checking over my shoulder to make sure Pen's in class, I say, "Sure."

Chapter 26

PENELOPE

"What are you looking at, Josh?" I ask, leaning over the geometry book he and I are sharing. His stare burns a guilty feeling hole in the back of my head, and I can't act like I don't know he's looking.

"Why don't you wear your sunglasses anymore, Penny?" he questions instead of giving me an answer.

A flash of heat reddens my cheeks, and I drop my pencil to the wide-ruled paper I'm copying math problems onto. I almost forgot colored shades weren't on my face, shielding anyone from looking at me in the first place. Letting my hair drop from behind my ear, it acts as a curtain between the ringleader who makes me feel more comfortable than he should and me.

"They broke."

Josh leans close enough for me to smell the spearmint gum in his mouth. "All of them?"

I nod.

"Why haven't you gotten more?" he asks, catching my pencil when it rolls off my desk. He holds it between the tips of his pointer finger and thumb until I pluck the orange painted wood from him.

"Because it's not sunny out," I lie with a sarcastic smile he can't see.

He pushes my hair over my shoulder so it's out of my face. The backs of his fingers brush across the pulse point in my throat, and I look up into eyes that are the same color as mine.

"You look pretty without them," he says, smiling so big the mint green piece of gum between his back teeth is visible. Josh reaches down into his backpack. "But it's August. The sun's out. Wear mine if you need them."

The boy they call risky drops a pair of black Ray-Bans in front of me. Over a month has passed since my dad snapped my sunglasses in half with his bare hands.

"We've enabled you long enough, Penelope," the man who gave me life said as he crushed the colored plastic. "I can't sit back and watch this happen to you anymore."

Dillon hasn't offered me the pair of heart-shaped glasses I gave him on our birthday a few years ago to ease the endless anxiety I suffer from. Everyone assumes they're helping me deal by holding them out of my reach, but no one knows what the heavy dread that constantly hangs over my head feels like. Panic coats logic with fear when I'm forced to face the public without my sunglasses, and I'm expected to function as it pecks at me all day long like a bird.

Since I'm no longer invisible, people see past the fake hair color and pretty clothes at the real me—lowdown and dreary. They whisper to each other and back away when I'm near, as if my instability is contagious.

Dillon says it's all in my head, but what does perfection know?

I push Josh's shades away and copy down the next problem. "No thanks. The day is almost over, anyway."

"Keep 'em. I have another pair at home," he says, like they're nothing special. The underlining tone in his voice is clear. "You need them more than I do."

"I said no thanks, rez boy," I fire back, daring him to act like he knows anything about why I wore sunglasses in the first place.

Unaffected by my anger, Josh picks up the pair of sunglasses from my desk and pushes them into my chest softly.

"I've always seen you, Penny. You don't need to hide from me."

"Don't," I say, fighting back tears. "There's no part of this you want, Josh."

"My mom was diagnosed with bipolar disorder when I was nine. I live with a crazy person, so I know one when I see one. You're completely nuts, Penny. But I dig it." He slides his large arm on the back of my chair.

Unable to stop myself, I laugh out loud and actually don't mind when the entire class looks back at me. There's an odd comfort in danger's confession, and I trust his sincerity. It's the same natural kindness he's always shown me that makes it easy to ignore rumors about drugs and gang banging. The Joshua Dark everyone talks about isn't the Josh I know.

Sliding the black frames over my face, it feels like coming home.

"ARE YOU SURE I CAN keep them?" I ask again, more comfortable in my skin than I have been in weeks.

I never wore dark lenses before because they're hard to see through, but these are by far the nicest and most expensive pair

I've ever owned. Sturdy frames hug the side of my face perfectly, and they're weightless on the bridge of my nose. No one stares at me or walks by to see what color shades I'm wearing. I'm not treated like I'm infectious or weird.

I'm truly invisible.

Josh ignores my question and lifts a lock of my hair. "You forgot to curl this piece."

I slap his hand away and tuck the straight pieces back as I walk past the boy I shouldn't like so much. He reaches out for my wrist before I get too far and pulls me toward his large body, blocking the sun and towering over me entirely.

"Tell me not to kiss you, Penny," Joshua says.

He doesn't give me the chance to.

His mouth is too big, too soft, too warm against mine, and every nerve in my body fires off, shooting white-hot fever through my veins. It's the first time I've felt anything but numb since Dillon took me into the woods and undressed me slowly.

Selfishly soaking it up, I can't bring myself to jerk away from feeling alive until his tongue parts my lips and a jolt of disgust straightens my spine. Sickening remorse creeps under my skin, slithering like a snake over hollow bones and weak muscles toward my worthless beat.

As I wipe the wrong kiss from my lips, carelessness smiles over my shoulder and says, "Your boyfriend's looking."

Removing sunglasses I'm suddenly ashamed of and wouldn't dare look at him through from my face, I let them slip from my fingers before turning to face consequence. Dillon's at the end of the hall with his hands at his sides and his breaking heart on the floor.

I take a step forward.

Dillon takes two steps away.

"Stay the fuck away from me, Pen," he says before finally backing out of my life.

I feel love fade as the boy next door disappears between an ocean of students just trying to get home. The place my heart normally palpitates falls silent, not allowing even an echo of the beat Dillon gave me. Emptiness makes a home deep within my soul, hardening what little self-respect and saneness I had left. Color literally loses vibrancy, and the air I breathe tastes like poison.

I suck in lungfuls.

"Do you need a ride home?" Joshua asks.

Dropping my book bag, I chase after happiness desperately. Tears that never leave me alone flow as warm air blows through hair I've hated since I changed it. I push through bodies and trip over my own untied laces. Searching for Dillon through blurry eyes, I stop in the middle of the courtyard and shout his name.

"Penelope, you have to calm down," bad news grabs my

arm and tries to pull me away.

Total fear seizes logic, and I drive my small fist into Joshua's chest. Unable to tug my wrist from his hold, I scream and scratch at his face and neck until he finally lets me go.

I run home with his skin under my fingernails.

Risa's standing outside their house when I come running down our street. Strands of my hair stick to my chapped lips, and salty sorrow continues to blind me. I try to run past my boy's sister, but she captures me between her thin arms and holds me hostage.

"You have to leave him alone," she says, restraining me against her body.

Fright shoots violent strength through my limbs, and I shove Risa so hard she falls back and doesn't come after me when I run up to her front door and pound until my knuckles split.

No one answers, but I hear the back door slam shut and follow its sound.

I come around the house as Dillon lifts the sledgehammer my dad has leaned against the back porch.

He points it at me and says, "I told you to stay away from me, Penelope."

Stopping at the end edge of the driveway, I search for the right words to say.

"I'm sorry," I cry. It sounds cheap on my traitorous lips.

Dillon stands where we pressed our hands into my dad's wet cement. Where we committed our love permanently—two hands and a heart.

He lifts the hammer over his head and smashes it.

"No!" I scream as he slams the iron into the concrete again.

Grabbing the back of his shirt, I try to pull him away. Stitches snap and cotton stretches. Unhappiness shakes me off and brings the hammer down again, splintering our palms.

When it's completely crumbled, and as our mothers come running from our houses to see what's going on, Dillon drops the sledgehammer and looks at me with red-rimmed eyes.

He says, "Now you mean something to him."

Chapter 27

DILLON

I turn seventeen years old on a hazy day in September and celebrate it alone for the first time in five years.

"Come on, D. Let's go get a cupcake or something." Risa leans in my doorway. She crosses her arms over her chest, nervously digging her black painted toenails into the carpet.

Lifting my AP Environmental Science book, I say, "I have homework."

My sister rolls her eyes and throws her arms in the air before stepping into my room and plucking the textbook from my hands. She closes one thousand pages of boring and sends it flying into the corner. Risa then smacks the blue binder from my desk and breaks my pencil.

"Give it up, smarty-pants. It's Saturday. Besides, truckloads of college acceptance letters will come soon enough, and then engineering science won't matter."

"Environmental science," I correct her.

"Whatever." Risa jumps on my desk and kicks her feet back and forth. She waves her hand toward my boarded-up window. "It's okay to be sad, but that is pathetic."

The day I caught Pen kissing Joshua Dark and after wrecking cement hearts, I went into my dad's garage and found an old sheet of plywood. I nailed it to the wall, covering the window I spent so much time at before my girl crushed my love.

Three weeks have gone by, and despite my parents' concern about the drywall, my bedroom remains sunless and as dark as my mood.

My blue-haired sibling pulls the keys to her Beetle out of her pocket and dangles them in front of my face.

"I'll let you drive," she sing-songs.

Since the breakup with madness, priorities I previously neglected because I was caught up in caring for a girl who took me for granted are slowly being taken care of. The DMV gave me a driver's license, I'm not late for class anymore, and my grades have quickly gone back up. Herb and Kyle come around more, and I didn't realize how much I missed them until they showed up at the front door after they heard about what happened with Penelope.

"One cupcake," Risa taunts, dangling feathers, charms, and the key to her vehicle from her pointer finger.

Pushing my chair back, I snag the key ring from her hand and say, "Let's go."

The house next door seems bigger than it used to. Every time I see it, my heartbeat picks up, and I feel sick to my stomach, but it's impossible to avoid. Walking around Risa's Volkswagen with my gray hood up and my hands tucked into my dark denim, I keep my head down and try to pretend the white two-story home doesn't hold my heart's breaker.

"You do know how to drive a stick, right?" my sister asks. She buckles her seatbelt and pulls it tight.

Checking my mirrors, I make a mistake and glance at the reflection of Penelope's bedroom window. Purple curtains twist the knife in my back, and I shove the rearview mirror up so that I can't see Pen's space. Slipping the key into the ignition, I push the clutch in and start the car. It stalls when I try to drive away.

"Hey." Risa swats my arm. "Be careful with my baby. She's old."

My pulse flies, and I turn to my sister before dread and burning hurt blow the top of her car off.

"Start the engine and slowly let go of the clutch and push

the gas pedal at the same time." Risa pulls back my hood and scratches the back of my neck as she carefully says, "Just because she hurt you doesn't mean you have to stop loving her, D."

Successfully driving the car out of the driveway, I keep my eyes on the road ahead of me and pretend my sister never spoke.

We pull up to the Cake Shop, and a smile spreads across my face when I see all my friends and family waiting for me out front with balloons and a banner that reads *Happy Birthday*.

I park the car, and Risa grabs my arm and shakes me.

"Surprise!" she shrieks. Her multi-pierced ears and studded nose glisten in the setting sunlight. "Dad didn't think I'd get you out of the house."

"What are you guys up to?" I ask, looking toward the group of people who love me unconditionally.

Risa gets out of the car, popping her head in before she shuts the door and says, "You'll have to come and check it out for yourself."

Following my sister up to the best bakery in town, Herbert sounds off a loud horn, Mathilda throws a handful of confetti at me, Kyle stares at Risa, and my parents gather me into their arms. I sink into an embrace I wish was hers, but soak up genuine affection and do my best to push back soul ache and thoughts of dark brown eyes and the colored sunglasses that used to cover them.

"We were going to throw you a party, but we didn't think you'd show up," Mom says, squeezing my fingers.

"This is cool," I say. "It's all I need."

Dad pats my back and guides me into the bakery. "There's cake inside. Let's celebrate."

Chocolate cherry doesn't stand a chance against us. After our stomachs are full and only when a single piece of cake is left, it doesn't go unnoticed to me that my dad nods at Herb. Cake crumbs fall from my best friend's shirt when he gets up and runs out the door. I ask what that was all about, but my parents just smile.

"You're a good kid, Dillon," Mom says. "We want you to know how proud we are of you. This was supposed to happen last year, but since you didn't get your license…"

A car horn honks three times from outside.

I sit up straight and look out the wall of windows toward the parking lot. Herbert's standing next to a black Pontiac with his arm in the window, pressing the horn three more times. He waves when he sees me looking.

"We got Risa a car when she got her license, so it's only fair that we get you one, too," Dad says. He stands when I do.

Risa scoffs. "Yeah, but I didn't get a freaking GTO."

I run out to the parking lot where Herb hands me the keys to my car and get into the front seat. The scents of old leather and pine from an air freshener hanging from the blinker fill my lungs. My family exits the Cake Shop as I start the engine, bringing the car to life with a vibrating rumble. The navy headliner hangs low, and the leather's torn in the backseat. Yellow-orange sponge-like cushion sticks out of the opening.

But I love it.

The only thing missing is Pen.

"IT'S YOUR BIRTHDAY," KYLE SAYS. "Don't spend it at home wallowing over a bowl of ice cream, heartbreak boy."

My parents and sister took off, leaving me with instructions not to drive over the speed limit and to always count to three after I stop at a stop sign before proceeding forward. I insisted I would be right behind them, but my friends have other plans.

"I'm not in the mood," I say, leaning back against my car door. "We can catch up tomorrow."

"Not a chance," Herb says. He jumps into the front seat of my Pontiac. "I need a ride."

"You have your own car here."

My oldest friend slaps his hand on the dashboard and answers, "But I like this one better."

The glowing blaze from the bonfire at the base of Castle

Rain is visible from the end of the lot where I park my car. Silhouettes gather around burning tree branches and chopped wood, holding cups or glass bottles. Laughter and music drift into the air with white smoke and small embers, and the salty ocean breeze sweeps it all away.

"Is that Dillon Decker?" I hear someone say.

Herbert and Mathilda head toward the water holding hands, and Kyle mumbles something about grabbing a brew before he walks away. I'm left on the sand alone as a shadowed figure makes its way closer to me.

Pepper Hill appears out of the shadows holding a red Solo cup, barefoot and barelegged. She's wrapped in a red zip-up sweater, and the strings to her black bikini hang out from under it.

"I've never seen you at one of these parties before," she says, kicking sand up behind her as she walks toward me. "Why are you way over here?"

"I'm probably going to head home," I say. "My parents got me this car…"

Her big blue eyes light up, and her lips spread into a big smile. "You got a new ride? Can I see?"

Pepper steps closer to me, kicking sand on my shoes. Liquid spills out of her cup, dripping off her fingers. When the blonde girl who led me to a horrible habit is close enough to touch, the stinging scent of booze is heavy on her breath, and I notice she doesn't have any makeup on her face.

"I'm a mess." She dries her hand off on red cotton. Pepper blinks slowly and grabs onto my arm to stay standing.

"It's cool," I say, leading the helpless to my car.

"Do you want a drink?" she asks, holding her cup for me over the center console.

I lean my head back against the headrest and decline. My passenger shrugs, dropping the sweating plastic into the holder and touching everything she can put her hands on.

"This is seriously the coolest car ever, Dillon. I bet my uncle can fix the headliner for you," she says, turning her attention to the old stereo dials.

Eventually she takes a hint that I'm not interested in small talk and sits still. I haven't been to the beach or the cave Penelope and I hid out in so often since we broke up. Being here without her feels wrong, and guilt weighs heavy in my chest.

Pepper places her small palm on my leg. I look down at her perfectly painted nails, but don't ask her to move it.

"I'm sorry about you and Pen," she says, reaching for my hand. Her thumb rubs small circles over my knuckles.

"Thanks," I reply in a shaky voice.

"Breakups suck," she continues. "But I feel like everything happens for a reason."

Staring at her tender hand in my larger one, the same guilt I feel for being here without Penelope flares and triples in size because I'm drawn to Pepper's soft skin. I turn my palm over and open my fingers so that hers fall between mine. Holding tight, for the first time in three weeks, I don't feel so alone.

When Pepper Hill's soft lips touch mine, I know I'm not.

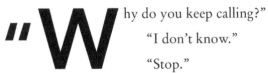

DILLON

"Why do you keep calling?"

"I don't know."

"Stop."

"I can't."

"My mom is getting mad."

"I can't stop calling."

"Are you going to the dance?" I give up and ask.

"Yeah."

"With him?"

"Yeah," she answers in a soft voice.

"Sometimes I wish you were invisible. I wouldn't have to

see you or love you."

"You can't say that, Dillon. Besides, I heard about you and Pepper. I saw you with her at school."

"How are you doing?" I change the subject.

"Bad. Does that make you happy to hear?"

"No."

Two months later and she still makes me cry.

"Don't. Please, please, please don't. Stop crying, I can't take it."

I clear my throat.

Hopefully, my next words sting.

"Stop calling me, Penelope."

Chapter 29

DILLON

"Dude, what are you doing?"

I hold up the overpriced corsage and lift my eyebrows. "Buying Pepper's flowers. These are the ones she told me she wants."

"I'm not asking about the flower, smartass. What are you doing with Pepper Hill?" Herbert leans against the counter beside me, waiting for my answer.

"She's my girl. We're going to the Winter Formal." I shrug and pass the cashier my dad's credit card.

Outside, I light a cigarette and blow dense white smoke into the cold January air. Herb stares at me like I've lost my mind.

"You can't smoke," he says, trying to grab the cig from between my lips. "This is wrong. Pen messed up, but Mathilda says Josh kissed her first."

"So that makes it okay?" I flick my cigarette into the street where it rolls end over end, throwing ashes until it rolls into the gutter and burns out.

"No, but you're not happy, and she's not happy. Pen's our best friend. You can't give that up."

"You don't even know what you're talking about, Herb."

Standing outside the florist shop, one of my oldest friends shakes his head at me with a knowing look on his face.

"Man-to-man, D, I know Pen's sick," he says, staring down to his feet before looking in my eyes. "Mathilda talks to her every day. They hang out on the weekends, painting nails and braiding each other's hair and shit."

A rush of anger surges through my body, and I have to step away from Herbert to catch my breath. My friends get to keep her, and I can't deal with even living next door to sadness.

"What's your point?" I ask, running my hand through my hair.

"You could have told us. We knew something was up. We just didn't know what."

Pressing my lips together, I turn to face him and hold my hands up. "What do you want me to say? Penelope's with Josh now, and I'm with Pepper. It's what she wanted, or she wouldn't have kissed him in the first place."

"Joshua Dark is bad news, Dillon. She hangs at the reservation with him. Pen told Mathilda he's dealing meth."

The only thing that stops me from driving home to be with her is the image of when she was my girl kissing the drug dealer she chose over our relationship. The moment Pen did that, she threw away everything we went through together and all I sacrificed for her like it meant nothing.

She isn't my problem anymore.

"You're wrong, Dillon. Penelope needs you."

"DANCE WITH ME." PEPPER POUTS her pretty lips, pulling on my hand.

The girl I came here with stands out in the room full of people decked out in their best formal wear. Pepper's hair is tightly curled and pulled back, pinned all around her head. The corsage I slipped on her wrist while our parents took pictures matches the loose tie around my neck and her red dress that brushes the floor when she walks.

She loves the attention.

I want to go home.

"You smell like whiskey and cigarettes. It's seriously gross."
My date gives up, holding her manicured hands on her hips.

"Want some?" I offer my punch cup.

"No thanks, dick." Pepper rolls her eyes before she walks
away.

Swimming in a liquid haze, my drunk eyes search around
the room for the girl next door. She's been the only thing on my
mind since Herbert filled me in on what she's been up to lately.
I stole the whiskey bottle Risa keeps under her bed and drank
most of it, hoping to ease my worries. It made them worse, and
it pissed Pepper off because she had to drive.

"Have you seen Pen?" I ask when Kyle takes the seat next
to me.

He nods toward the gym turned winter wonderland
entrance.

Madness walks in under Josh's arm, expressionless and
beautiful in a simple white dress. The group of reservation kids
she's with is loud and flashy. All of them with the exception of
their ringleader are dressed casually.

I put my cup down to go talk to her, but Kyle pulls me back
into the chair.

"Don't do it, D," he says. "Wait until she gets away from
him."

Sitting through another hour of annoying beats from the

stereo and my girlfriend giving me dirty looks as she dances with her friends, Penelope finally gets up from her table on the other side of the room, and I follow her to the bathroom.

"Does Wayne know Josh is a drug dealer?" I ask, taking her elbow and yelling over the music.

"Why do you care? You don't want me, remember?" She pulls away from me and straightens her dress.

"You know I do, Pen," I say.

I'll never stop.

Tears pool in her eyes, but before I can comfort her, Josh shows up and does it instead. I thought watching them kiss was hard, but it's nothing compared to seeing him care. To stand here and watch him brush her hair out of her face and wipe away sadness only I used to understand creates a stinging bitterness in me I can't bear to deal with alone.

He took everything from me.

"Take your hands off of her," I say, squaring up.

Josh looks away from Penelope and steps toe-to-toe with me without making sure she is safely out of the way. Instead, he smiles in my face and dares me with his dark eyes to make a move.

I shove my hands into his chest.

Rez boys aren't that fucking big.

"She doesn't want to be with you, Dillon," my worst enemy

says, unbuttoning his cuffs.

Herbert and Kyle run up with Josh's crew behind them. My boys hold me back and I allow it, but when I notice Mathilda shove Pen into the girls' bathroom, I fight them off and rush after the kid dumb enough to mess with my girl and me and expected me to go down without a fight.

Before I have a chance to break his face, I'm pushed out of the way and told, "Move your feet, boy."

Stumbling to the side, Coach Finnel shoves me over and over until I crash through double doors out into the cold Washington night. I breathe in mouthfuls of icy air, hoping it will clear the blind rage coursing through my veins.

It doesn't work.

"Do you have any idea who he is?" I ask, pulling at the front of Mr. Finnel's shirt. "Who you're letting your daughter be with?"

Wayne doesn't budge or stop me from taking my aggression out on him. He just looks down at me with a sympathetic stare I wish I could rip from his face.

"What are you going to do anyway?" I push my fist into his chest before releasing him. "You're a washed-up football coach chaperoning a high school dance."

He cracks a smile.

"She needs to learn for herself, boy. We can't do everything for her." The man I've grown up fearing reaches out for me. "But you should know I would never let anything bad happen to Pen."

I shrug his hand off my shoulder, but his fatherly affection frees pressure behind my eyes, and I start to cry. When Wayne reaches for me a second time, I let him wrap me in his furry grip and soak his shirt with my self-pity.

He's right.

There's no saving Penelope from her own mind.

I need to let go.

Chapter 30

PENELOPE

Months go by and eventually Dillon and I start to pass each other in school hallways like there was never anything between us. Sometimes our eyes meet, and my muted heart comes to life and thumps like it used to, but one of us always looks away and my beat goes silent.

As gloomy weather parts the sky and allows the sun to shine down, graduation day gets closer and closer. They tell me I'm going to get a diploma, and I'll be able to walk with the rest of my class in a cap and gown.

"But going to a university isn't an option, Miss Finnel," the school counselor says. "Here are some pamphlets on our local community colleges and trade schools."

My therapist thinks I should give my future more consideration than I do. She gives me pamphlets about the advantages of having short-term and long-term goals.

"There's no reason why you can't be successful in life, Penelope. The fact you continue to see me each week is proof you want more."

"Or that my parents force me here," I say with a smile, shoving the pamphlets into my book bag with the ones she gave me during our last session.

Dad and Mom have come to an agreement about the medication I've taken sporadically since I was a kid.

"It does more good than harm, sweetie," my mother says, dropping two pills into the palm of my hand—one white, one yellow. "You've done so well lately."

I throw the mood stabilizer and anti-depressant to the back of my throat and swallow them dry.

My parents stand back and wait for me to open my mouth and lift my tongue, which is the direct result of them catching me when I used to spit them out before bed.

"Good?" I ask, after having shown them proof their drugs are now dissolving in my stomach.

Dad uncrosses his arms. "You don't have to be so sarcastic all the time, Pen. We—"

"Only want what's best for me," I finish his sentence, heading toward the stairs. "I know."

Mom locks the orange prescription bottles back inside a box she hides from me anyway, and I take two steps at a time up to my room. I close the door behind me and pull off my shirt and kick off my pants as my lips start to tingle and my head feels light.

Changing into a pair of pajamas, I open my now yellow curtains in case Dillon's taken the board down from his. Tears used to break from my eyes every time I looked and it was still up, but they don't anymore. Maybe it's the pills doing their job, or because I'm used to him treating me like I don't exist, but I'm able to walk away dry-eyed.

I slip under my covers and grab the cell phone my parents gave me for my seventeenth birthday. There are a voicemail from Josh and a text from Mathilda, but I turn the phone off without responding to either one of them and find myself brushing my fingers over the Deckers' home number, knowing I'll never dial it again.

As my eyes grow heavy and my bedroom begins to fade away, I wonder if the boy next door ever does the same thing.

DILLON'S CAP AND GOWN ARE as green as his eyes, and from my spot two rows back, I can't help but appreciate the man he's truly becoming. His hair is cut short, and it makes the angle of his so-sharp jaw more predominant. Something causes him to laugh hard enough he tilts his head back, showcasing the most perfect Adam's apple I've ever seen.

When he looks over his shoulder and catches me staring, the right side of my mouth curves up. Dillon doesn't reciprocate, and his eyes pass over me like I'm another stranger in the crowd.

Normally being treated in such a way from the only boy I have ever loved would crush me and send my mind into an episode of self-hating and near insanity, but the medicine coursing through my bloodstream puts a wall between heartbreak and reality. Madness swarms below a false cure, waiting for me to slip up.

Until then, I'm … numb.

"Dillon Timothy Decker," his name is called over the loudspeaker twenty minutes later.

The alumnus walks onto the stage and accepts his diploma with a gracious smile. Our graduating class erupts into a loud buzz of cheers and claps. Herb throws a beach ball—he must have snuck under his gown and blown up while we sit here and wait for our name to be announced—at his best friend as he walks off stage. It bounces off Dillon's shoulder back into the awaiting hands of the commencing student body where it's bounced around until a teacher is able to deflate it.

"Penelope Georgia Finnel," my full name is broadcasted. I follow the designated path taped onto the stage and receive what I didn't work hard enough to earn.

After shaking hands with the principal, we take a photo before I'm led away with a smile and a nod, and just like that, it's over.

Once the platform is cleared and we flip our caps into the air, Castle Rain High School's graduating class is officially released to become productive citizens of the world. I share a quiet good-bye with the very few friends I made through the years, leave Mathilda Tipp with promises to get together soon, and meet up with my only family I have here to support me—my parents.

Dad slings his arm over my shoulders, Mom slides hers around my back, and we go home to start the rest of our lives.

"I DON'T WANT TO MAKE anyone uncomfortable," I say, falling into bed with my phone at my ear.

"Don't be silly, Pen. You know Kyle. He wants you to come," Mathilda replies. "I'll be in front of your house in two minutes. Be ready because I'm only going to honk."

"But Dillon's going to be there. He should celebrate graduation with his best friends. I'm the one who doesn't belong."

"Penelope, you're one of us, and you're my best friend. Shouldn't we be able to celebrate together, too? We only have the summer."

"Okay, you're right." I sigh. Looming panic fights to break past my chemical resolve. "I'll wait for you downstairs."

"Good," my redheaded friend says. "And if Pepper Hoe-Bag Hill tries to mess with you, I got your back. I've been waiting to chew her face off."

"Thanks." I laugh and hang up.

Quickly checking my reflection in the mirror, I rub smeared mascara out from under my eyes and run a brush through my colored hair. True to her word, the sound of Mathilda's horn follows the echo of squeaky brakes coming to a stop in front of my house.

"Is it okay if I go to Kyle's for a party?" I ask, standing before my parents in our living room.

Mom glances up at the clock on the wall and hums.

"It's eight o'clock, baby. You're supposed to take your

medication in a half hour, and I'm not sure if it's a good idea to miss a dose."

Dad shakes his head. "Be home at eleven. You can take them when you get home."

Kissing them each on the cheek, I run out the door into the humid summer night and jump into Mathilda's Camry. Herbert reaches forward from the backseat and messes up my hair.

"We could have walked," I say as she pulls away from the curb. Yellow-orange headlights illuminate the road ahead.

"I'll just pretend you didn't say that," Mathilda says, making a sour face. "I haven't walked anywhere since I was twelve years old."

Dillon's car is parked in Kyle's driveway, and Pepper's white Jeep is behind it. A dozen or more other vehicles I don't recognize are lined up and down the street, and loud music booms from the small three-bedroom house.

"This will be fun," my friend insists before getting out.

I follow her and Herb through the front door I used to spend summers walking in and out of when we were younger. Kyle's house looks the same as I remember it, and it helps me feel not so out of place.

Until I see Dillon with Pepper in the kitchen, smiling and talking in quiet voices only to each other.

"Remember, I'll eat her face," Mathilda says, walking me

past the kitchen to the living room and passing me a beer. "Drink this and relax. I leave for college in six weeks, so let's make the most of it."

I hold the icy silver can, but don't take a single sip. Three brews in, Mathilda doesn't even notice. She controls the room, animated and fun with conversations she makes a point to include me in. Redhead retells stories about when we were younger—holding hands while we rode on handlebars and dirty faces as we explored the woods—and it's truly not until this moment that I realize I've always been important to her.

"It was back when Pen wore colored sunglasses every day. One of the lenses popped out, and she wouldn't stop crying until we found it. Turns out some freakin' squirrel snatched it. Dillon literally chased it around all afternoon. Meanwhile, I walked Pen back home to grab a new pair of shades, and we were making mud pies when D showed up a few hours later with a squirrel bite on his hand and the purple lens."

We all laugh, and Dillon comes out of the kitchen at the sound of his name.

"Remember that?" Mathilda asks him. "Your mom rushed you to the ER for a rabies shot, and you couldn't play outside for a week."

The boy next door looks at me and actually smiles. "Yeah, I remember."

The tension eases with his simple statement, and as the conversation continues, Dillon and I don't directly speak to each other, but his presence isn't horrible. I finally let my guard down and enjoy myself.

It isn't until I excuse myself to use the bathroom that I realize my cell phone has been ringing. Joshua's name shows up five times under *Missed Calls*, and he's left a few text messages.

Where are you?

Why haven't you called me?

Heard you're at Kyle's.

His last one sends me running out of the bathroom door, but it's too late.

I'm here.

Josh and his friends are already inside, and the mood of the party has dwindled significantly. Instead of caring about my boyfriend's reaction at seeing me here, I wait for Dillon's. His response doesn't surprise me.

"Mind taking your trash out, Pen?" He nods toward the party crashers lingering in front of the door.

A true troublemaker, Josh pushes past me like I'm not here and attacks the boy he's held a grudge for since the day a bus dropped him off at our school four years ago while his friends go after Herb and Kyle.

Everything after that goes by so fast.

Josh hits Dillon, and he falls.

Dillon fights back.

Both boys bleed.

Everyone shouts.

Mathilda pushes me into a corner and won't let me move.

Dillon's hit in the stomach. He's doubled over and looks up at me as I cry for Josh to stop.

"Please! Please, stop!" I scream.

It's not until blue and red lights start to flash through the front window do Josh and his friends bolt out the door they came in through. Left in the wake of their destruction, no one has to say anything. I know they blame me.

Chapter 31

PENELOPE

"**Y**ou're not staying in bed all day again, Pen." My mom yanks the covers off my body before she walks over and opens the window. "Stop feeling sorry for yourself. Millions of people live with depression and don't sleep their lives away. Get up."

Blinking against gray light brightening my room through parted curtains, I give my mind a second to catch up to an ache buried deep within my bones and stiffness weakening my muscles before I say anything. That's all the time it takes for anxiety to realize I'm awake and strike straight through my deadened heart. Panic rises next, lodging itself in my throat so

I can't take a decent breath. I turn over on my back and stare at the white ceiling above me, praying today is the day this goes away.

I missed one dose the night of Kyle's party. Two weeks later, I'm still fighting to get back on track.

"Why don't you understand it's not that easy?" I say in an uneven tone.

If she'd leave me here, maybe I could get decent sleep and feel better when I wake up on my own. Instead, she barges in here every few hours with the same demands, sparking the same argument.

"I started the shower for you," she says.

We've been here before. Mom and I have had this conversation during this identical situation hundreds of times, but she still doesn't get it.

I'm broken.

A shower isn't going to help me feel better.

All I want is to be left alone.

Mom sits on the edge of my bed and rubs her hand up and down my leg. I gasp for air, clawing at my throat and chest, crying and frustrated. There's not a thing I want more than to disappear, but it's impossible because I'm made of nothing.

The woman who brought me into this hell holds my face in her hands. "Is it never better, Penelope? You can't live like this."

Tingles swell from the tip of my nose to the ends of every stand of hair on my scalp. Collapsing lungs push shallow gasps of air between my clenched teeth and cracked lips. I dig the balls of my feet into my mattress and bunch the fitted sheet into my white-knuckled fist.

"Go away," I cry, pulling the white cotton from my bed completely.

Mom kisses my face, mixing her tears with mine. "Tell me what to do, baby. Tell me how to fix this."

Dillon.

I haven't seen my boy in so long and miss everything about him: his face, his hands, his voice. I miss his laugh, his love, his arms, and his strength. I miss him between my legs and all around my body. I miss his presence and his conscience. I long for his kindness and caring. I miss him so fucking much it hurts. So I cry, and I fight, and I scream until my mom leaves my room and shuts the door.

Pulling the covers over my head, I block out any light and curl myself into a tight ball. Panic continues to rage, alive inside my chest, but slowly my body calms and my breathing regulates. Burning eyes drift from open to closed, and my aching jaw rests. One by one, my stiff fingers release their hold on my sheet, and sleep sweeps me into its embrace.

My only company in this void is my longing for Dillon.

In the blackness of unconsciousness, I miss him so much.

Tomorrow I will try. Tomorrow will be better.

For now, I need to sleep.

Chapter 32

DILLON

"I overheard Coach Finnel talking about Penelope last night. Do you want to know what he said?" Risa asks, sitting at the kitchen table.

Pouring myself a glass of orange juice, I shrug my shoulder and look at my sister over the rim of my glass as I take a drink of the cold citrus. It's taken twenty-three years, but the girl born a half-decade before me has finally grown up. She didn't spend this summer following some band going nowhere around the state, sleeping in the back of a van, or getting tattoos with unsterilized needles. The dreads are gone, and her hair is its natural blonde color. Risa still lives at home, but she got a job at the diner in town and even started taking a few online college courses.

Much to my parents' dissatisfaction, it's more than I'm doing.

"The medication she's been on for the last year stopped working, and her doctor is having a hard time finding something that does. Wayne said she's on her third prescription in three months, but it doesn't look good, so he's not coaching this season to be home with Pen more often."

I set my empty glass into the sink and place my hands on the edge of the counter while what my sister tells me soaks in. Dropping my head, I squeeze my eyes shut and remind myself that it isn't my responsibility to go next door and force madness out of bed.

More than twelve months have passed since she broke my heart, but I have to tell myself this daily.

"What do you want me to do, Risa?" Clearing my throat, I stand straight and turn to face judgment.

The same person who lectured me about taking care of myself when I was in the thick of sickness with Pen stares back at me with bright green eyes that reflect my own yearning for her. I look away and swallow the responsibility loving Penelope requires and force one foot in front of the other before my sister layers blame on top of guilt I already live with.

"I only said something because I thought you would want to know," she calls after me.

"All right," I say quickly.

It's hard when my family loves her as much as I do. None of them appreciated the turn our relationship took, but our families are close, and they come to me with her conditions and diagnoses. What do they expect me to do? Run over there and somehow save her? I couldn't before, and I won't now.

"Dillon, you owe Penelope some of your time," Risa says, conflict thickly laced in her voice. "I know she hurt you, but this is larger than that now. She's not doing well."

"You have no idea what she's done to me."

Despite the pain I could easily run away from and regardless of my refusal to face sadness, I'm still in Castle Rain while college acceptance letters sit unanswered in my room. Goals I've had since childhood fall further out of my reach as everyone I know moves on with their lives. I live with my mom and dad's disappointment every day because I'm afraid to leave the girl next door behind.

It's a purgatory I can't escape.

Risa snatches her keys from the counter in haste. "I have to work, and Mom and Dad won't be home tonight. Can you hang here alone until I get home?"

"I'm eighteen." I smirk. "You don't need to babysit me

anymore."

"I know, but I worry," she says. "If you're not going to school, you should get a job or something. It's not good to sit around the house all day. Ask Kyle if he can get you on the road crew with him."

Rolling my eyes as I take the stairs up to my room, I've heard that same line from my life-givers all summer long. They don't agree with my decision to skip a year before continuing my education. Ending up in medical school will put a hold on my life long enough without prolonging it by twelve months, but neither one of them needed me to actually spell out the reasons behind my choice.

Pepper put on a show before she left a month ago, complete with smeared mascara—because of some one-sided tears and claims that she *thought this was love.* I felt I owed her my time after stringing her along, so I sat through her breakdown and apologized when she threw an empty shoebox at me and asked, "How could you do this?"

She knew.

Before I left her house that night, Pepper Hill's last words to me proved it.

"Your Penelope is with Joshua Dark. She doesn't love you."

Upon opening my bedroom door, my space is colder than the rest of the house, lightless—thanks to the board hammered around my window. After staring at it for a moment, knowing the thin piece of plywood never did anything to block sadness out, I walk over and slip my fingers between it and the wall. Metal nails easily slip out of the dusty drywall as one corner at a time comes free.

Gray October light fills my room again, and I squint against its brilliance. Old metal blinds, bent and broken, fall free, shaking dirt and dust into the air. Tearing them down entirely, I unlock the window I haven't seen or touched since I nailed it shut and lift the rickety panes of glass to let in some fresh air.

Penelope's yellow curtains are open, but she's nowhere in sight. I can't bring myself to go over there yet, but I hope she sees the board down and knows I'm still here.

"HERB AND MATHILDA ARE HOME for Thanksgiving," Kyle says, breaking off half of his sandwich and taking a large bite. With food in his mouth, he asks, "They're having a party tonight. Wanna go?"

I took a job filling in potholes and repainting the lines in the streets with Kyle and the rest of the Castle Rain road crew when my dad wouldn't get off my back about school and my inability to support myself. Sitting on the curb along our worksite, decked out in an orange reflective vest, old jeans, and work boots, I have calluses on my hands and a new respect for manual labor. This is it for my oldest friend who decided a long time ago that another four years of school wasn't for him, but grinding this hard has solidified my decision to work toward earning an MD.

"I don't know," I say, kicking gravel into the middle of the street.

With the second half of his turkey on rye in his right hand, Kyle swallows his last bite and says, "Penelope's going to be there."

I heard the girl next door got a part-time job at the grocery store, and my mom mentioned that she saw her driving Wayne's Chrysler in town a few times. Pen and her family go into the diner where my sister works at least once a week, and Herbert told me she and Mathilda have kept in touch after their move to Seattle. But despite living in such a small town and being neighbors, my path doesn't cross with hers any more than that.

Even with the board covering my window down.

I stand at the mention of her name and lean back against our work truck. Squinting against rare November sun, I say, "It's probably not a good idea."

"When's the last time you talked to her? Maybe it'll give you some closure or something." Kyle wipes crumbs from his hands on the front of his dingy white T-shirt.

The right side of my mouth curves up, and my friend shrugs his shoulders.

"You guys split up over a year ago. How long are you going to avoid her?" he says, placing his hard hat back over his blonde hair. "Besides, seeing you out here breaking a sweat and popping blisters instead of learning how to save lives breaks my heart. Get this shit with Pen figured out so you can start living life, my man."

Grabbing my shovel, I follow Kyle out to the street where we were working before we broke for lunch and ask, "What do you know? You've never even had a girlfriend."

"I went on a date last night," he says, shoveling a scoop of asphalt into the hole.

"With who?"

Kyle stands straight and pushes his hard hat back. With a crooked smile bowing his lips, he winks and says, "This older chick."

I PARK DOWN THE STREET and smoke a cigarette to calm my nerves on the walk up to Mathilda's parents' house. With the moon covered by storm clouds, the streets are dark, and a light mist starts to fall from the sky onto my face. Blowing burned nicotine into the air, I flick my cigarette butt into the gutter and pull my hood over my head before knocking on the white security screen.

Herbert answers, flooding the porch with light and the sounds of laughter and music from inside.

"Get out of the rain," he says, moving to the side so I can come inside.

He pats me on the back and hands me a cold beer bottle, but my attention has already fallen on madness. Everything but wavy brown hair and uncovered sad eyes dissolves into a blur of nothing important. My feet carry me over to where Penelope's sitting on the couch alone, and I lean down and kiss her cheek.

"Hey," I whisper.

"Hi." Sadness pushes her hair behind her ear.

She's smaller than I remember and uncomfortable in her own skin.

Rubbing my thumb over the roundness of her cheek going red, I stand over the only girl I've ever loved and wonder how I've gone so long without touching her. Holding my gravel-scratched, road-rough hand out for hers, she slips her small bones covered in soft skin into mine without hesitation. Lacing our fingers into a mended fist, I pull Pen up from her seat and lead her to the first room I come across.

This isn't the girl who used to draw peace signs on her cheeks or write me notes across our lawns in the middle of the night. The softness in Penelope's eyes has hardened with the fucked-up deal life has dealt her. She doesn't cover obvious sleeplessness with thick layers of makeup anymore, but allows the world to see the dark purple stained beneath her lower lashes.

Lifting regret onto a dresser along the wall, I spread her knees and shove her skirt up her skinny thighs before standing between them.

"Tell me not to," I say breathlessly, staring at her parted lips.

Penelope scoots to the very edge of the stained wood and jerks me closer by the front of my hoodie. Her round chest expands and contracts against mine with every heavy breath entering and existing lungs that won't work fast enough. Wrapping her arms around my neck, Pen circles her warmest part against where I am hard.

"Please, don't stop," she says, turning her face into my neck. "Don't leave me here."

Kissing the side of her heated face, I reach between us and unbutton my jeans. Penelope cries out as my knuckles brush against her tenderness, and in an attempt to hear it again but louder, I push her underwear over and enter her in one harsh thrust.

We melt.

"Do you feel me now?" I ask, pulling almost all the way out and slamming back in.

Shaking around every part of me, madness pulls on my hair and sinks her teeth into the base of my throat. My knees crash into the drawers, and my fingers get caught between the edge of the dresser and the wall as our bodies send groaning wood into the semi-gloss finish. Practically climbing on top of her, I cover every inch of sadness with my bursting need to be nearer and more inside.

"I love you. I love you," I say before attaching my mouth to the thin skin of her neck and suck.

I empty every emotion I've had since this girl broke my soul inside her and pull her thin veins and flimsy tendons between my teeth, breaking blood vessels with my lips. I leave her throat black and blue by the time we finish, marking Penelope with my incapability to control my need to be with her. Brushing my fingers across marks she doesn't deserve, guilt slices me open when I look up and watch her eyes spill devastation.

Pulling out of her, I tuck myself back into my dark denim and sit on the bed across the room.

Pen sits up, tugging her skirt down her thighs as she slides off the dresser. Her navy knee-high socks are bunched around her ankles, and her shoelaces are untied. Standing with unsteady legs, she straightens her sweater and wipes her mouth on the sleeve before letting tears fall.

"Penelope, I'm sorry," I say.

She holds her hand up and shakes her head, closing her eyes as she turns and leaves the room.

Chapter 33

PENELOPE

"I don't know if working so much in your condition is a good idea, Miss Finnel. We've made progress over the last five months, but these things are unpredictable at best."

Dropping my head back, I blow a large, pink, watermelon-scented bubblegum bubble and let it pop over my top lip and nose. Sucking the gum back into my mouth, I snap it between my teeth and say, "I'm not quitting my job."

"No one said you have to quit," Dr. Judgmental Eyes says, jotting more notes down onto her yellow pad. "But you should consider cutting back the hours you're working. Your mom said you picked up an extra shift last week and suffered a setback that night. She said she felt like you overworked yourself."

"I took the extra shift because I can't stand being locked in the house with her every day. I'm almost nineteen, and she won't even let me go to the bathroom without knocking on the door every five minutes to make sure I haven't offed myself. I'm not suicidal."

Dr. Consistently Nodding nods and asks, "And the setback she mentioned?"

"I wanted to help out and make dinner and needed to chop onions. They made my eyes water, and I accidently cut my hand with the knife. She thought I was trying to slit my wrists or something," I say, blowing another bubble.

"She explained it a little differently than that," Dr. Monotone replies, setting the notepad down onto her desk. She pushes her wire-rimmed glasses through her middle-parted hair. "She said she walked into the kitchen, and you were bleeding with the knife in your hands."

"My mother didn't give me a chance to explain. Like I said, I'm not suicidal."

"Maybe you should leave the chopping to your parents so this doesn't happen again," Dr. Know-It-All says, picking her notepad back up.

The left side of my mouth lifts, and I say, "Maybe you

should mind your own business."

Dr. Nods keeps on nodding, scribbling down more notes about me. "Have you noticed a difference in your mood swings lately, Penelope? Do you often become angry for no reason?"

"I'm not angry," I say.

My therapist purses her lips, but doesn't give me any other indication of what she's thinking about. Stone-faced and scratching her lead pencil across the yellow paper, she messes up and flips the pencil around to erase her mistake.

More writing. More writing. More writing.

She flips the page.

I start to bite my nails as heat rushes up my spine, and a bead of sweat pools on my lower back. The curve of each letter she writes and the sound of every T she crosses feels as if it's being carved into my bones. Clenching my jaw, I grip onto the edge of my seat with bitten-raw fingertips and bleeding cuticles just to keep from running out of this room screaming.

"What about the boy next door, Pen? Do you want to talk about him?" Dr. Write Master asks. She stops her pencil and waits for my reaction.

"Why would you ask about Dillon?" I choke out, fighting inner burning and thrashing to seem uncrazy.

"Because I was told he's finally leaving town next month."

"So?" I ask as tears burn my eyes.

"Well, you had that run-in with him—"

"I don't want to talk about it," I interrupt her.

"Your parents are afraid Dillon's absence is going to devastate your headway. What do you think?"

Swallowing my gum, I keep my grip on my chair and say, "I think my parents should stop talking to you and start talking to me."

"PENELOPE, WE DIDN'T TELL HER about Dillon to upset you. We only mentioned it in case it becomes an issue," Mom says. Her brown eyes briefly meet mine in the rearview mirror before returning to the road in front of her.

Sitting in the backseat with the windows down, the near-summer breeze leaves my hair salt-scented and windblown-textured as we cruise through town after my therapist appointment. The sun's warmth soaks through my skin, heating me from the outside in. A spark of excitement about the pending summer—my first with a driver's license—sends a rush of anticipation though my veins, flushing out dread and self-disgust. I daydream about days spent on the hot sand, swimming though the salty ocean, and leaving Castle Rain completely for a road trip.

Then I remember everyone I know has moved on with their lives, and it'll just be me this year.

The crazy girl.

Pulling into the driveway, Mom shuts off the car and turns around to face me.

With my hand on the door handle, I ask, "What?"

She beams, lighting up her round face with forced happiness. Dark hair turning gray with age and years of stress—thanks to giving life to a daughter like me—my mother has worry lines set deep around her eyes and fingernails bitten down like mine. I can't remember the last time I saw her smile and mean it or heard her laugh until she cried.

"I want you to know Dad and I are proud of you, Pen," she says. A few strands of hair fall free from her ponytail.

"Thanks, Mom," I mumble, getting out of the car.

I shut the door, about to walk around the back of the Chrysler when the Dillon comes out of his house. With his keys dangling from his hand, dressed in a pair of board shorts and a white T-shirt, the boy next door stops cold at the edge of his porch and stares at me until I can't take it anymore and move forward.

"Penelope," he calls after me.

Saving us both from the awkward conversation we never had about what happened at Herb and Mathilda's party and sparing myself from having to listen to Dillon tell me himself that he's finally leaving, I rush through my front door and run upstairs where I lock myself in the bathroom.

Resting my hands against the edge of the sink, I look into the mirror and stare at the reflection of a person I don't want to know anymore. The girl glaring back at me with dark circles under her eyes and a permanent scowl on her face is the same one who chases everyone I love away.

"Be normal," I say to her. "Act normal."

My heartbeat speeds up as anger tenses every muscle in my body. I slam the ball of my palm into the mirror, sending a ripple through my unchanging reflection.

"Be fucking normal!" I scream, smashing both of my hands into the looking glass.

A crack breaks through the center of my face, but nothing else changes. My eyes are detached, my skin looks sick, and my insides feel like deadweight.

Sending my fist into the glass one more time, it splinters completely until my reflection is unrecognizable. I'm nothing but razor-sharp fragments, a kaleidoscope of wreckage … and he said he wouldn't leave me.

Chapter 34

DILLON

've spent the last few months trying to figure out where we went wrong, wondering what I could have done differently and questioning if any of this can be fixed.

I miss the days when we were kids.

Young love is so untouchable.

I long for how simplistic things used to be. When Penelope would ride on my handlebars or when she would get excited about a new pair of sunglasses. We used to play until the streetlights came on and go into the house kicking and screaming, dirt-cake faced and grass-strained. I miss building jumps with Herb and Kyle and hanging with my friends without having a care in the world.

I miss madness.

While I was struggling with the decision to finally leave, Dad did a lot of threatening. He threatened to take away my car and my stability at home. He threatened not to pay for school at all and gave me the summer to decide. When none of that worked, he convinced me.

"Do you want her back, Son? If it works out, what will you have to offer a girl like Penelope without an education?"

My heart's in Castle Rain, but I'm leaving for college.

It's been months since Herb and Mathilda's party, and I hadn't seen Pen until yesterday in the driveway. If how fast she ran away is any indication of her feelings about out last encounter, I'm not surprised.

I fucked her, literally and hypothetically.

Betraying her trust in the worst way possible, I took advantage of the only girl I've ever loved and let her walk away from me without an apology or explanation, broken and bruised. I should have chased her out of the room, past the party of people who heard everything, and out to her car before she drove home alone. The words *I love you to death* never passed my lips when they are the only ones I should have said.

With my room mostly packed and my days in this small town numbered, I look up at open yellow curtains, and I'm tired of being without her.

Penelope is all I have. All I need. All I have ever wanted since I was twelve years old.

I take a hit from the cigarette of a habit I can't kick before I drop the butt to the floor and snub it out with my shoe. Inhaling a deep breath, I go to her.

That's what I do.

It's what I've always done.

For her, I will stay awake forever.

"SHE'S IN THE BACK, SWEETIE."

"Thank you, Mrs. Finnel."

I pass between our houses and step in wet grass through her backyard. Penelope's rollerblades, old and dirty, collect dust on the wooden porch I helped Wayne build years ago. A smashed slab of concrete—our hands and a heart—lies beneath it.

I don't have to go far to find her.

Stepping past the tree line, she's where we spent entire summer days digging up worms or hiding from our parents. Left down and naturally curly like it was the first time I ever saw her, Penelope's long hair fans around her head as she spins in a circle, dancing to a slow playing song on an old portable radio. Pink painted toes dig into the damp ground beneath her feet, getting stuck under her nails.

Sitting against the base of an old tree, I cross my arms and watch Pen's white dress sway across her thin body and sweep against her skinny knees. Penelope sees me and smiles, but she doesn't stop twirling. She tilts her face toward the sunlight peeking through tree branches covered in thick leaves and closes her eyes as it warms her pale skin and tired eyes, extending her arms and spinning.

She was born for me to love.

As one song ends and another begins, the girl next door sits next to me and wipes dirt from the tops of her muddy feet. She looks up at me under her long lashes and smiles, momentarily dismissing the time we've spent apart. There are so many words and explanations that need to be said, but none of them feel important enough to say.

Penelope needs to be taken care of.

"Dillon," Penelope whispers. "Sometimes I'm so sad."

"That's okay."

"I don't know how to fix it," she admits. Emotion pools in her brown eyes.

"I'll help you," I say.

Rising to my feet, I offer her my hand, and she takes it easily. Salty sadness drips to the muddy ground as I wipe her tears away, and we step through them as I lead her out of the woods. Gray clouds cover the bright sky, and small raindrops start to fall by the time we walk through the Finnels' back door.

The familiar aroma of just-brewed coffee takes me back to times when I treated this place like home. Sonya looks up from her mug as her daughter and I pass through the living room, hand-in-hand to the stairs. She doesn't mumble a word, but her relief is apparent by the smile on her face.

Shutting her bedroom door behind us, my girl climbs into bed and slides under her heavy blankets. I slip out of my shoes and take off my jacket before getting in behind her, noticing that multi-colored marbles and yellow feathers rest on top of her dresser.

Pushing her wavy hair away from her neck, I hold my girl's body against mine and kiss her temple before resting my head on the pillow beside hers.

There aren't many words for the mending of two broken hearts. It's as natural as breathing. We lie in the dark, in the middle of the day, making silent promises and voiceless convictions. She holds my hand and kisses my wrist. We fall in and out of sleep, and the entire day passes without a single word spoken.

"DILLON."

I open my eyes to the sound of Mrs. Finnel's quiet-spoken voice. She stands at the foot of the bed, dimly lit by the yellow-orange light shining in from the hallway. Shifting my heavy-lidded eyes toward the clock glowing from the nightstand, I'm surprised to see it's after midnight.

"Is she okay?" my girl's mom looks toward the sleeping form next to me.

Nodding my head, I sit up and stretch, prepared to be told to go home.

"Stay," Sonya whispers. "I'm sorry I woke you."

She leaves, quietly closing the door and turning off the hallway light. The glow under the doorjamb goes dark and so does the room.

"I deal with that every night, and she wonders why I sleep all day," Penelope says.

Lying back down, I turn on my side and face restlessness. With prayer-like hands under her freckled face, she blinks heavily and yawns.

"Parents worry about their kids," I say.

Pen closes her eyes and takes a deep breath. "When are you leaving?"

"In a week."

"Why are you here, Dillon?" she asks in a shaky voice.

"Because I want you to come with me."

Chapter 35

DILLON

Changing out of the white dress she slept in, Pen sticks her bare feet into a pair of beat up sweats, and I pull a shirt over her head. She runs her fingers through her unruly curls and blows stray hairs out of her face.

"Ready?" I ask, taking her hand.

"Yes."

Penelope and I spent most of the early morning talking about time we wasted and how to make the most of our future together. Apologies weren't necessary, and we easily agreed between soft kisses and light touches that the past is the past.

It was that easy.

Listening to Wayne walk by the bedroom door more than once, we waited until nine to get out of bed, hoping he wouldn't be inclined to murder me in the light of day.

"They can't say no, Dillon. I'm nineteen. I won't—"

Pinching her lips between my fingers, I smile. "Don't freak out before we hear what they have to say."

Like any other typical weekend morning in the Finnel home, Sonya's cooking breakfast in the kitchen, and her husband is sitting on the sofa, cleaning his shot gun.

"What are you doing here, boy? Did you forget my house rules in your absence?" He looks down the barrel of his weapon. "Do you need to be reminded, boy?"

I push Penelope in front of me and head toward the door. My girl shrieks, but Wayne and Mrs. Finnel laugh. My girl's father puts the gun down on the table beside an open book about adolescent depression and invites us to sit with him.

"Did I scare you, boy? Don't be such a pussy, Dillon."

Did he just call me Dillon?

Cautiously sitting on the recliner across from pending demise, I pull Penelope into my lap and hold her tight in case we need to make a run for it. Coach Finnel offers me a beer, and I decline, knowing it's a test.

"Pussy," he mumbles again, popping the top and taking a drink.

"Why do I have a bad feeling about this?" Sonya takes a seat beside her husband. She wrings a red dishtowel in her hands.

Dressed in yesterday's clothes, I bounce my foot up and down as the four of us sit in an awkward silence. My eyes shift back and forth between my girl's parents and the gun I hope Wayne only has out to scare me with. Waiting for Penelope to speak up and tell her life-givers what she wants, my hands start to sweat, and I can feel my heart's beat in my fingernails.

Thirty tension-full seconds that feel like decades pass, and sadness still hasn't pronounced a single syllable, so I say it for her.

"I'm leaving for Seattle in a week and want Pen to come with me."

The college Nazi stands, and his face turns red under his thick eyebrows and salt and pepper colored mustache. His knees hit the old wooden table in front of him, knocking it back a foot, and the black metal weapon tips over and falls to the floor.

While I wait for it to accidently fire and shoot me in the face, Sonya screams and Penelope starts to cry.

"I'm only asking out of respect, Coach Finnel. If she wants to leave, she can. But I don't want it to be like that. Your blessing is important to us."

His face turns three different shades of inflamed before

ultimately turning purple. "Seattle? Do you realize how far from home that is, boy? She can't be alone."

"She won't be," I reply, having thought about this since asking her to move with me. "Herb and Mathilda have been there for a year. Among the three of us, maybe we can work out a schedule so that someone is always with her. Or she can take classes at the community college while I'm at school. We'll work it out."

"You're my baby. I worry about you." He shakes his head, directing his dark eyes toward his brittle-hearted daughter. Anger wrinkles and fiery skin color soften and return to normal the moment he takes in her small frame.

"I know, Dad," she says softly.

"Help me understand this, baby," he says, falling back onto the sofa. "How did I not realize you and the boy are back together? Why do you want to leave?"

"I love him," Pen simply answers, wiping tears from her face.

After the initial shock of our announcement passes, Wayne starts to ask questions about school and how I plan to support his only child and myself. Describing the one-bedroom apartment my dad has agreed to help pay for as long as I keep my grades up, I think he understands that we won't be living like royals, but exactly like stereotypical college kids.

I'll receive money for living expenses through financial aid, but since I have a year to make up for and a loaded class schedule, I won't be able to work for extra money.

"It won't be easy, but I want to be a doctor," I say. "And I want to be with Pen."

Uneaten breakfast goes cold as morning burns into afternoon. We talk for hours, and eventually call my parents over to join the discussion. They're as surprised as the Finnels and justifiably nervous. Dad wants me to take the responsibility living with someone with chronic depression requires into consideration.

"There's no need to rush, Son," he says. "Why not wait a semester or two until you adjust alone first?"

"She doesn't remember to take her medications on her own, Dillon. If you're going to take care of her, you can't let her stay in bed all day. What about therapy and other doctors' appointments? It's not like you'll just be down the street. I won't be able to help…" Sonya trails off, turning toward her frightened-looking husband for support.

"I can't spend another year without her," I say honestly. "She'll be okay with me. We'll be fine together."

Ultimately, they accept that this is our lives and our decision, and reluctantly, agree to be supportive.

Even Wayne.

"Don't think I won't come out there, boy," he huffs.

"Seattle isn't that far," he puffs.

"You mess around, boy, I'll come after you, boy."

Chapter 36

PENELOPE

Dillon closes the last box and writes *Pen/Fragile* on the side before shoving it in the corner with the rest of them. After tossing the packing tape and marker onto the mattress, he falls to my side on the floor and rests his head in my lap.

I tickle my fingers over his scalp, resting my palm on his forehead before gliding my hand along his cheek and his jawline. After packing all week, tonight's our last night under our parents' care in Castle Rain. My walls are bare, the closet is empty, and in the end, ten boxes are all it took to sort my life.

Dillon yawns, closing his eyes and rubbing his hands over

his face. "We're finally packed."

Dad walks by my room, throwing a blue peanut M&M at Dillon before making his way downstairs.

"Watch where you put those hands, boy," he mumbles.

Taking my room apart after living in it for nine years was grueling, but I found things I forgot I even had, like old pairs of sunglasses and a sweater Dillon lent me when we were in junior high. I rediscovered pictures, music, and old yearbooks. Every single time I found some lost treasure, it had a story that usually connected to Dillon.

They were nice reminders.

Despite turning my life upside down, I've had a near-normal week mentally. Dad hasn't let the freak kid next door spend the night again, but sleep comes easy knowing Dillon's no longer out of reach. Our reconciliation was simple. There was never any other choice. We just are.

"Nervous?" my boy asks. He takes my hand and kisses my knuckles.

Tilting my head back against the wall, I close my eyes and say, "Not even a little bit."

"Are you sure you're ready to live with me? I can't always promise to leave the toilet seat down."

"Just don't let me fall in," I whisper, feeling calmer than I have in an entire year.

Dillon rises from my lap and situates himself in front of me. I sit crisscross, never opening my eyes. Loving the way my blood rushes under his touch, I can feel as his lips hover above my face and his fingers dance over my eyes. The hairs on my arms stand straight and follow his lingering trace. My eyes flutter and dance, wanting so badly to open to see how perfectly beautiful he is.

"You're such a dream," he says softly into my ear, caressing the back of his fingers across the roundness of my cheek. "Do you know how much you mean to me?"

I pull my bottom lip between my teeth and turn my face into Dillon's, rubbing my nose along his too-perfect jawline. Drowning in the faint scent of aftershave and toothpaste on his breath, I sink into affection and open myself with hopes that we can shut the door and be quiet enough to make up for lost time.

Climbing onto his lap, I spread my legs around his waist and hold on to his strong shoulders. Sweet kisses softly sweep along the curve where my shoulder and neck meet, up the side of my throat.

"Can we?" I ask, tilting my head back and swaying my hips.

Hard beneath me, the boy next door sighs and answers, "These boxes need to get into the moving truck, Pen."

A prickling spark of anxiety pierces my heart, catching my breath and turning my warm blood icy. It's a feeling of insecurity that disappears as soon as it comes, leaving me wary of its violent return and tendency to ruin entire weeks of my life at a time.

I won't sabotage this.

I'm stronger than my disabilities.

"Get my shoes and I can help," I say, sliding off Dillon's lap to catch my bearings.

He stands, adjusting his shorts with a wink before placing size seven faded black and white Chucks at my feet. I untie the dingy laces and slip them over my mismatched socks, retying the left with a loop, swoop, and pull, and the right with bunny ears. He takes in my appearance—holey cut-off shorts and a throwback band T-shirt—and smiles.

"I've seen this before. Moving trucks and first loves."

"Only loves," I say.

"Better fucking believe it."

Dillon lifts a box, kissing my cheek as he walks by. He doesn't make it out of the room before my dad is on his case.

"Watch your language in my home, boy," he orders.

"Don't think you're too old to spank. I'll give you the ass kicking of your life," he says.

"You better not be using that language around my daughter, boy," he warns.

Then…

"Fuck, no, I'm not helping you pack that truck so you can take my only daughter away from me."

OUR FULL-SIZED MATTRESS IS TOO small for us, and the toilet leaks. The refrigerator is always empty, and we've had ramen noodles for dinner every night this week. I swear the tenants in the apartment above us move furniture and host dance competitions all night long. I've broken two broomsticks banging on the ceiling, trying to get them to shut up.

In the four months since we moved here, and despite living three hours away, Mom has made the drive from Castle Rain to Seattle once a week like clockwork. She cleans, even though we don't have much space or furniture, and she cooks, even though we don't have much food. The woman who gave me life makes sure my prescriptions are full and called around until she found a therapist to take my case.

I don't have the heart to tell her it's wasted effort. Maybe I've grown out of it or maybe it's because Dillon's given me a fresh start, but I mostly feel better and have stopped taking the medication.

With the exception of some anxious moments here and there, I haven't suffered a depressive episode once since we moved out on our own and truly believe that part of my life is behind me.

Miracles happen.

I'm just not willing to share this enlightenment with my parents yet.

"Taking your meds every day was part of the deal, Pen. Don't you think you should talk to your doctor before you stop taking them?" Dillon circles spaghetti noodles around his fork, suspiciously eying the only meal I know how to cook before shoveling it into his mouth.

"They make me feel loopy and tired all the time," I say, pushing red sauce covered pasta around on my plate. "Why doesn't this look like it does when my mom makes it?"

"Because it's missing meat and seasoning, and I'm pretty sure you didn't boil the noodles long enough." Green eyes I adore look up at me, and he takes another bite of tasteless, undercooked spaghetti like it's the most delicious meal he's ever eaten.

"There are other ways I can deal with this," I say. Not willing to brave the food I spent minutes making before my boy got home from school, I set it down onto the coffee table and lift my feet onto the couch. "I've never felt this good, Dillon. It's different this time."

Chapter 37

DILLON

Our apartment smells like cinnamon and spice and Christmas trees. There are cheap cardboard cutouts of a fat Santa and Frosty the Snowman hanging from the walls and fake out-of-a-can snowflakes on our one window Sonya stenciled on to make our small space less struggling student-like and more winter wonderland.

My mom sent up a few boxes of old ornaments and strings of twinkling lights Penelope hung up in our room because our bulb burned out until her Dad showed up with a tree we don't want.

"What do you mean you're not getting Penelope a Christmas

tree?" he yelled hours before he unexpectedly arrived with a noble fir that's too tall for our living room ceiling. "The top needs to be cut off. I'd do it, but I don't have a saw."

"Neither do I," I said, already freaking out about the needles all over the place.

Wayne looked at me from under his fuzzy brows and said, "What kind of man doesn't own a saw, boy?"

It's not decorated. I don't have time with school, and Penelope doesn't even remember it needs water. It's already turning yellow, so I spend more time worrying about it catching on fire than enjoying the nostalgia and tradition the stupid tree is supposed to provide.

Our first Christmas on our own won't amount to much, anyway. We agreed not to get each other gifts this year because times are tough. Penelope wants to get a job, but I disagree.

"There's the coffee shop down the street, Dillon. We can use the extra money," she says.

"We have everything we need," I say, picking a Christmas tree needle out of her hair.

"Except good food and shampoo. We ran out," she replies, brushing needles off the front of my shirt.

She needs more time to settle, and school is more important than working. Penelope starts classes at the community college after winter break, and if the tree doesn't spontaneously combust and melt us both in our sleep, I want to make sure she's able to handle one responsibility, not two.

I'm pretty sure our intake of chicken-flavored ramen is dangerous, but it's my responsibility to make sure Pen is mentally sound, especially since she's not taking her medication.

My girl shakes her curls loose. "I had to use dish soap on my hair this morning. It was weird."

We made this agreement about the gifts, but it's not one I could abide by. I spent the entire week shopping at every store in town, and even looked online for what I needed.

Coach Finnel wanted us in Castle Rain last night, but with some convincing, Penelope talked him into a morning arrival instead. Now it's five in the morning, and I'm sneaking out of bed so I can put her gifts under the dead tree. There are boxes hidden under the couch and in the stove she doesn't use. Presents are in my dresser drawers and in the trunk of my car.

I may have gone overboard, but I love her.

She doesn't wake up, so after a couple of hours of waiting, I start being purposely loud. I take a shower with the door open and shut the closet doors with extra force. After turning the volume on the TV loud enough that the people above us start pounding, I'm surprised she doesn't come running out of the room. Breaking broomsticks on the ceiling is her favorite.

"Penelope, wake up," I give up and say.

"Go away," she mumbles. She swats at me, rolls over, and groans.

"I got you something, but you have to get up."

"It better be in the form of an orgasm because we agreed not to get each other anything, Dillon."

The girl with tired eyes follows me out to the living room and sits on the couch, scowling at her pile of presents. I happily watch, and my heart beats steadily as she chooses the poorly wrapped gift on the top and peels back the candy cane striped paper. I got her a sweater and a backpack for school and a few notebooks and other supplies she'll need. I also got her a new pair of green Chucks, a blow dryer, and a few books she wanted.

When she reaches for the last box, I become nervous and sit at her feet.

"Is this the spice rack I really wanted?" Penelope shakes it.

I don't remember her ever saying anything about a spice rack.

"Just kidding." She laughs, ripping the paper apart.

I watch carefully as she opens the box.

Madness sucks in a sharp breath and covers her mouth with both of her hands as her sparkling brown eyes start to water.

"It's been a while since you've owned a pair, so you don't have to wear them if you don't want to. But I thought they'd help since you're not taking your medication anymore." I take the box and pour out every single pair of colored and shaped glasses I could find onto the couch so she can see them all. "I'll never take these away from you."

Penelope chooses red heart-shaped ones like the pair she had when we were kids and slips them onto her face.

"What do you think?" she asks. "Do they still make me invisible?"

"You've always been clear to me, Pen," I say, looking back at my reflection in her shades.

"I JUST GOT OFF THE phone with your sister," Pen mumbles around a mouthful of suds and bristles.

Hot water rains from an old showerhead and pours down my back, easing some of my stress, but low water pressure and a full schedule prevent every ache from washing away.

School's hard, and with one year in, it feels as if this shit will never end. The road ahead of me is too long, and it feels like I'll always be a student. Dad promises all hard work pays off in the end.

In seven to ten years.

Pen tears open the plastic shower curtain, standing in front of me in nothing more than a pair of panties and a tank top that her right nipple is kind of sticking out of.

"You don't care?" she asks, talking out the side of her mouth.

Her hair is in a high, messy ponytail and a pair of pink sunglasses sits low on her nose, displaying her round eyes.

"I'm just trying to shower." I cover my junk, laughing as the shampoo bubbles slide over my shoulders.

The right side of her lips bends up, and color flushes her cheeks. Nothing is perfect, some days are better than others, and some months are better than most, but no matter how she's feeling, she's always into sex.

Dad says it's because of endorphins. When she has an orgasm, it's like having a natural, instant anti-depressant.

So we do it a lot.

It's part of the process.

Pen removes her glasses and sets them to the side. The hair tie is next to go. Then the tank top is over her head, and the panties are off. She's naked and stepping into the water with me.

I wrap my arms around her small frame, pulling her under the water. Pen kisses my chest, under my chin, and on the corner of my mouth. She tells me I'm sexy and that she loves my hairy thighs.

"Hairy thighs are not sexy, Pen," I say, kissing down her neck, down her chest. She leans her head back.

"Yours are," she whispers, gripping my arms.

Hooking my hand underneath her slippery knee, I lift her

leg over my hip. Pen stands onto her tiptoes before she wraps both legs around my waist and covers my mouth with hers, gasping against my mouth as I enter her fully.

I watch through hooded eyes as a blush spreads from Pen's cheeks down to her chest. She whispers my name, tilting her head back and parting her lips.

This is a far cry from two punk kids crying over stupid shit, smashing cement and boarding up windows.

It's love.

Always has been.

Always will be.

When my sexy, hairy thighs start to cramp, I lean Penelope against the shower wall and use it to push harder, love deeper. She pulls my hair and begs for more … begs and begs and begs until she screams for me to stop, but I don't.

As she whispers sweet nothings into my ear, I come undone inside of madness. Pen pushes my wet hair out of my face and forces me to look right at her as I come.

She smiles and bites her lip.

When we've both calmed down, I feel right. She sets herself back down onto her feet, pushing me away playfully so she can wash her hair. I kiss her back and her shoulders. We laugh and everything is good. Then she drops the bomb.

"Like I was trying to tell you earlier, I spoke to your sister.

She had some news."

"What?" I question skeptically.

"She and Kyle eloped last weekend."

Chapter 38

DILLON

She's not better.

There's no cure for this.

Sunglasses don't make sadness invisible, and sex only does so much.

Madness is back with a vengeance, and we're going crazy.

I left her this morning when I shouldn't have. She can't be alone unless she's feeling aware, bright, and content, and Penelope was none of those things when I walked out the front door of our apartment before class.

I called my sister and asked her if she could drive up to Seattle to be with my girl for the day. She couldn't, but promised to call in and check on her with exhaustion thick in her tone. Penelope's depression has held Risa hostage for the better part of a month. She's made the drive more times than I can thank her for.

"Can you stop?" the girl sitting next to me in class says.

Tapping the tip of my pen on the top of my small desk and bouncing my foot under it, I look up and come face-to-face with bothered eyes.

"Sorry," I mumble, marking off pages in my textbook I'll have to reread later tonight.

After sitting through an entire day of lectures, this is my last class, but a heavy sense of dread coats me from the inside out. The thought of Penelope lying in bed alone, a ball underneath a mound of blankets, makes my skin crawl and I can't concentrate.

Has she gotten out of bed yet?

Did she eat?

Is she breathing?

This inability to control her emotions and sadness paralyzes me. All I can do is worry, wanting so badly to make her life easier and feeling guilty because I can't.

Running my hand through my hair, I scope out the clock on the wall.

Five minutes.

Five more minutes and I'm free.

I watch as the second hand makes its way around the clock over and over, taking its time. I listen as each minute ticks and tocks by. My foot bounces, and my pen hits the desk despite the girl's dirty looks.

My stomach twists, and my heart clenches.

Four more minutes until I can go.

Three more minutes.

Tick, tock, tick, tock...

Two more minutes.

One more minute.

Thirty seconds.

Five seconds.

I slide my key into the knob, slowly and quietly unlocking our front door. It's bright outside, but inside the apartment is pitch-black and silent. I drop my backpack onto the couch and head back to our room, bringing the container I brought with me.

"Hi," Penelope whispers, lifting the comforter so I can fit in beside her.

"Hey." I kiss her forehead. "Are you okay?"

She shakes her head, smiling despite tears running from her eyes. I open the container and light the pink and white candle. Penelope smiles, knowing.

"Happy twenty-first birthday," I whisper, holding the cupcake for her to blow out.

The candle burns, but neither one of us blows it out. Our dark bedroom is illuminated with the slight orange light the flame gives off. Penelope and I stare at each other, hearts beating and breaths shaky.

"We're supposed to be out living it up. We're twenty-one," she cries softly.

I make a wish—the same wish I always make—and blow out the candle. Reaching for her, I hold her so fucking close. So fucking tight she'll never, ever, ever question my devotion. I kiss the top of Penelope's head and allow her to cry into my chest.

"No, this is good." I smile, leaning back and closing my eyes. "This is perfect."

Chapter 39

DILLON

"**W**e're moving."

Penelope dumps chopped potatoes from the cutting board into the crock-pot with the pot roast. She took a cooking class, so gone are the days of eating raw spaghetti noodles with red sauce. We now live in the times of overcooked proteins, lumpy mashed potatoes that taste like a salt lick, and garlic sautéed everything.

"What do you mean 'we're moving'?" she asks, wiping her wet hands on the back of her shirt. Pen maneuvers around our small kitchen in a pair of purple-rimmed sunglasses and bare feet.

Plucking a carrot from her meal, I pop it into my mouth and immediately turn away so I can spit it out into my hand. Who knows what she's done to make a carrot taste like soy sauce, but Pen's done it.

"I want to get you a bigger place, somewhere with a backyard." We've been in this apartment for almost four years; I'm ready to move on.

"That's dumb." Penelope pushes me away, knowing I'm inspecting her food. "We can't afford to move, and you still have quite a few years of school left."

I've been accepted into medical school here in Seattle. The next few years of my life will consist of residencies and fellowships. Not to mention a shit ton of money and a hell of a lot of stress.

"We're getting a dog," I offer instead.

Penelope laughs, chopping the onions. "We can't have a dog without a backyard."

"Then we should move."

"What is with you today?" My girl pours a handful of onions into the mix. She looks up at me and smiles.

"I don't know. I feel like we're stuck. We've reached some kind of dead end."

"It's all a part of the process, Dillon," she says, shaking paprika over tonight's dinner.

Since when has pot roast needed paprika?

Our relationship—that's what's stuck. We move along at the same pace, doing the same things day in and day out.

"You're going to love me forever, right?"

"No. I've met someone else and have fallen madly in love. I was going to tell you, but I figured killing you softly with poisoned pot roast was a better idea."

"Good to know." I laugh.

She kisses my lips, slipping something into my hand. "Here, take this."

I look at it and laugh. "What is it?"

It's a heart-shaped radish. Odd but completely fitting.

"If that's not a sign of our undying love, then I don't know what is." Penelope winks, setting the lid onto the crock-pot.

Penelope's pot roast didn't kill me. It was actually very good, and we ate two servings each. Penelope had some trouble going to sleep, so we stayed up a lot of the night. When my alarm went off in the morning, I already knew I wouldn't be going to class.

I make the room dark, covering her completely, helping her to feel safe. "Not today, Penelope?"

"Not today, Dillon."

Chapter 40

PENELOPE

"**A**re you feeling okay? Do you want to head home?" I ask.

"No!" Dillon rubs his palms over his face before pulling the collar of his shirt away from his neck. "No, I'm okay. It's just warm in here."

He nervously runs his hands through his hair, pushing his messy blonde strands away from his reddened face. Our waitress comes by and delivers edginess another soda, even though he hasn't touched the last two she brought by.

"What's the matter with you, boy?" My dad laughs from the other side of the table, eating his steak, looking with a smug smile and knowing eyes.

Mom swats him with her cloth napkin, Timothy and Dawn smile, and Risa glows, staring at me with a smile spread across her face. Kyle elbows her, and the grin falls, but pops right back up a second later.

"I'm sure it's just stress from school, right, Son?" Tim offers, almost like he's leading the conversation.

"Yeah, Dad, whatever," my guy answers, scooting his seat back.

Dillon stands.

The entire table takes a breath.

Meeting our families for dinner to celebrate our birthday was his idea, but he's been avoiding and completely on edge all day. Looking up at the boy in question, dark green eyes meet mine, and goose bumps rise on my arms.

"Take me somewhere where we can be alone," I whisper, needing some space.

He nods, capturing my hand in his and telling our families not to follow us. Dillon leads me outside, inhaling a deep breath and blowing it out between his straight lips once we're out in the open.

"I should have done this at home. This is stupid," he mumbles to himself before addressing me. "You're everything to me, Penelope."

"I know," I answer timidly.

"Who knew it would be so hard?" he whispers. Dillon takes another deep breath, brushing my hair away from my shoulder. "Stay here, okay?"

After running back into the restaurant to pay the bill, the love of my life walks me to his Pontiac, and we drive back to our childhood homes, where we're staying for the weekend. The end-of-September night smells like incoming rain and is quiet enough to hear waves crashing against Castle Rock a mile down at the beach.

When my parents' old Chrysler and the Deckers' vehicle pull into the driveway behind our GTO, I'm surprised to see they left dinner when we did. Dad was still buttering his roll when we excused ourselves for some air.

"What are they doing here?" I ask, motioning to open my door.

"Let me get that for you." Dillon places his hand on my knee, stopping me before he gets out and rushes around the back of the car.

The tremble in his body doesn't go unnoticed when he opens my door and stands back to let me by. My confusion only grows when I see everyone standing on the lawn, staring at us.

Risa gives me a thumbs-up.

Turning around to ask Dillon what the heck is going on, I'm stunned to find him down on his knee, shaking, crying, and speaking.

He says forever and always.

He says be mine, and let's grow old together.

The ring shines like his watering eyes in the moonlight.

Families cry, Moms hug, and Dads look happy.

"Marry me, Penelope."

I cover my mouth with my hands as tears fall from my eyes. Dillon waits patiently for an answer as the world around fades away, leaving only us.

He's so handsome. So strong. So entirely forever.

I think back to the very first day I saw this boy. How the sunlight lit up his hair. How cute I thought he was while he sat on his bike watching me move boxes from the moving truck to the stairs. I remember blowing the biggest bubbles I could, knowing boys thought bubble gum was awesome.

We spent years writing letters across lawns, and he traded M&M's for smiles.

He gave me yellow feathers and kept our heart-shaped radish.

Dillon brushed my hair and taught me how to use tampons. He brought me coffee and kissed me for the first time.

"Say yes," eternity whispers.

So I do.

I say yes.

EVERYTHING'S DARK BEHIND HIS HANDS, but I let him guide my way, knowing he will never let me fall.

"Your eyes better be closed, Penelope," Dillon warns.

"They are."

I hear the sound of a door being opened and smell wet paint. We slowly shuffle forward until the ground under my feet softens, and we're no longer outside.

"You can look now."

We're alone in an empty house I've never been in before. The living room opens to a large kitchen, and Dillon's excited to show me the master and three other smaller bedrooms. The bathrooms seem bigger than the one-bedroom apartment we've spent the last five years in. A pool and spa are in the backyard that I can't wait to dip my toes into.

"I got in at the hospital, Penelope. This is yours. Anything you want you can have."

Dillon is a doctor.

This is what the last few years have been for.

"I love it." It's the absolute truth.

He sweeps my feet out from under me and runs toward the pool, and I know there's no point in doing anything else but holding on.

We cut through the air, and as we drop, I take a breath so big my lungs burn.

I release it the moment my skin touches the frigid water.

Sinking fast, bubbles blur my vision, and I kick free from my captor.

Dillon catches me, and we kiss beneath the water, stopping time so this airless moment lasts just a little longer.

The true love way.

Epilogue

DILLON
PART 1

I f you freeze a heart-shaped radish, it will still shrivel and
grow roots.

If you wrap a heart-shaped radish in plastic wrap
and stick it into the far corner of your freezer where it's safe,
protected, and loved, it will still go bad.

Despite all my efforts to keep this radish safe from itself,
from its nature, from the reality of its sad existence, my heart-
shaped radish is still only a radish.

All my hard work and dedication will never change that
simple fact.

"You should have let the radish go in the crock-pot,

Dillon," Penelope says, shaking her head at my poor heart-shaped radish.

"Maybe, but I love this radish more than anyone, and I wanted to keep it safe."

"It's only a radish, a plain and dirty radish," she says, laughing as she jumps onto the kitchen counter. "Besides, that radish has real, real serious problems. I've heard that radish, the one you love so much, is a little bit crazy."

Penelope winks, turning the page of her cookbook, kicking her feet out in front of her.

"Watch your mouth, woman. I love my radish, and I won't let you talk shit." I kiss it before sticking it back into the freezer, confident that it will last as long as I keep cutting off the roots. Turning back to my girl, I kiss her face and her neck. Running my hands up her thighs, I whisper into her ear, "Besides, we're all a little bit crazy."

"Maybe, but your radish—she's crazier than the rest." She wraps her arms around my neck.

I nod, not disagreeing with her.

"What are the chances that I'd be lucky enough to find that particular heart-shaped radish? Out of all the radishes in this world—all the *normal* radishes—I was the one chosen to have the heart-shaped one? Pretty small, I'd say." I kiss along her jaw. My thumb rubs over her nipple through her shirt. "I'm pretty lucky, and I'll never take that for granted. Even if it does have roots."

"Your radish is defective."

"Take that back. It isn't even close to being true," I whisper against her skin, pulling her shirt over her head.

Penelope sinks back onto the kitchen counter. Her arms fall above her head, and her legs wrap around my waist. I kiss up her collarbone and touch the side of her breast.

"Your radish loves you, too, you know?" She squirms, laughing when I bite her nipple over her bra. "It's grateful for all you do for her. She sleeps well at night because she knows you'll always be around to help when the roots get a little out of hand. And when your radish goes a little bit crazy, she is well aware of your love. Your radish told me to tell you that."

"Does my radish know that she has great tits?" Unhooking her bra, I throw it behind me.

Penelope bites on her bottom lip, closing her eyes and nodding her head. "Yes."

Hooking my fingers into the waistband of her shorts, I pull them down her legs and die when I see my radish isn't wearing any underwear.

Once I situate myself between her legs, chills run up and down her naked body. She touches the side of my face, and I turn and kiss her palm, loving the way the diamond around her finger binds her to me.

"Does my radish know that she drives me wild? Does she know I've loved her since I was twelve? That I would die for her?"

"She knows. That's why she's going to marry you."

"I'm going to be late for work," I groan, pushing inside her.

Six months without an episode, Pen's edgy, and I can feel it coming. She isn't as quick to get out of bed in the morning because she's not sleeping at night. Madness is easily distracted, and her mood swings are unpredictable.

When I love her like this, giving myself to her to take and use in whichever way she needs, she seems better. Our bodies move together, heavy breaths and clinging limbs. I want to be here, in the now, enjoying her skin against mine. All I can manage to think about is whom I can call and have come over to watch her while I'm at the hospital.

"Love me. Love me," she whispers.

"I do. So much."

As I kiss over her flushed cheeks, Penelope smiles and hums. Her closed eyes open, looking at me with her dark browns. The depth and the significance of the brief stare is enough to let me know she is thinking about the same thing I am. Neither one of us says a word about the inevitable—the silent condition that rules our lives.

THE NEXT COUPLE OF DAYS pass slowly, and I have no choice but to leave for the hospital every day. With new opportunities come new responsibilities, and obligations at work don't care that my fiancée is dying inside.

Balancing on the edge of hopelessness, it's a battle she has been losing since she was a kid.

She doesn't have any more fight to give.

"You treat me like I'm a fucking child, Dillon!" she snaps, walking past me into our bedroom and slamming the door.

Before I follow her inside, I take a step back and remind myself that the girl I love isn't upset with me; it's the monster inside her.

"I'm coming in," I warn her, cautiously turning the knob.

Taking off my tie, I slip out of my shoes while Penelope sits in the center of our bed with her face in her hands. There isn't anything I can say that will make her feel better. She'll use my words against me, so I remain silent while changing out of my work clothes.

"I'm alone all day," she cries. "I miss you, but you're always gone."

"This is how it has to be for a while." I hang up my shirt and step out of my black slacks.

"I don't want your sister here. I don't need a babysitter."

"She won't be here to babysit you. I promise." I sit on the edge of the bed, careful to give madness space.

She cries harder and harder as the minutes pass—shaking the bed and hurting my ears, my pride, and my heart. I should be able to fix this. I'm a doctor. I've studied about treating and curing people and their aliments, but there is nothing I can do for the one person who means everything to me.

I'm helpless.

I can only sit back and listen to her ear-shattering sobs, knowing this is only the beginning. Tonight, she won't sleep, but tomorrow, she will sleep all day. Penelope won't eat, and she'll stop talking. She'll lose weight and manipulate me into having sex. She'll feel so bad afterward that the crying will start all over again.

Who knows how long it will last? A few days. A week. A month. A few months.

"Penelope," I whisper her name. "We have to do something about this. We can't just sit back and let it happen to you."

Taking a chance, I look over at the love of my life. Her green circular sunglasses block the view of her red swollen eyes. She doesn't even attempt to smile, laying her cheeks down on her knees. I scoot closer, then closer again, until I'm right next to her and my arms have her safely pinned against me.

"I hate feeling like this. It's like I'm dying."

"You're not. I swear you're not."

"My heart is beating too fast. I can't catch my breath." Her feet start to kick, and her fingernails dig into the skin of my arm.

"Everything's okay," I assure her.

Looking back at our lives, this type of depression is a condition that was passed down to Penelope through genes and birth. Symptoms showed themselves as early as age two. By five, she was hiding behind her glasses, unemotional. At twelve, she'd met me, but nothing about her personality had changed. Penelope was awkward and overlooked because of her unsociable personality. She was detached to everyone except me, and around age twelve, the symptoms really began to show. She was consumed by fifteen.

I'd like to think I did something to help—that any of us did—but the reality is we did nothing more than contain and treat, again and again. We got Penelope by.

Maybe it's our fault it's getting worse.

Maybe it's my fault.

I'm her worst enabler. I gave her the new glasses after she went years without them. I allow her to sit around all day and do nothing. I'm the one telling her that everything is okay, even though it's not. Not even close. It's always there, lurking and teasing. Not only affecting our day-to-day life, but also our future.

What if we want kids? Will they be born with it, too?

As I lay Pen down on her back, she fights against my grip. Trying to convince me that she can't breathe, she hits and pulls on my clothes. Her hands shake, and her eyes tremble. Her mind's betraying her body. It's so sad I can cry.

"You're having a panic attack," I whisper into her ear, unsure if she's even listening. "I won't let you die. I will never let anything happen to you."

It seems like hours before her breathing returns to normal. My skin burns from where she scratched and hit me. Her glasses are broken, and her face is swollen. A few shaky breaths and some leftover tears, Penelope apologizes.

"I can't live like this anymore. I can't do it."

What do you say to something like that?

Sorry, but you were born this way? Your brain is messed up, and there is nothing you or I can do about it? Get used to it because this is your life, Penelope.

Our life.

I don't fucking think so.

PENELOPE
PART 2

"Remember when you went through that phase?"

"What phase?" Risa blows smoke out of her mouth in O shapes.

I take the joint from her hands, puffing once, twice, three times before handing it back. "When you tried to quit smoking pot and left your hair one shade of blonde."

"God, yes." She rolls her eyes and laughs, putting her feet up on my lap. "Don't mention that to anyone. I'm sticking it to the man with reefer and pink hair."

Risa moves her pink bangs out of her eyes.

"Dillon is going to be home soon," I warn, tickling the

bottom of her feet.

"I know; he just called." Risa smokes what is left of the weed and puts it out. "I have to head back to Castle Rain tonight. Kyle can only go so long without me."

Dillon has Risa come up a few times a month to stay with me so I won't have to be alone when he's working. Sometimes she'll rotate with my mom or even my dad. Dawn came up for a week a few months ago, but with Risa comes herb, and with herb come peace and laughs.

She's utterly the same as I remember her being when we were kids—wise beyond her age, spiritual, and free. Stupid, non-essential tattoos scatter her body; her nose is pierced on both sides, and her fingers are littered in different sized and shaped colored rings. When Risa is here, she wears my sunglasses, claiming to feel "left out" because I wear them and she doesn't.

My partner in crime sucks on lollipops all day, bounces around the house, and recycles everything. It's impossible to feel bad when she is around. Doesn't mean I don't, but she makes it easier.

I smile, light-headed from the high. As I shake Risa's foot, she looks over at me. "I can't wait to marry your brother."

"You guys should just do what Kyle and I did. Go to the courthouse. Let it be done."

"No, I want to make a huge deal out of it."

"You do?" Looking at me skeptically, Risa sits up and drinks an entire bottle of water.

"I do."

"White dress and everything?"

"White dress and everything."

"Your love is such a fairy tale, it's sick." She sits back, bringing my head to her lap.

"I am hardly a fairy tale," I say.

"Oh, but you are." Her fingers run through my long brown hair. "You're such a sad girl, Pen. I wish you weren't. There's so much to be happy about."

"I can't help it, Risa."

"I think you can, or you can try," she says carefully. "When was the last time you were evaluated?"

"A couple of years ago, before Dillon and I moved into the house."

Sometimes I feel like a child who is kept inside a bubble. Like Dillon's radish, he keeps me wrapped up so tightly, afraid that I might get hurt. In the end, I still grow roots. My disease, my condition, and my stipulation keep me prisoner.

On the outside, I am normal—a twenty-four-year-old girl who's engaged to the most beautiful person in the entire world. Most days I can go out and do normal things. Risa and I like to go jogging. It usually ends with her coughing on the side of the road, but we try. I attend classes at the community college, content with the fact that I may never have a real career.

Dillon's given me the gift of indecisiveness; I never have to be sure of anything if I don't feel like it. One day I can be a cook, the next I can be a photographer, a teacher, a painter, or a writer. He indulges in my indulging, supporting me every step of the way.

"Guess who?"

Risa giggles. Dillon laughs under his breath.

"Umm …" I play. "Is it … oh, I know… is it the cute guy who works at the hospital with my guy? What's his name? Lance?"

Dillon removes his hand, cigarette hanging from the edge of his lips. "What? You think Lance is cute? Pierce me through the heart, why don't ya?"

I sit up from Risa's lap, feeling a little loopy from the pot. Dillon's there to steady me, laughing while smoke seeps from his cig.

"Careful," he whispers.

His eyes reflect so much adoration and devotion. I am the center of his world, his debilitating center.

Throwing my arms around his neck, Dillon laughs and falls back onto his butt. He warns me about cigarette burns, but I couldn't care less. I would burn all the way through if it meant I could touch him like this for always.

"WE DON'T HAVE TO DO THIS."

Dillon, being a doctor, doesn't mean he uses his knowledge to diagnose or cure me. Together, we have turned a blind eye to how severe my depression has become. I don't think a reassessment will fix this. I won't ever be rid of it. It's my second forever. But I have to try to truly manage it.

"Dillon," I say. "Just trust me."

With reluctant eyes and hesitant kisses, he does.

For six hours, I go through the ropes. I speak about my routine and my actions. How often this happens to me, and do I have suicidal thoughts? Dillon finds it hard not to defend my helplessness. He's easily angered and quick to block me from any type of grief. He doesn't want these doctors asking me personal questions about my sexual activity or inability to be close to anyone else but our immediate family. He's protective, but it's time for him to step back.

I don't like everything the doctors have to say. They call me *dependent* and *clinical*—words I have heard before, only this time they include *bipolar* and *manic*.

Dillon cries. He tries to hide his face, but I see him.

I don't. I refuse to cry. Instead, I act.

"Help me fight this," I say. "Tell me what to do."

"Mood disorders are hard to treat." One doctor hands Dillon a pamphlet on manic depression and bipolar affective disorder.

He goes on to describe rapid cycling and mixed episodes. His words about isolation, self-loathing, and sadness describe me perfectly.

It's not easy hearing that I have a classified mental illness. I am unstable, and while there are worse cases than mine—cases where people cannot function or live properly—it doesn't make it any easier to hear.

Dillon takes my hand and winks, having wiped the tears from his eyes.

He is on my team: Team Penelope.

They want me admitted for further observation. Dillon refuses, and I don't find it necessary. We thank them, take the pamphlets and a new understanding on my condition, and leave, but not before my meds are changed and also reevaluated.

With an array of anti-depressants and mood stabilizers, Dillon and I drive home in a comfortable silence. He reminds me that everything is okay, that I'm not alone. He won't ever leave me.

"No more caffeine," Dillon repeats what the doctor said, rubbing my cheek as we sit at a red light.

"But I love it," I whine, playing along.

When the light turns green, Dillon goes on and on about stress management and ridding the house of caffeine. We're going to join a gym and get a dog, because dogs make people feel better.

"I'm going to be this way forever, Dillon," I remind him, loving the idea of a puppy but not deterred from the fact of the matter.

"And I'm always going to be like this." Dillon looks at me with crossed eyes and a stupid smile while speaking about toast in a French accent.

My laughter echoes throughout the cab of his car.

Epilogue

DILLON
PART 3

I take a breath, looking into Penelope's eyes, holding onto her hands with sweaty palms and shifty fingers. All our family and friends are watching. My sister stands behind my girl with hair braided and dreaded, up and curled. A daisy decorates her ear. Penelope's bouquet is in her hand.

Risa winks as Penelope and I say, "I do."

She cries and wipes away her tears, always knowing that this is where we would end up.

In the front row sit my father and mother, Coach Finnel, and Mrs. Finnel. My parents look up with shiny eyes and proud smiles. The Coach's normal "boy" look has transformed into subtle content.

Kyle taps on my shoulder, passing me her ring. He smiles, hugging me before stepping back into his place in front of Herb. Mathilda, who stands beside Risa, sniffs loudly. Everyone laughs, including Penelope.

My love's lips are colored a deep ruby-red. The rest of her makeup is left simple. Her hair is curled loosely and pinned up on the left side with a barrette given to her by my mother. Her nails are painted red. A heart-shaped necklace, a present from her dad, surrounds her neck.

Penelope is godly and unfairly beautiful today. By tradition, I wasn't supposed to see her until she walked down the aisle.

Fuck tradition. I snuck into her room before I even came outside.

I put the barrette in her hair and whispered against her flushed cheeks. I helped clasp the button on her dress and slipped her shoes onto her feet so she wouldn't wrinkle her gown. Penelope ran her fingers through my hair, because she likes it better when it's messy. She loosened my tie and smeared a little lipstick on my collar. I tried to talk her into running away together, skipping the ceremony and going straight into the honeymoon, but she declined.

"I want everyone to see how much I love you," she said before Risa came running into the room with a pointed finger and a joint between her lips.

Now we're here—me, slipping a ring onto her finger, and Penelope, sighing with completeness.

"We can run away now," she whispers, looking between her ring finger and me.

"Not yet," I whisper back, saying my vows and listening to hers.

The priest tells me to kiss my bride.

My bride.

I take her into my arms while the crowd whistles, claps, and cries, and I kiss her. Red lipstick smears, more hands in the hair, and a few cleared throats, but I kiss her relentlessly.

This is officially forever.

Penelope's head leans back, her laughter causes my heart to swell.

I kiss her again.

At twilight, Risa gives a speech about rollerblades and hearts in the cement. She mentions broken souls and boarded up windows, but reminds us that we are stronger than our faults.

"You guys have what most people only dream of. You've been in love since you were kids, unconditional and irreversible." She wipes her eyes, taking a gulp of her champagne. "Remember the first time we all smoked out—"

Dad takes the microphone from Risa and gives his own

speech about proud parents and fulfilled expectations. His words about overcoming struggles and long-roads-defeated choke me up. Penelope smiles with glossy eyes, kissing my cheek.

Coach Finnel is the next to speak. His speech is in the form of grumbles and mumbles. "Boy, you better…" and "Boy, I always knew you were the one," and "Boy, I'm not buying any more M&M's." Ending his speech with a failing voice and, "Dillon, I know you will take care of her, because you always have."

Everyone watches while we share our first dance as a married couple.

I dip Penelope before continuing to sway in my parents' backyard. "This is so cliché."

The trees are decorated with twinkling lights, and white tables with candles and white linen tablecloths decorate the reception area.

Penelope laughs, laying her head against my chest. "Shut up. Give me my moment."

Her hair smells like vanilla and almonds, bare feet on top of my shoes and ears over my beating heart.

We dance in tiny circles. Penelope's dress brushes along the grass. We don't talk. We only move and sigh, until a tap on my shoulder and permission to cut in is asked proudly from Coach

Finnel.

I kiss Penelope on her forehead, then her cheek and the corner of her mouth before handing her over to her dad and taking my sister by her hand. My sister smells like weed and lilacs. She has the giggles and bloodshot eyes.

Risa and I spin in playful circles, laughing until we cry and hug until we can't breathe.

"I know that I'm not the smartest person in the world, Dillon, and I didn't do much with my life, but for what it is worth, I am entirely proud of you and Penelope."

"Risa, shut up. You have done more for Penelope and me than you could know. If it wasn't for you—" I drop my forehead onto my sister's, trying to keep my composure. "I don't know where we would be without you."

She laughs. "Together. You were born to be together."

Kyle is the next to tap on my shoulder, asking to cut in. He offers me a small smile and a pat on the back, but he only has eyes for Risa. The two of them just work, meshing and gravitating in a way that is so intimate I walk away with my hands inside my pockets, without a look back.

On the sidelines of the dance floor, I'm able to steal some time alone. I order a beer from the bar and hide in the tree line, leaning against the trees Penelope and I used to play in as kids.

The music is loud, voices echo, and laughter floats. The cold beer is relief on my warm lips. I loosen my tie and unbutton a few buttons of my shirt before untucking it from my pants and rolling up my sleeves.

I can see Penelope with the Holy Matrimony Nazi from here, dancing in circles song after song. Beside them are my parents, looking more in love than I have ever seen. Herb and Mathilda, who have been together longer than Penelope and me, whisper playfully before he spins her away from him.

But it's Penelope whom my eyes always return to. Her father's cheek lies on top of her head. His black and gray mustache moves as he gives her advice and words of love. Penelope cries, wiping her face clean. Her lips are stained red, but the lipstick has long been gone since I kissed it off during the ceremony, and green grass stains are on her train.

I give them one more song before I head back toward my wife.

"I'm ready when you are," I whisper, taking her back from Wayne.

"We can't leave yet. The wedding isn't over." Penelope kisses my cheek, allowing me to pull her away from the dance floor.

I spin her a couple of times; she fits perfectly under my arm. Before Penelope has a chance to figure out what I'm doing, we're running away from our wedding and heading toward my

Pontiac. She giggles and runs, holding her dress up. I'm right behind her, lifting the train so she doesn't slip.

We run until the music is a distant noise and the car is in our sight.

Penelope laughs, dropping her dress and gasping for air. "You did this on purpose, hiding the car around the block."

With lips at her ear, the other on the car door handle. "I can only share you for so long. I was beginning to lose my mind."

Running around to the other side of the car, Penelope and I drive back to Seattle with our cell phones off and the stereo blasting. I smoke a cigarette, and Penelope pulls at her dress. She releases her hair from the barrette and reaches back to loosen her corset.

Three hours later, we are running to our front door. Penelope has given up on holding her dress up and concentrates more on getting out of it as fast as possible.

Once we are through the front door, both she and I work on the string and lace until it falls to her feet and Penelope sighs with relief. She stands in the entryway in white panties and bra. I give her about ten seconds to catch her breath before I'm on her.

My hands are in her hair, her back is pressed against the wall, and her legs are wrapped around my waist.

"I love you," I whisper against her lips.

Penelope's head falls back and hits the wall with a thump. "I love you," she whispers back, circling her hips.

Slowly making our way back to our bedroom, we are undressed and a tangled mess of limbs and heavy breaths in no time at all. Her smooth legs run up and down mine. Penelope's back is arched, and her mouth is open. I press into her, slowly and fully.

With the sounds of her love in my ear, the memories of our past flood my mind.

The first time I saw her.

Same birthdates and peace signs on her cheek.

Rollerblades and feet pushing my bike.

I kiss along Penelope's neck, her hands run up and down my back, and I dip into her.

Love consumes. Love conquers.

Penelope whispering with Risa on the couch. I only ignored her because I liked her so much.

Notes across the lawn.

Saving all my M&M's in a box under my bed.

"Dillon," Penelope moans, her chest pressed against my own.

"Shhh…" I kiss the corner of her mouth, diving into her.

Everything about our childhood flips through my mind, one thing after another.

Teaching Penelope how to use tampons and our first kiss. Hiking in the woods and holding hands.

She wanted to have sex and finding out she was depressed. Starting high school and a rainbow of sunglasses.

Stolen feathers and staying awake all night long.

Penelope pushes me onto my back, climbing on top and dropping herself slowly onto my length. She moves her hips back and forth, head tipped back. I touch her legs, her stomach, her chest.

"You took it down?"

I look up at my sister and nod, not interested in talking about it.

Risa sits next to me. "Penelope seems happy about it."

Taking a chance, I look up from my book and out the window, over to Penelope's. I haven't had the balls to look yet, too afraid to see what I would find, ashamed that I put it up in the first place.

But there she is, with a small smile and an even smaller wave, she closes her curtains and walks away.

I sit up, wrapping one arm around Penelope's back, placing my other hand on her hip. She moves back and forth with closed eyes and raised skin. I touch her, feel her ... remembering everything.

How it felt to see her with Joshua Dark at that party. How

it felt even worse to fight him and lose, again. Living every day in a haze and staying away, despite wanting nothing more than to go to her.

I will always regret not going to her sooner, but I'll never regret the lesson learned.

I run my hand along her face, lips touching and tongues gliding. I grip into her skin and rock back and forth as she comes. Penelope holds on to my shoulders, confessions of love and forever exchange until tears leave her eyes and our bodies collapse.

Penelope smiles, hooded eyes and flushed cheeks. She runs her hands though my sweaty hair and locks her legs around mine so I can't pull out.

"Happy Wedding Day, Dillon," she whispers.

"Happy Birthday, Penelope."

Epilogue

DILLON
PART 4

I drop my keys onto the counter, blow out a candle Penelope left lit, and sift through some of the mail that was left for me to see. "I'm home, Pen."

Bills, junk, and congratulation cards are still coming in from this weekend's no-shows.

"I'm back here!" she yells over splashing water and loud reality television.

I take off my jacket and empty my pockets before heading toward our bedroom. The TV is on, blasting so Penelope can hear it in the bathroom. When I turn it off, Pen says, "Hey!"

I turn the radio on instead, and she shuts up.

I lean in the doorway of the muggy bathroom. Penelope sits in the bathtub, bubbles up to her neck and candles lit on every surface.

I laugh, unbuttoning my shirt. "I've been telling you since we were fourteen about these candles, Penelope."

My wife looks up at me, lifting her knees so I have room to get in. "Oh, I know. I just love them so much."

I drop my shirt to the floor, step out of my shoes, and get into the water. Bubbles overflow, and water spills onto the floor. Penelope laughs loudly while she sticks her feet on my lap and lies back, not caring that I just got in with my pants still on.

She sighs, lifting her hair and tying it into a knot. "You're silly."

I don't stay on my side of the tub for long; I'm up on my knees, between her legs and over her belly. I kiss her lips, then her cheek, her chin, her chest ... our growing miracle.

I rub my hand back and forth over our baby girl. "How are you doin' today?"

"Tired, hungry, and a little bit moody." Penelope closes her eyes. "I thought of a name, though."

"You did?" I stand and take off my pants so that I can sit behind Penelope. With her back pressed against my chest, my knees up on each side of her body, both of our hands lie on top of her swollen belly.

"Layla," she says, playing in the bubbles.

"Like the song?"

"Yeah, like the song."

I kiss the top of her shoulder, watching as goose bumps spread along her skin. "It's beautiful."

"I went through the rest of the gifts from the baby shower." She smiles. "Your sister got the baby one of those pacifiers with crystals all over it. It's so, so pretty."

I kiss her neck and the spot right below her ear. "That's nice."

The bathroom is dark, candles being our only light. Pen goes on and on about the baby shower she had last weekend. We got almost everything we need, with the exception of a few small things. I tell her about the cards that came in the mail.

After she tells me about cribs that need assembling and about so much pink she wants to puke, we fall into a comfortable silence.

Penelope looks back, and I smirk. "I mean, just because she is a girl doesn't mean she has to wear pink all the time, right?"

"Right," I assure her.

"I said no pink on the invitations, and still, it's all we got." She giggles, rambles, and laughs.

I smile, already knowing her reaction. "I like pink. It's gentle."

Penelope scoffs. "Gentle?"

"And soft."

"And cute." Penelope sighs, defeated.

The bath starts to cool; Penelope uses her big toe to turn the hot water back on. We fill the tub until it's spilling over the side. The bubbles are long gone, and our skin is pruned.

I could fall asleep.

"Dillon?"

I clear my throat and open my eyes. "Yeah?"

"I'm afraid."

I nod, knowing already that she is. It's a conversation we have had over and over since Penelope found out she was pregnant.

Will her depression be passed on to our baby? Does it really even matter?

Our girl will be here in three months, and our fears will become real life. Fears we've always had, fears that keep Penelope from being able to sleep or eat, but fears we cannot allow to run away the happiness of the larger importance— Penelope and I are going to have a baby.

A healthy and happy baby girl.

Layla.

"Everything will be okay."

"Promise?" she asks, voice small.

Regardless, everything will be okay. "I promise."

With my hand on her belly and Penelope's head on my chest, I close my eyes again. I drift in and out of sleep while Penelope sings along with the radio and the water cools. One by one the candles go out, being lit for too long.

In the dark and in a tub full of cold water, Layla starts to kick.

Penelope holds my hand on her kicking tummy. "Did you feel that?"

With closed eyes, I nod. "Yeah."

The baby kicks again and again. Proof of life, a life Penelope and I made together. Proof of love and proof that everything will be okay.

No matter what.

Epilogue

PENELOPE
PART 5

He said this would be good for us. For her.

Especially her.

We have to trust everything he says, because he's never wrong.

I lean my head on the cold glass, looking as we pass under a covering of trees. Sunlight shadows over my face when a break in leaves allows it to shine through. This drive has always been peaceful. We make it on weekends and holidays. Only this time, we aren't leaving.

Dillon was offered a job at the hospital, and it didn't take much to convince me it was time to leave Seattle.

He said, "This is what she needs, Penelope."

And I said, "I know."

Layla's ten now. She's a lot like Risa. It's probably why they're so close. She's also the spitting image of her father. I don't know when, or why, but Dillon and I silently agreed that Layla would be our only child. Having more kids wasn't an issue or something we worried about. Layla's everything we ever wanted.

And feared.

"Tired, baby?" Dillon reaches over and touches my arm. Age has done wonderful things for my husband. Sometimes I think back to when we were kids; he has such a soft face ... always strong, but he had the most precious skin. Now, he has laugh lines and a few gray hairs he won't admit to. His eyes reflect wisdom and understanding. He's a fantastic provider and caretaker. I'd be lost without him. I always was.

"A little," I say, brushing my fingers over his hand.

He looks in the rearview mirror and calls out his daughter's name, "Layla."

She doesn't answer, and I smile.

He calls her again. She blows a bubblegum bubble.

Dillon turns to face her, doing his best to keep his eyes on the road. Our only girl sits in the back with a pair of Hello Kitty sunglasses on her face, earbuds in her ears, and multicolored fingernails tapping in the air to whatever song she's listening to.

She notices him looking. "What, Dad?"

"Quit kicking my seat," he says, sitting up straighter, giving our baby dirty looks in the mirror. But he smiles and ruins it. Layla half-smiles before placing her earbuds back into her ears.

"Your daughter is rude," he mumbles, half-smiling like she does.

It didn't take long before we saw the signs in her. Like my own case, Layla showed symptoms as young as age four. By kindergarten, Dillon was whispering sweet words into her ear, promising school wasn't bad. He insisted she'd make friends. Then he handed her a pair of sunglasses and swore that behind her shades, she was untouchable.

It was probably a bad decision, but we didn't know what else to do.

As she grew older, we realized it wasn't something she was just going to develop out of. It wasn't a social anxiety, or nerves about friends, or the dark. I had passed my worst trait down to my daughter.

We've done everything we could since. Dillon and I try to make good decisions for Layla; we make sure she eats right, and we don't allow her to wallow. Sometimes we have to give in and let her sleep, or cry, or scream. She sees a child psychologist regularly, and knows that her parents are here for her.

What else can really be done?

We can move to Castle Rain. And we are.

Our family waits curbside for us. Layla sits up as soon as she sees Risa and starts shaking the seat for her dad to let her out.

"Hold on." He laughs, taking off his seatbelt. He opens the driver's side door, and Layla practically jumps out, into the arms of her favorite aunt.

I stay in my seat, smiling at my mom and dad. I wave. They wave back. Kyle smiles, walking around the truck to welcome Dillon.

"Baby…" Dillon ducks back inside the moving truck. "Are you coming?"

I nod, slipping my sunglasses off my face. I shove them into my pocket and say, "Yeah, I'm coming."

We chose a house on the other side of town from our parents. Dillon and I haven't lived in Castle Rain in fifteen years, and we like our privacy. Our new home is cozy and typical for our town. We have a few neighbors, but they're down the road. Dillon's made sure, once again, that I have plenty of room to be … me.

My dad waits at the back of the moving truck, holding a box with my name on it. I take it, stick my tongue out, and carry it inside. "Penelope, quit daydreaming and grab a box."

Inside, Risa and Mom put dishes away in the kitchen and clean out cupboards. They ask me where I want things, and I shrug. After dropping the box off in my new bedroom, I head outside.

What I find is hilarious and awfully familiar.

My ten-year-old daughter, wearing her shades and blowing her pink bubblegum bubbles, stands near the front of the truck holding a box. Her dad, with the sun in his eyes, stands at the opposite end, trying to find his words.

In the street, on a bike, is a boy.

"What are you looking at?" Dillon calls, taking a few steps forward. "Get away from my daughter, boy."

I laugh.

Layla shrieks, "You're so embarrassing, Dad!" and "I can't believe you, Dad!"

The boy, the one on the bike looking at my daughter with puppy-sick eyes, sits up straight. He waves at Layla and spins his bike around to join his friends. My baby girl stomps her way toward the porch, giving her daddy nasty looks the entire way there.

I laugh. "That was ironic."

"Shut it, Pen," he says, watching the boy pedal away. "That was bullshit, you know?"

"Why?" I ask, wrapping my arms around him. He hugs me

back. "Because it's so well-known?"

Dillon looks down at me. "It was nothing like that. We were different."

"It was exactly like that," I whisper. "Puppy-dog eyes and bad intentions."

Dillon lifts me, setting me inside the back of the moving truck. He joins me, closing the door. "I'll show you bad intentions."

My guy pushes me down onto the bare mattress.

I laugh out loud as Dillon finds me in the dark. He crawls between my legs, kissing my neck. Outside the truck I can hear my dad and daughter wondering where we are.

Dad hears me giggle.

"Boy, you better not have my daughter in there!" he yells.

"Okay." Dillon sighs. "You're right. It was exactly like that."

ABOUT
MARY ELIZABETH

Mary Elizabeth was born and raised in Southern California. She is a wife, mother of four beautiful children, and dog tamer to one enthusiastic Pit Bull and a prissy Chihuahua. She's a hairstylist by day but contemporary fiction, new adult author by night. Mary can often be found finger twirling her hair and chewing on a stick of licorice while writing and rewriting a sentence over and over until it's perfect. She discovered her talent for tale-telling accidentally, but literature is in her chokehold. And she's not letting go until every story is told.

"The heart is deceitful above all things and beyond cure."
JEREMIAH 17:9

For more information, follow Mary on:
Reader group: Facebook.com/groups/167289490301046/
Amazon: Amazon.com/Mary-Elizabeth/e/B00MW8Z81Y
Instagram: @maryelizabethromance

ACKNOWLEDGEMENTS

My very first thank you has to go to my husband. You make it possible for me to live out this crazy dream of mine and never hold my occasional madness against me. Thank you for always being there to trim my roots when they grow too long.

There's a whole team of people who helped bring *True Love Way* to life:

Amber L. Johnson—man-handler of my insecurities and self-loathing—thank you for encouraging me to be the very best writer I can be and for believing that I can do it alone when I didn't.

Paige Smith—my editor who made crazy beautiful. I look forward to a long working relationship together. Thank you for handling my inconsistencies with grace.

Debbie—my life-giver—thank you for making a bunch of numbers make sense. And just thanks for being my mom.

Kelly V.—my friend and keeper of all things Realist—thank you for getting the word out and keeping me on track. You pick up my slack when I'm busy making up stories, and for that, I'm forever grateful.

Christina and Jennifer—without your help, none of this would happen. Thank you.

Dee and Silvia—because I've never appreciated lists so much in my life.

To the readers—a million times, thank you.

And lastly, to anyone who read this and thought, *That's me*. It's me, too. We're all a little sad sometimes, but remember life is too beautiful to ever give up.

Made in the USA
Monee, IL
02 August 2021

74805623R00197